SKY ROBERT

A Fated Mates Alien Romance

Broken Books
Kent, WA 98030

First published in the United States of America by Broken Books LLC, 2023
Second Edition 2023
Copyright © 2023 S.M. McCoy, Sky Robert
ISBN: 978-1-7322475-4-3
Cover Design by Taurus Colosseum
Proofreading by Green Proofreads, Jeff Bennett, and Volunteer Typokillers

Dedication:

There is something magical about exploring a world without the constraints of societal norms. To explore the what ifs about things some people are shamed for.

Enjoy what you enjoy without judgment. From vibrating peens to exhibitionism.

What would society be like if there was no shame about things that are simply biological? Who cares if you don't want to wear shirts, or pants anymore? What's wrong with being excited by the beauty of copulation?

Nothing.

Nothing is wrong with that.

Enjoy your monster alien porn.

Praise for the Trillume Universe

"Excellent book, good intro into this series. Well-paced, excellent descriptions and world building, realistic and fascinating characters. Very good balance between internal dialogues and action, also very hot sex scenes. Reminds me of Viola Grace and Loki Renard, two of my favorite authors. Waiting with bated breath for next books!" **5-star Review of Her Alien Exchange - Terri**

"Loved it!
Running from a bad relationship, Violet jumps into a situation that could be termed jumping from the frying pan to the fire. Luckily she meets Roe-el who is everything Violet wants in a man. Roe-el's people look at humans as mere pets, not a species they would mate with. Then he meets Violet and all his misconceptions are put to the test. These two are absolutely perfect for each other." **5-star Review of Her Alien Exchange - Jeanéva**

"Oh my goodness, I wasn't sure what to expect because this is my first time reading anything from Sky Robert. I was very pleasantly surprised by how vivid the characters are and by the detail of the world building. I'm so intrigued to see what is going to happen in the rest of the series." **5-star Review of Jewel of the Alien Bandit - Jenna**

"It's got fated mates, forbidden romance, action, political intrigue. The love story between Trent and Mabel is beautiful. Fighting for what you believe in and a coming of age story since Mabel doesn't know who her family is. I highly recommend this book if you read the first." **5-star Review of Her Alien Prince - Melissa**

"I have to say the more I read this, the more I love the story. One thing you do that I enjoy is you don't make the female heroine stupid. I see this often in other stories and I usually can't finish them due to frustration at the blatant silliness of the characters. Tis is not how you write your characters (thankfully). In fact each of the characters here act according to the personality you showed us throughout the story. Well done. I wish I could write as well as you do. Your imagination and storytelling is wonderful." **5-star review of Her Alien Prince – Tori**

Join Sky Robert

TABLE OF CONTENTS

Chapter One... 1
Chapter Two.. 16
Chapter Three.. 23
Chapter Four... 44
Chapter Five.. 58
Chapter Six.. 75
Chapter Seven... 83
Chapter Eight.. 96
Chapter Nine.. 105
Chapter Ten... 112
Chapter Eleven... 125
Chapter Twelve... 136
Chapter Thirteen.. 146
Chapter Fourteen... 156
Chapter Fifteen... 160
Chapter Sixteen.. 171
Chapter Seventeen... 183
Chapter Eighteen... 191
Chapter Nineteen... 197
Chapter Twenty.. 212
Chapter Twenty-One.. 227
Chapter Twenty-Two.. 234
Chapter Twenty-Three... 238
Chapter Twenty-Four... 244
Chapter Twenty-Five.. 253
Chapter Twenty-Six.. 266
Chapter Twenty-Seven... 278
Sneek Peek.. 281
About the Author.. 291

Chapter One

Mabel

Three loh jewels: one tiny jewel on my forehead and two larger ones on my shoulder blades. That's it. That's all I had to absorb the moon's radiation. Because of that I'd grown small and weak in the eyes of my peers. No male had looked at me with more than pleasant acknowledgement, since coming of age to participate in the mating ceremony.

They weren't mean, not overtly.

I was simply ignored, and it wasn't difficult to be distracted by more accomplished estrelds that glowed in the moon's light.

The mating ceremony had been open to off-worlders for twenty cycles now. I didn't even know who my father was. Nor did I really care to. I'm different from most multi-species because female offspring usually take more after estreld genetics, having just as many loh to absorb the moon's rays as their mothers. Me, well, I only have three.

Three loh… and a freckle on my temple that glowed sometimes.

It was a sign of health to have many loh and, since most female offspring took after their mothers... Well, it wouldn't be wise to choose someone like me with so few loh to help an offspring grow and be strong. With the only mother I knew gone, the craving to have a family of my own burned inside like a cyclone of sand that my skin could hardly contain. I was one of many to my mother. She ran the offspring training center, raising hundreds, thousands even, of young. My only chance to raise even one would be to lure an off-worlder during the mating ceremony this cycle.

This year was my chance. According to all of my research as part of the M.R., Mating Research, team there has been a great correlation between offspring and an estreld's twentieth renewal cycle. I'll be twenty cycles this mating season, one of the first offspring spawn from an off-worlder. There was bad data collection that first cycle. My estreld foster mother didn't even know what species my father was, and my birth mother… well, it was easy enough to disappear into the fabric of duties and never return to the training center again. She could be anyone.

Sometimes, I'd look into the faces of females as they passed, searching for similarities between them and myself. Paying close attention to whether they were taking pity on the girl that had few loh, or if there was something more. Guilt, perhaps? It was foolish, and over the years I cared less about finding either parent. There were many to get to know, and there were many who faded the same way my blood parents did. Estreld males took turns caring after me in hopes of becoming my foster mom's sired mate. She never chose any of them. And I learned not to get too attached to any of them.

"Mabel, I'm glad you're here," Elder Ezra said without looking up from her microscope scanner. "I have your results back from your egg samples. Every estreld is required to be examined before participating in the ceremony, as you know."

She was always very clinical in the way she spoke about the mating ceremony. The future of our species depended on her, and she relied on my data collection from other estrelds by interviewing them before, during, and after mating. That was my job. The more we knew about the intangibles, the more it could guide Ezra's research on the offspring decline.

I correlated the data, and provided statistical probabilities of the likelihood of factors contributing to successful offspring.

"Did you do the tests yourself?" I asked.

Pressing her lips together flat, never a good sign, she clicked off her tablet. Again, not a good sign, prying her away from her work was never easy. Ezra took a deep breath preparing herself, she had never been great with the communication bit of her job. That's why she relied on me to do the social interaction necessary for the job.

"I reran the tests several times myself after hoping there was a mistake with the synthesizer. I wanted to inform you personally before Almder summoned you, as all results are automatically uploaded for her this close to the ceremony. She likes to review them personally and verify electronic data with verbal acknowledgements to confirm their accuracy." She was rambling and relying on facts to help her get through what she needed to say. My heart pounded in my chest, waiting for her to reveal what needed her direct attention. This build up didn't do me any favors, but I couldn't blame

3

Ezra for that. "Mabel, you know as well as I do that we've yet to see any estreld establish offspring with no endometrium to attach to. There is simply no place for the eggs to secure themselves should they fall."

"What are you saying?" My voice quivered with fear for what I knew she would say but didn't want her to confirm. This would mean I failed my examination and would be disqualified from joining the mating ceremony.

"Mabel, if you meet a compatible mate... you would be risking your life. Dropping your eggs without a lining is dangerous. They could try to attach anywhere to seek purchase, and that anywhere could kill you and the unborn offspring. The safest thing for us to do would be to remove your sack from beneath your shoulder glands. You could still have some fun without risking your life," she explained.

I stared at her, stunned. I was twenty cycles... Perfect estreld age for offspring, for starting a family, and she wanted to remove my eggs. Gulping back my fear, I asked, "There's no way to wait until they drop and then safely transfer them to someone else? Or perhaps keep the eggs and test to find a compatible donor to incubate?"

Her eyes lowered and distracted themselves with a spot on the wall, not wishing to look at me directly. "So much technology," she said wistfully. "So much advancement, but I can't risk it. I can't risk you. Of course, there are tools out there," she motioned to the stars outside of Estreldez, "but we don't have an alliance with Trillume directly. We are on the outskirts of the galaxy. Everything we get outside of our planet is from Krelis, and we can't risk trade with Necias Delta Fal. They are outlaws from even their own kind. There's no telling when trill enforcers will return to bring order to this sector, or if we even want them to."

"What do you mean, 'if we even want them to'?" My eyes

were stinging as I held back my emotions about being told I was broken. That I wouldn't have a family of my own.

Ezra quieted when she leaned in to say, "Sometimes being left alone is better than the cost of being 'helped'."

But the trill could help me, I thought rebelliously. "Allow me some time to process this," I said, trying to sound stronger than I felt. I knew she would want to perform the surgery to remove my egg sack sooner, rather than risk meeting a compatible mate when all the off-worlders joined shortly. Their ships were already orbiting our largest moon, and they'd be landing once their examinations were verified. It was my job to interview the mating candidates, and Ezra wouldn't want me around any mates if I might be compatible.

"Please return before the ceremony begins," she directed, her usual monotone, business-as-usual voice back in place.

I left the labs and went to meet with the leader of Estreldez, Almder, to see if I could get her approval to continue being her advisor despite my new status as infertile. There was more at risk besides not being able to have my own offspring; my whole career was on the line. Not only was I half estreld and half unknown, I only had three loh and had now failed my mating exam. I would be cast to a new position outside the palace, because it would be seen as a bad omen to have a mating advisor to be infertile. Perhaps I could convince Almder that I could at least train my replacement for a time being.

When I arrived at the central alcove carved from black tarnpul deposits to focus the moon's rays, Almder was busy speaking with a tall male with blonde hair... and horns. A krelin... in such close proximity to our leader, and her guards so far away? Whatever concerns I had for myself vanished as I watched with curiosity and a bit of fear. Luan would be appalled to see such trust shown to the krelins after what

5

they pulled with our last import trade. I'd worked so hard to become an advisor to be of use to Luan when she took over as Almder one day. We were going to change Estreldez together. She'd risk going to the trill to help our planet, if need be. I knew she would.

"And the queen has agreed to this already?" Almder asked the krelin representative.

"Queen Kai seeks resolution to the tension between our trade agreements. It is reasonable to believe sharing biological ties between our species will bridge the gap we've found ourselves falling into of late. Krelin warriors are growing restless with our increased male population and are in need of females to calm their minds.

"As you well know, the hive shares a connection that all of Krelis feeds from. Many do not have the patience nor the desire to cull that connection when it overwhelms their sense of self. This has caused avarice to spread through the hive, infecting many warriors with a need to claim more than what is owed to them. Our export ships have taken advantage of their supply, and, without something for them to latch onto, they will continue to increase their efforts."

"Are you threatening Estreldez?" Almder thundered back, and I took a step back, feeling the increased tension in the room.

"Of course not. I am merely stating facts. I aim to prove the krelins are compatible mates with your females and promise you peace should you grant me the opportunity to prove the same to my species. To all of Krelis. Give me time with a strong leader of your clan. Should she reject me, I will respect her decision to do so." He bent down on a knee and bowed his head to Almder. It was very unlike a krelin to posture themselves in such a manner. To bow to someone other than their own queen was unheard of. It was almost like begging for them; their pride would never allow it, but there he was, kneeling at my Almder's feet.

"Very well," Almder conceded. "You've proven yourself to be reasonable for your species, and I agree with your queen that a union between our clans would solidify peace for many generations. I will allow you to join the ceremony, since you've passed all of our examinations. However, as you said, the final decision is not yours. It belongs to any female that is compatible with you. I will even grant you a single offering to spend some time with our strongest female this mating cycle, on the condition that you discuss other ways our clans may seek peace together once a union is formed."

"Agreed." The krelin male stood, and his back muscles flexed and bulged before straightening. He clicked his tongue, making noises that bounced within the stone carved dome. "You have company," he said without turning to see me there.

"One of my advisors," Almder explained my presence, and I flushed with embarrassment at not removing myself as soon as I saw she was already with someone. Something about the krelin made my feet plant where they were, and all I could do was stare. All I saw was the back of his head, but he was very handsome. I shouldn't have thought like that at all, considering what he was, but my skin heated as I watched his shoulder blades move, and I gasped as I noticed something reflective that shifted along the leather strap across his back. He wore armor coverings all over—except for keeping his back exposed—but as the moon's light moved across him, it was almost like there were iridescent bones twitching as he moved. How could no one else see this?

He had wings!

Only the most powerful of the krelin warriors had wings, the ones that led the armies of their fleets. Not a single delegate had ever come to Estreldez with wings before. He was escorted out of the alcove by one of Loric's best trained guards, Gaven. Whenever Loric went off-world, he always took Gaven with him. It was a relief to see they wouldn't give the krelin free range around the palace.

Golden eyes captured me as the krelin passed, and like one of the glilor reptiles near the waterholes they blinked with a second lid that watched me with curiosity. I sidestepped and plowed towards the Almder with purpose, not wanting to embarrass the Almder further, should the krelin think I didn't belong amongst dignitaries. Of course, he'd have been right. I shouldn't have been here while she was discussing diplomacy with Krelis, but I *was* an advisor, and I wouldn't shame the Almder by letting the krelin know I wasn't summoned.

It wouldn't be the first time I'd gone somewhere I wasn't supposed to. The trading post on the farthest moon, a favorite of my excursions, was where I acquired nectar from a krelin called the Chief. The thought was almost enough to distract me from what I was doing here to begin with.

"Almder," I addressed, bowing my head. Her crystal, silver eyes dulled as she shook her head at me. As soon as the doors closed behind Gaven and the krelin with a thud, I cringed.

"I understand why you are here." She sounded sad. "You've always been like a seventh daughter to me," she explained, and my heart sank even farther into my gut. Luan was her only living daughter. Five others did not survive gestation. To be her seventh daughter was a great honor, and the sadness in her tone broke me. All I've ever wanted was family. Luan and my Almder were all I had left.

"I didn't mean to interrupt—"

She stopped me from continuing with a lift of her hand, I

bowed my head once more to accept whatever punishment she saw fit for my intrusion. I took liberties with my role as advisor because of her affections. Being around her daughter since we were offspring, made me feel like I was family. A point that was often dismissed by others, but it was times like this one where the Almder looked at me with those caring silver eyes that I believed it to be true.

"Mabel, I received your exam report this morning." I flinched at the quick shift in the conversation. "This was going to be your first official ceremony as a participant, and not merely as a researcher for the M.R. team, and I recall how excited I once was as a fledgling into mating age. This must be extremely tough news to take, but I've already discussed things with Elder Ezra. Your life is priority, not that of life yet to form." Almder stood from her black, polished throne of tarnpul, carved with intricate murals of our history at her back.

Wearing flowing, black robes of the sheerest threads so as not to hinder her absorption of the moon's rays, Almder's every jewel shone and gave her an ethereal glow no other estreld but Luan, her own daughter, could match. She was mesmerizing to watch. So much so, I could forget why I was there, and why so much sadness tainted the brilliance of her eyes for me.

She bent her knees to be eye level with me, her delicate, long fingers leaned on her thighs. I was shorter than most females—a runt. It was unusual for the Almder to stoop for anyone, let alone someone like me, yet she still did it so gracefully and maintained a regality about her.

Almder continued, "It is the strongest of us that must bear the heartiest of burdens. It was not long after Luan that I was told the very same thing. I did not listen to my elders, and I suffered such great loss of sons and daughters I will not meet again until the end of my days. Their lives cut short before they even began.

"The souls of your offspring are out there in the stars. You need not suffer their loss, but embrace their new futures in their next life, as we all return to the moon's dust, and are born anew. Mabel, I will not make you relive this feeling with every mate you interview. Hearing of the futures you will now not be able to obtain yourself; it is a burden I will not add to one I care for so deeply. I will devise a suitable position after you've had time to process this new phase of your life."

Her arms wrapped around my shoulders, and she kissed the top of my head as she would her own daughter. A warmth from her radiation flooded from her loh and through my body, giving me all of her love and a great sense of comfort, though I knew it was temporary relief from the weight building in the carved out cavity that once held my heart.

My Almder, my second mother, was removing me from my position as advisor of the mating research team. I feared this would be a possibility, but I didn't think it would happen so soon. After the ceremony perhaps, as all of our resources were stretched to the limit with the largest off-worlder invite to date.

I was not only told I could not participate in the mating ceremony I had been eagerly anticipating this cycle, but I lost the very position I had worked so hard for, despite not having many loh and being deemed weak and small.

Where would I go? What would I do?

Would I be sent outside of the palace?

Would the only family I had left send me outside of the city in some misguided attempt to keep me from harm? I was stronger than that. I was good at my job.

No, I thought with anger brewing deep in my gut, I was more than good. I was her best research advisor when it came to finding correlations in the efficacy of successful matings. Since I joined the team, our spawn rates have been steadily increasing. Marginally, but my research was bringing more offspring into the world. I knew it was.

But what proof did I have? Many could simply dismiss the small increases to other changes in the program. What proof was there that it was because of my efforts directly?

"My Almder... I can still do my job," I insisted, and she pulled away.

"I wouldn't hear of it," she dismissed as if she were doing me a favor, and perhaps she thought she was doing me a kindness.

"Please..." I choked, feeling the pressure build up behind my eyes. Fresh tears threatened to shed themselves at her feet.

She smiled warmly, pity in her silver eyes. "Take some time to consider your options. We can discuss after the ceremony."

That was the best I was going to get for now. I bowed and backed away. A sob struggled free from my throat, and I didn't want her to hear me cry. She would only use it as more evidence she was doing what was right. I was processing more than one kind of loss, and I'd already pressed more than any other estreld would dare with the Almder once she'd made a decision. My short legs walked briskly back the way I'd come. By the time I reached the doors, I felt close to running. The guards slid the doors aside for me, and water sloshed from my unruly eyes. I wiped away at them vigorously before colliding with Luan.

I cleared my throat to calm myself. Luan's hands grabbed my shoulders, but I kept my head lowered to hide my flushed cheeks with the strands of black hair that had escaped from my tie.

"Mabel?" she asked, gaining my attention with her silver eyes wide. They were so much like her mother's that it broke me further before Almder summoned her inside.

Forcing a smile to my lips, I shook my head at Luan dismissing my behavior, and rushed down the hall to be alone. I could hear Almder's voice carry through the halls before the doors closed, "Mabel has been informed by the M.R. that she is no longer eligible..."

My throat choked up as I steadied myself against the wall. If only it were as simple as Almder's words. Joining the ceremony was my chance to build something all my own. But my heart broke into painful shards that split and cut their way down my icy veins from the knowledge that it wasn't just a family lost, but my very purpose on this planet. I'd been dismissed from my duties to help the clan in the only way I knew how. Would I even be an advisor after this ceremony? Was Almder telling Luan at this very moment that I would no longer be acting as mating research advisor? How would the optics look, having an advisor being infertile? Broken?

"Those tests." Loric's voice startled me, and I wiped at my eyes once more, hardening myself for a conversation I didn't want to deal with. He was the Pride of Estreldez, Almder's favorite advisor on security and off-worlder politics. Loric had a lot of sway with Almder, and I had no choice but to listen to what he had to say. Running away from Luan was one thing; she was distracted, and, even though she'd be the next Almder one day, she was my friend, and she'd understand my need for some time to process before talking with her.

"I can still do my job, Loric. It isn't a debilitating

diagnosis," I interrupted with a determination driving me to defend myself from being removed from the M.R. team.

His face softened. With a kindness he was known for throughout Estreldez, he nodded before replying, "I know how much you wanted a family. Luan spoke many times of solving the food shortage with Krelis being our main trade, so your offspring need only worry how to sneak out of the palace when she was watching them for you. You and Luan will always be family."

I sniffled, once more feeling my emotions overflow. It touched my heart to know Luan spoke of our futures together. I knew she relied on me to divert some of the attention away from her mating by spawning enough young for the both of us. She feared she'd be just like the Almder, like many of our clan, and have trouble conceiving. Stillbirths, miscarriages, and... infertility.

Almder would be even more insistent on Luan mating this cycle with my exam results on her mind.

"Perhaps, she'll have enough for the both of us," I replied lightly, forcing a smile that didn't quite reach my eyes.

"What I was going to say," he glanced over his shoulder to the window that looked over the palace gardens, "those tests aren't conclusive. The scientists can only work with the data they are given. Much is still incalculable. Elder Nen has spoken of how our loh are capable of healing great wounds when their essence is complete."

Covering my mouth, I chuckled through a hiccup. "Loric, I never knew you were such a romantic. It isn't often these days I hear an estreld speak of the fated mate bond, even in all the interviews I've had over the last few years."

He cleared his throat. "Yes, well, you scientist types tend to overlook the undefinable. Even Elder Ezra explains the fated mate bond in technical terms of pheromones and chemistry compatibility ratios, describing it as a reaction between two compositions."

"Well, isn't it?" I lifted a brow, already smirking at the welcomed distraction from my own issues.

Loric folded his firm arms over his exposed chest. His blue skin was covered in loh jewels, more than even our toughest warriors, a sign of his strength with the moon. Any female would be drooling to have his attention, but I'd grown up with him. His eyes were always on Luan. Whatever attraction I had for him when I was young was long since buried as I resolved that one day Luan would realize he'd always been there for her. The Pride and the Jewel of Estreldez were the perfect match. Both of them worked so hard to help the planet in their own ways.

"Our loh are more than simply biological compositions," he said impassioned. "They are our connection with the moon, with our own souls. You can explain away the warmth as radiation energy conversion, but you can't explain the fact that it feels different for every estreld. When the Almder shares her radiation with us, it isn't merely her energy, it is her essence, her soul, speaking to us. Wishing us well. Giving of her love for her clan. You cannot tell me it feels the same when the scientists share loh energy with you versus when Almder shares it, or even when Luan shares it?"

The way he said Luan's name towards the end, I could sense the way his mood shifted to a different kind of passion. Ever since Luan had led the ceremony the last two cycles, Loric has been even more eager to have her participate. His loh glowed even brighter, and he was certain to be fertile this cycle if she joined.

Being curious, I'd already snuck a peek in the M.R. lab to compare their files. They were a very close match. Nearly perfect.

I never told either of them; regardless, it was their decision to mate or not.

"You're right," I placated him, but it didn't change my results, "it does feel different. Any scientist will tell you that we can't prove anything. All we can say is our data has yet to be disproven."

"Mabel," he chided, knowing I was deflecting. He was just trying to give me hope, but even that would be gone the moment Elder Ezra removed my egg sack for my safety.

"Fine. Until new data disproves historical results, there is a lack of evidence that some fated mate out there could heal a lack of lining to help support viable spawning of offspring." There was more bite to my statement than I intended, but it was a bitter hope to cultivate, knowing Estreldez didn't have the technology to do anything but perform preventative measures for my health. Estreldez didn't...

"I can already see the glorbins swirling in your mind. You are not like Elder Ezra, simply taking data for fact. Perhaps you need only find that new data yourself," he encouraged, then left me with my thoughts to go join Luan in the Almder's alcove.

My eyes were puffy, but who was I trying to impress? I rushed to the transport control to meet with Hazel, the lead advisor of the shuttle and space traffic control. She knew everyone and could help me find some potential off-worlders to interview. Until Almder officially removed me from my position as an advisor on the M.R. team, I still had complete access to all mate candidates.

Chapter Two

Trent

My wings bristled behind me. They refracted light, camouflaged until necessary. I didn't know the exact science of how each wing had its own frequency that created some kind of temporal hole in the way our eyes perceived wavelengths, but I didn't need to. Many couldn't see them when they were folded back. It was uncomfortable to restrain the leathery weapons, but that's exactly what they were, and it didn't help political matters to display them unless my intention was to intimidate. Estreldez was running out of time with my queen. She was set on conquering this land for the quarry deposits of the rare Ordin Crystal, which the estrelds called Glorbin Flower. I had very little time to sway the hive of Krelis away from forceful takeover. My queen has been busy stirring up the warriors' interests in the many females of this planet as our own females dwindle in number.

A cunning maneuver, but I'd use it against my queen's interests. If my plans succeeded in swaying the leader of Estreldez, I could convince the hive that the females would be available for their mating needs without invading. I would claim a strong mate for myself and prove to all, bonds can be formed without taking things by force. In time, even what my queen seeks will be hers by other means. The Ordin deposits can be negotiated, and our own warriors will aid in the extraction.

Finding a strong mate on Estreldez was my last resort to preventing the hive from following my queen's plans to invade.

Even now, I could feel the buzz in my head of royal influence trying to dig around in my mind seeking out my motivations. Like the nits that eat the molt before we add it to the hewve lard to preserve it for transport. Swat at them, and they scatter. My queen never did like my preference for disconnection, independence. Most warriors welcomed the intrusion and the several pleasure glands that activated when the queen, in particular, gave attention.

I was anything but a sycophant, stroking the glands as the queen's tendrils of influence wormed through their minds. There were plenty of other ways to relieve myself; listening to her 'check in on me' wasn't it. Since the last potential queen of our hive died of the Molt Fever without gifting the hive with spawn, my queen has become increasingly desperate to appease the hive's needs. No matter the cost.

The one I needed was Luan, the Jewel of Estreldez and future Almder of the clan. With her at my side, I could sway the hive, and she could lead both of our planets to victory against the coming war. There wasn't much time; Necias

Delta Fal had already sensed the impending change in this sector of the universe, and many of their warships were approaching Estreldez, even as I knelt at the Almder's feet.

King Sylve had the same idea as our Queen Kai. Conquer Estreldez, gain control of the exports, and leverage against the trill. My queen had no intention of me finding a mate while here. Participation in the mating ritual was all a guise for me to acquire intel on how best to invade, but I had different plans.

My back bristled and I clucked my tongue to confirm the occupants of the room. I was a commander of the Krelis war fleet, first and foremost, and that feeling had never failed me in any battle I'd fought. The vibrations made it back to my horns' receptors, as I suspected, another had joined my meeting with the Almder.

I informed the leader of Estreldez, "You have company." It was preferable to distract her from our conversation as I had already received her permission to court her daughter, though not in so many words.

Whoever this newcomer was, they were not unwelcome. A softness filled the graying eyes of the Almder. My wings flexed as I rose to my feet from prostrating before the Almder in hopes she would trust that I wasn't as prideful as my queen. It was merely good politics to show my respect. Kneeling before her did not diminish my strength, nor my reputation among my warriors.

My second in command, Gho-ran, would agree, though he may not find it as easy to bear with a smile on his face. At no point in our time together had Gho-ran ever knelt at my feet, nor would I ever ask it of him. He was prideful, and popular with my warriors. Often, he was more dismissive of circumstances than I would like of a second, but he had never let me down either.

A hum lingered in my horns that I couldn't shake since I'd scanned the room. It wasn't all that unpleasant like a warmth that spread from my horns to my toes. It reminded me of when my mother was less concerned with the hive's wellbeing and still proud of her first born. It had been a while since I'd had the touch of a female and being in a room full of them had me susceptible to a kind of nostalgia I'd rather forget. It was as good a timing as any to be in need of that touch when courting Luan to be my mate. Perhaps, finding an estreld attractive would be easier than I had once thought.

I'd made the decision to seek Luan as my mate the moment I'd caught my Chief of Trade smuggling home-brewed nectar at the trading station on Estreldez's farthest moon, Bina. They had chatted like old friends, and I felt like I knew her. Having never seen her directly, it was an odd feeling to have. I was worried over the disruptions of trade and I didn't need to be. Smiling at that thought, of course the future Almder of Estreldez would already be crafty in her efforts to keep peace between our planets. Then and there, I knew she'd make a wonderful queen.

Turning to take my leave, I spotted the guest. She too stirred an excitement within me I hadn't known was possible outside of the hive. Stunning. Her eyes were as green as the mountain tops of Krelis, and so bright. A roguish tie couldn't keep her black tresses secured, strands fell across her face obscuring those green gems as she commanded the space to stride past me without another glance my direction. Were all the females of Estreldez so fierce? I smiled to myself, looking forward to meeting Luan at the mating ceremony tomorrow.

I caught the movement of my escort, a warrior called Gaven, as he glanced over his shoulder back at the female who'd passed. It could simply be part of his training to assess all surroundings—estrelds didn't have horns to sense this themselves—but I felt myself tense at the extra attention he was giving to this advisor. Who was she?

The doors closed behind us, and whatever I saw on his features was expertly masked with a stoney expression.

"We will introduce all eligible mates during tomorrow's ceremony. Until then, you may rest in your assigned quarters, or be escorted around the palace gardens," he said, clearly indicating that he would be with me at all times during my stay, aside from when I was guarded within my quarters. At least the estrelds weren't completely ignorant to my potential betrayal. I'd have been disappointed if they weren't a bit cautious with my proposed peace agreement.

"Wonderful, and will you be joining the ceremony as well?" I knew he wouldn't be. He would always be within striking distance of me, or someone he trusted to do so. Seeing how he reacted to conversation was important to help me know who I was dealing with. I needed to know whether there were things I could take advantage of, or if he would be a hindrance to my successful mating with their future leader. My mission wouldn't be well received by all of Estreldez, just as it wouldn't be easy to sway the mind of the hive without a powerful mate.

He said nothing. We kept walking as he guided me to what I assumed would be my living quarters for the time being.

So, he was that type. That could be a good thing, if he was more focused on his job and less on intervention. It also meant it was unlikely he would leave any openings in his duty to keep me observed during my stay.

Passing the gardens, I noticed that the windows throughout the hall gave an ample view of the collection of foliage and rock. The palace was a fascinating structure that appeared carved from tarnpul and a strange dusky white stone that must have been one of the few tough minerals they didn't eat on this planet. A moon stone of some kind the estrelds held in high regard, called pan. Such a strange term; there wasn't really a translation in Krelis.

The whole palace was a large, open air dome with the center garden connecting it all. Weather on this planet was humid, making my wings feel sticky and creating the urge to unfurl them to feel even the slightest wind. It would provide relief from the heat that reminded me of the hatcheries for our spawn... suffocating. Though that was to be expected by keeping on my armor while all the estreld, even the warrior at my side, wore a sheer fabric barely covering much at all.

Estrelds were like walking radiation packs. The windows were everywhere to not only let in the moon's rays but amplify them. Their bodies were capable of storing the radiation and utilizing it in blasts that could char the skin or even morph those pretty jewels into vicious weapons. I grinned. Yes, they were beautifully deceptive in their lack of clothing. It meant nothing of their defenselessness. Krelins were merely lucky that their radiation was harmless unless harnessed with a focused precision. Even their moons were armed with nanonets that could refocus the radiation at will and, with great accuracy, melt an invading warship. It wasn't flawless, though.

"While I'm here, I thought it prudent to take care of other matters before the ceremony. Would you care to escort me to the import station? There is supposed to be a final exchange planned before the rest of the off-worlders are granted access tomorrow. I'd like to overlook the process and make sure there are no incidents."

"We'll have to have it cleared with the head of transportation. The meet is on our farthest moon, Bina, as you already knew."

"Yes, it should keep us busy for the evening."

Gaven quirked a brow in curiosity. "You have no desire to snoop around the palace or sneak off to the quarries?" There was disbelief in his tone. He had expected some kind of subterfuge, which was what my queen wanted of me, but I fully intended to make sure the final trade exchange between our planets didn't screw up my plans to secure the future leader of Estreldez as my mate. I had suspicions of my own that my queen would have backup plans in place that didn't involve waiting to see what kind of intel would come her way.

"Should make your job easier," I said with humor.

He grunted, unconvinced. The warrior was right to be skeptical; I had no idea what we might be getting ourselves into by checking on this shipment. It could be nothing, or it could be an ambush that would take advantage of the stretched resources due to the mating ceremony and the influx of off-worlder ships surrounding the largest moon.

It was possible my future mate would be checking on the exchange, since my Chief of Trade had informed me of her increased visits to secure more nectar, and the last time she was absent... Ong decided that everything was solved with his crew and didn't oversee the trade directly. Mistakes were made that could jeopardize the peace we were both working towards.

I could say that my desire to make sure this exchange went smoothly was solely for peace, but a part of me knew that I hoped the future Queen of Krelis, my mate, would be there, and I could finally see her in person, instead of through Ong.

22

Chapter Three

Mabel

Hazel sent over the list of mate candidates to my implant, and I connected my tablet, downloading it so I could work through the mate's files without my access being revoked. As long as I didn't reconnect the tablet for any updates, I was safe to read the files without Elder Ezra getting in the way. This was more Luan's area of expertise, knowing about different planets and researching what kind of technology was available there. Each mate brought an offering from their planet when they signed up for the ceremony.

Strange trinkets, nope, not what I'm looking for.

I wrinkled my nose at some of the things these off-worlders considered food. It was important to include in their evaluations just in case we had a successful spawning of offspring with them.

Flipping through the mating candidates, it was always their image that popped up first. My finger stilled over the screen.

This was the krelin from before. Trent. I smiled, liking the way his name felt on my tongue. He was one of the few males that did not take the advice of the technician to remove his leather coverings for the image capture. It didn't matter much, the leather flaps formed to his torso nicely. The image rotated, and I stared at his back muscles, revealing a distortion that made me squint.

It wasn't important what he looked like, I told myself, but he wasn't someone to blink away from either. I shook my head to clear my thoughts and stared at his bio markers. How was a krelin's bio marker only half a percentage point removed from an estreld? Could they actually be more compatible with us than many of our prime mating candidates this season? Only the unGor showed a closer match from previous cycles, and their delegate was a no show to their exam.

My comm buzzed, and I tapped behind my ear to connect.

They didn't wait for me to answer before saying, "Mabel, my mate candidate will not be able to make their interview tomorrow before the ceremony. I'll need you to do their evaluation on the shuttle to Bina. You'll return before dinner. See you at the transport deck."

I sputtered to reply, but he ended the transmission, not even giving me the chance to say whether I could make it or not. Typical. Gaven was always so abrupt, but the fact that he, of all estrelds, didn't know I was no longer an active advisor for the M.R. team spoke volumes about how busy everyone was, preparing for the ceremony. I had an uneasy feeling settling in my gut.

When I arrived at the transport terminal Hazel's projection appeared at the gate. "Oh good, it's you," she said with relief.

"It's me...?" I agreed in confusion.

"I thought Gaven was sending some dry spawn out there with him. We're spread thin on security, and I don't trust the krelins after what they pulled at the last exchange. You've been trained to handle yourself if something should happen, and Gaven could use the backup." She sighed and tossed her light pink braid back over her shoulder as she cleared me to board the shuttle.

I wasn't completely sure what was going on. Apparently there were krelins involved, and Gaven needed assistance with more than just an evaluation of a mate candidate. It was just then that the information clicked, and I gasped. What was Gaven doing, going off-planet to one of the moons? The last time I saw him, he was escorting the krelin delegate.

Suddenly, I was nervous and delayed entering the shuttle, holding my tablet tight to my chest. I hadn't had much use for my warrior training outside of practicing in the arena from time to time, and knowing that Hazel was relieved someone with training would be boarding the shuttle set my hairs on end.

I knew enough about krelins from my interactions with them at the trading post on Bina to know I didn't want to fuck with them. The spores in their musk could knock an estreld out before they ever got a chance to defend themselves. There were stingers in their forearms that could spring from their skin so fast that it could pierce through armor. The mightiest of warriors had wings with talons on the ends, and horns on their heads that could impale their enemies.

Every time I ever went to Bina, the chief was always there

to greet me. My nectar was always brought personally. Though I always kept my face covered, the old krelin would always insist I sit with him and share a sample of the nectar to ensure I was satisfied with the trade. It was a krelin custom, and he always brought small bowls for us to sip from. There was a fondness between us over the many visits.

The Chief of Krelis Trade wouldn't harm me, but that said nothing about what krelins who didn't know me would do.

Throat dry, I gulped my saliva, feeling no relief. What was Gaven thinking asking me to join him like this? With an intake of breath, I entered the shuttle. Unsure if the Chief Ong would be at the exchange today to ease my worry. The krelin delegate sat with a direct view of the entrance. His golden eyes seemed to penetrate straight through my core, and I had to force myself to take the next step.

Many estrelds would shame me for thinking it, but he was more handsome than his holo-picture. Even all the males I had ever interviewed, including Loric, the Pride of Estreldez, didn't compare in my mind. The hardened edges of his jaw, the decorated blond braids along his scalp that highlighted the black horns on his head, and even the way his eyes seemed to glow with a fierceness I wish I felt within myself. He was eye catching, and I'd been so focused on avoiding his attention at Almder's alcove that I hadn't given him a second glance. If I had, then I would have made a fool of myself for not being able to take my eyes off him.

"Will you be conducting your interview from the boarding deck?" the krelin teased. Heat flared up to my cheeks, but I kept my expression unamused. This was business. I would ask my questions and then leave.

"If that would make you feel more comfortable," I replied smoothly. If staying in the loading deck of the shuttle meant this would be over before we departed then that would have been preferable, though I kept that to myself. I wasn't normally the "bite back" type, but something about him put me on edge. And I refused to think this had anything to do with how attractive I found a krelin upon further inspection.

Gaven didn't say anything, and neither did the krelin, as I sat down. The silence made me feel even more awkward about my initial reaction to seeing the krelin delegate.

"The pre-interview is to gauge correlations between the data from your exam and your mental state before and after the ceremony. There are no wrong answers, nor is anything you say during this interview going to be used against your participation. Please be as honest as possible," I prefaced as I normally would. "We'll start with what drew you towards participating in the ceremony?"

He lifted a brow, as if that should be obvious without his input, but he answered anyway, "I plan to acquire a mate to merge our species in peace."

I smiled politely and nodded. "Yes, that's one reason. I'm more interested in the draw beneath political interests. Unless," I paused to consider that perhaps that was all it was to him, "there is no attraction, physical or otherwise? It's fine if that's the case. Again, there are no wrong answers." My eyes wandered over his sculpted cuirass that molded perfectly to his toned pectorals. A thunder thrummed in my chest, and his lips quirked in a grin when he noticed how I assessed his own attractive features.

The krelin leaned forward. Those golden eyes did a similar scan of my own attributes, and I heated at the attention. "There is a certain appeal to the way an estreld's skin glows when they are interested in satiating their needs. I like how the mating process of your species is just as much for pleasure as it is for the function of spawning. I admit, I was concerned an estreld would be too small to take a krelin cock, but the files indicate your body stretches to accommodate like a freshly formed chrysalis. I find this is something I'd like to feel for myself with my mate." His legs opened as he ran a thumb along the top of his pants, bringing my eyes lower to the bulge below the leather flap. He smirked, and if I wasn't so used to the off-worlder's different anatomy, I might have been shocked to see that his cock was left vulnerable on the outside of his body. An estreld male sheathed his organs, including his cock.

"Right," I cleared my throat, feeling the tips of my ears burn. Clenching my thighs together in my seat, I adjusted, thinking about how big a krelis cock must be when it was fully masted if he was concerned that an averaged-sized estreld would not be large enough to accommodate him. I was a runt of estrelds. Many females were taller than me by a foot or more.

Gaven interrupted, "She won't be participating in the ceremony. The size of your cock is irrelevant. You can drop the theatrics." I blinked, regaining my composure. I wasn't sure why Gaven felt the need to interrupt the interview. It wasn't the first time I'd had an off-worlder flirt with me. The whole reason they were here had to do with mating, and it was natural for mates to have their hormones be overactive when approaching the ceremony.

"Is this true?" the krelin asked.

I nodded. It wasn't either of their business, but Gaven must have known I was ineligible already. "The ceremony is reserved for mates capable of spawning. And as Krelis is currently in a similar situation of needing more alpha females for the hive, you can save your flirtations for the ceremony tomorrow."

Spasms in my stomach revolted at the admission that I

28

couldn't have offspring, and I internally cringed at telling him not to flirt with me. I was still capable of sex, and the thought that no male would flirt with me again was a very real prospect. Where off-worlders had made me uncomfortable with their interest in previous interviews, I liked how the krelin was looking at me before he knew I couldn't spawn.

Pity calmed his libido, and he straightened up in his seat. "Without a new queen in our hive, many warriors continue to be infertile." A seriousness took over his statement. His replies were all business now. "Krelins require the musk of a fertile queen to trigger our mating hormones. My queen hasn't blessed many mates in her recent cycles. I'm one of the few male warriors with active glands, though that doesn't do much good without a fertile mate. Forgive me for projecting on you."

"The whole galaxy has suffered since the asteroid showers came through. Estreldez closed its borders, and—"

"Krelis waged war on the shol," he finished my thought for me, a sharpness to his tone that made me think he was not a supporter of the war that had nearly destroyed an entire species, completely decimating a planet. The tentative agreements between Estreldez and Krelis were out of necessity, due to the proximity of our planets. No other planet had the consistency of trade that Krelis could provide for food imports.

"Some would argue that Krelis intends to wage the same war with Estreldez rather than trading for what they want," Gaven added casually, saying what was on most estrelds' minds, including Luan's, but that most wouldn't dare say out loud. He wasn't really one to speak much, but when he did...

"Gaven," I admonished.

He shrugged.

"It's okay," the krelin dismissed. "He isn't wrong."

"He isn't..." I gaped at him. Was he saying Krelis intended war with Estreldez, or that his planet deserved the distrust based on past events? The hard set of his golden eyes was difficult to read.

"My queen is fully capable of changing her strategy between peace and war to protect the hive." I stared at him in shock. This was not the kind of interview I had expected, and we'd veered completely off topic into a dangerous political conversation that I was not trained for. Diplomacy was not the focus with these interviews, and I didn't want to be scolded by Almder or Loric for overstepping my bounds after I was clearly dismissed from my duties in the first place. This could be disastrous. "I assure you, I have every intention of making this mating agreement successful. Merging our species is my top priority."

"You are very transparent with your intentions... that is—"

"Unnerving," he completed for me.

"Refreshing," I corrected him. "I'd rather you tell me if you were going to stab me instead of being surprised when you do."

He quirked a brow. "There would be no surprise, should I impale you." I couldn't help the direction of my thoughts going right back to the large cock between his legs, detecting a dark undertone that had nothing to do with the horns protruding from his forehead. My throat went dry once more as I thought about being filled so completely I screamed, having nothing to do with fear, but pleasure. An ache built up behind my shoulder blades where my loh throbbed.

Fuck, was I about to drop my eggs for a krelin? Elder Ezra would murder me herself for putting myself in this situation. It was much too risky to find him attractive, but there was a reason why I agreed to interview a krelin. Before the decline of their alpha females, the krelin's fertilized eggs were dropped from their bodies and incubated outside of the females in their hive's spawn hatchery. They might have the key to how I could save my own eggs. Perhaps the same methods could be utilized for estreld females with no lining capable of bringing a spawn to term.

Now is as good a time as any, I thought, trying to distract myself from the lust building inside of me. "Could you describe how krelin females bring spawn to term? It's important that we know, just in case you produce any offspring this cycle. We need to be able to assist their growth."

"All of this data should be with your scientists already. From when I submitted my physical exam." He caught me in my curiosity, but decided to humor me by answering, regardless. "Copulation is a lengthy process." He watched me with an interest that had my cheeks coloring. I'd watched the mating ceremony many times, and there were couples that took all night to copulate. So, I wondered how much time krelins believed to be lengthy. "But once fertilization occurs, the eggs are harvested, then stored in kantos sacks within our hive's nursery. It takes the queen's germination to bless the eggs in whatever order she chooses, and the growth begins. We are hoping that with an estreld pairing, the final germination will not be necessary to begin the growth cycle."

I couldn't rely on him to know the details of how the whole larva sacks were prepared for the hive's nursery, but I was intrigued and needed to find out more. "And Krelis would be providing larva sacks for future generations, should they be needed?"

"Kantos sacks," he corrected. "That is something the mated pair build together," he said with a show of his canines. "Perhaps you'd like a demonstration in private?"

31

"She isn't interested," Gaven snapped.

"It's fine." I lifted a hand to calm Gaven. I'd never seen him so worked up before. He was usually so collected and aloof. "Really. So, you're saying this larva," I stopped myself to use his terminology, "kantos sack can be created even if I'm not a krelin?" Finding out more about the larva sacks was all I cared about, but the way his tone darkened made me think it was part of the copulation process of the krelins, making my skin heat. Perhaps, it was the males who produced this incubation sack for the fertilized eggs?

I'd spent plenty of time asking questions about krelins before, but it was hardly appropriate to talk about procreation details with the Chief of Krelis Trade when I was negotiating for nectar imports.

His smile broadened, and he leaned forward to whisper in my ear, "Why are you so interested in something your scientists should already know? This has nothing to do with your questionnaire, does it." That last one wasn't really a question, it was an accusation. "I'll tell you what you want to know little estreld, if you help me secure my mate."

I blustered. "I, well, I have no control over whether a compatible mate chooses to be with you or not."

"Ah, but that isn't the point, is it?" He leaned back and stared out the window of the shuttle into the vast darkness with bored disinterest. "You have a personal reason for wishing to know more about my species that, for some reason, you can't ask one of your scientists to answer for you."

Gaven growled. "Enough. This conversation is over. Whatever he has to say about his opinions and 'feelings' before the ceremony won't help the M.R. team's data collection. We're almost to Bina, anyway."

What was up with Gaven? I'd never seen him like this

before.

"You're right," I admitted out loud. Both men stared at me, waiting for what I was going to say next.

Was I agreeing with Trent, or with Gaven?

My future family depended on me to be strong, to not let pride get in the way of what could be. So I continued, "My questions have nothing to do with protocols. I should have been asking you things like what your previous experiences have been when you've copulated, if you'd like me to reserve private space for the ceremony should a mate choose you, and if there are any particular needs you might have to assist with copulation. Most of our data comes from post questionnaires, rather than the pre-screening. I want to know about your kantos sacks because I think they could help estrelds who can't carry offspring to term themselves. Because of previous tensions with your species, it's never been considered and probably won't be until the Almder is certain your peace negotiations are truthful."

"But that doesn't help you, does it?" Trent added gently, an understanding in those yellow eyes as his second lid relubricated horizontally like the glorbin flighters that frequented the food mines. They were reptilian fliers that darted around, snatching jewels and eating them. Harmless, but sometimes annoying. I found myself associating Trent with the glorbins because I didn't like the pity I saw in his eyes, and I grew increasingly irritated.

My arms folded over my chest in defense, but I pushed past that feeling to respond. "No, it doesn't help me."

"You don't have to tell him your personal business," Gaven defended. Even his tone was softer. He knew. Somehow, he knew exactly why that didn't help me, even before I'd boarded this shuttle. His green skin darkened around his loh, showing he was ready to do more than defend me verbally, if need be. The large jewels along his arms would lengthen into sharp weapons that were strong enough to both protect and harm. His back loh would remain dormant unless triggered by a compatible mate. Trent ignored him, his full attention stuck on me, waiting.

"What is it that you want?" I asked the krelin point blank. "I have no control over whether a mate selects you," I added in haste, just in case he thought I had any sway on those kinds of things. But, no matter what, I wanted at least one larva, kantos, sack given to me in the negotiations. Elder Ezra may not approve, but she would help me try to implant one of my own eggs... I knew she would, right? Maybe... I'd test her interest before I told her I had one. If I could get one. She was a scientist. It would be hard for her to resist trying it out at least once, I thought logically.

And if Trent, a diplomat for Krelis, couldn't get one for me, then I could always try to convince Ong, the Chief of Trade, to barter for one.

"Mabel." Gaven said my name in a low growl of warning. Trent had to know that if he asked for too much, Gaven wouldn't keep it a secret. Whatever was said would be used against him. Against, Krelis, I thought sadly.

Keeping Trent's gaze, I gave him the same intense focus he gave me. What would he say?

"You want a kantos for yourself," he surmised correctly. "I need a queen for my hive." I gaped at him and he shook his head as if I were misunderstanding him. "I'm not propositioning you to carry such a burden. I need one of your strongest females to be my mate, but I knew coming into this that my goal was political peace, not attraction, nor even friendship, or otherwise."

It was the or otherwise that stirred something inside me. The state beyond friendship... love. Was he looking for love?

I stilled waiting for him to state clearly what he wanted from me. Could I give him that if it were asked of me? My heart fluttered. No off-worlder ever choose to stay with an estreld mate, would he be different?

"Then what are you asking of me?"

"You," he said simply.

"I don't understand," I stammered. Gaven stood from his seat, loh glowing a light yellow-green as they extended out. One loh pointed directly at Trent's unmoving neck. He merely blinked at the threat, dismissing it while replying to me. The gentle curve of his throat bobbed, a hair's breadth from being cut by the loh. Trent was fearless, unconcerned with Gaven's response, and I found myself growing both flustered and intrigued by this dangerously handsome krelin.

"It is exactly as I stated. You wish to have a kantos sack, and I enjoy the idea of making one with you. I cannot make one alone, and it's unlikely that one created with another female would be an appropriate home for your offspring, should you have any."

"Just like that, you'd give me a," I hesitated and used what he called it instead, "kantos sack as long as I assisted you with it, and you don't want anything in return?" It was too good to believe when krelins were known for extorting us when we needed something from them. Well, most krelins. Chief Ong was the exception, he was a sweet old krelin.

"Mabel, he is asking you to mate with him," Gaven gritted with venom. "I should slit your throat for daring to offer yourself without her approval first."

"Ah, yes," Trent mused. "You have a custom of having your males wait to be offered a token of interest from your females before discussing such things. I apologize if I've offended you, Mabel." I liked the way my name played on his tongue, and he let the sound resonate before continuing as if he too were contemplating how it rolled from his lips. "But is it not an offer of interest to ask for me to make you a kantos?"

I cleared my throat. "I haven't read your species full file. I'm unsure of the implications..." My cheeks heated, feeling I had a pretty good idea of what he meant.

"I have no misconceptions about my estreld mate being attracted to me, nor whether our union would be anything more than a political treaty to prove peace is possible," he stated plainly, with no emotional attachment to whether he'd actually form a bond with the woman he intended to make his mate. "But, I do not wish to be scorned my whole life. It is obvious you are attracted to me, and I find you delightfully forward in your appeal. You have no obligations to me. I merely ask that if we both enjoy our pairing, you would stay by my side."

"As what? Like your concubine?" I balked.

Trent pushed Gaven's loh aside with a stinger that protruded from the top of his wrist. "No." He kneeled at my feet as I sat. The black horns on his forehead were intimidating, but he scooped my hands into his own, the stinger now retracted. His thumb rubbed little soothing circles on my skin that made my insides flutter.

Wings spread out from his back, hiding us from Gaven like a shield. I stared at them in awe; they were beautiful. Black, iridescent leather stretched behind him, refracting the light of the shuttle around him, making it appear like he was glowing. He continued with a whisper that I hoped Gaven wouldn't overhear, "I know of the rumors of Krelis harems; they are wrong. I have never made a kantos with any other female. A male chooses one female to do this with. I'm unsure if I made one with you that it would be possible to make one with any other. We could grow in affection for each other. You would not be my concubine..." His words trailed off, but

36

I knew what he didn't want to finish saying.

"I wouldn't be your mate either," I clipped coolly, removing my hands from his. I knew what I got out of the deal: a chance at a family if the larva sacks, kantos as he called them, worked. But what did he get out of it except for some kind of one-night stand? Sure, he asked for me to remain at his side, but why? He still fully planned on courting someone stronger than me to be his mate and unite our species. He wanted someone like Luan.

I was used to being compared to her. She was beautiful, smart, kind, and her strength with the moons was matched only by the Almder.

He didn't have to confirm what I said. His silence was enough.

"And what of the one you choose to court during the mating ceremony? Will you not need the kantos for your actual mate?"

He shook his head and stood. The magnificent wings behind him flapped and folded back behind him, disappearing but for a glimmer if the light hit just right. That's what I saw last time, in the Almder's alcove. The distortion before was the camouflage of his wings. Why would he want to hide something so exquisite?

"You confound me." Trent paced the small aisle of the shuttle. "Our research has shown that estrelds mate and then discard their spawn donors once they've achieved offspring. None of your mates are allowed to stay on Estreldez, and you give me this look of pure disgust when I mention wishing to have something more for myself. My estreld mate will discard me once I've mated with her, but our spawn will give hope of peace to both of our planets. I do not wish to mate and then be done. No female would dare seek comfort in my bed once I've produced spawn with another. You seek something from me. I will give it to you as it so happens to align with something I seek as well. I want a second mate, one that will stay by my side."

"That's not how mates work!" My voice rose an octave. Now I was standing from my seat and glaring at him. He couldn't just purchase me with a larva sack offering. And he completely misunderstood Estreldez. We didn't discard mates. Every mate was offered the chance to stay, they simply didn't wish to. They gave their donation and that was that. The mates brought to our planet have their fun and never return! They are all given standing authorization to return to Estreldez if they've produced offspring.

They still leave. They still do not come back!

This was not on Estreldez, and he would not put blame on us. I fumed. Even my ears felt hot.

Gaven was at my side now, his hand enclosed over my fisted one. "We will find another way, Mabel," he whispered from beside me.

My attention went to Gaven, and I watched him curiously. Was he saying what I thought he was saying? He'd said we, and his chest was puffed out in a strange fashion that spoke more of determination than protection against the krelin pacing the shuttle.

"Gaven...?"

Now, it was Trent who interceded, "Seems my services are not required. It is unlikely I'll have need of making a kantos for any mate, so my offer stands, should this other way not work out for you both."

Wait what? That didn't make any sense. You both? Gaven and me? His offer stands? "But you'll have a mate..."

"One that does not require a kantos to spawn," he added, and I felt dumb for not thinking about that. Of course, any other estreld in the mating ceremony would not need a larva sack to attempt to carry their offspring to term. It was just me then. I wasn't giving up on the option just yet, but the terms had to change.

"We aren't mates," I pointed out. "I don't know you. You don't know me. I won't commit to being at your side simply because you create a *kantos* sack for me. And even if, for some reason, I grew to like you, I would not accept being a second mate. You can't just... You can't just, well—" I got flustered with the way he was watching me with those golden eyes of his. "You just can't." I didn't know what he couldn't do any more than he probably did.

I'd lost focus. What did I actually want from him? I mean, in one sentence, I basically said I don't want to be mates, I only wanted his larva sack. And in the next, I was saying I didn't want to be his number two choice. What was wrong with me?

"Can't be attracted to you?" Trent's voice shook as he took a step forward, and I bumped back into Gaven's torso. "Can't want to know more about you?" Another step. There was some kind of clucking sound coming from his throat that sent shivers down between my legs. "Can't want to find who my planet wants as my mate to seek peace, while also seeking someone I want as a mate for me?" He was toe to toe with me, and Gaven growled, yet he did nothing to stop him from approaching. I wouldn't have expected him to; he knew I was fully capable of defending myself if I wanted to. If I wanted to, I repeated to myself. Did I not want him to stop? He finished with, "Can't want someone that the rest of her clan has deemed unsuitable for mating?"

I flushed. It was like he'd stabbed me in the heart with the truth. Was that why I didn't want him to get to know me? Why I immediately thought it was impossible for him to want more than to take advantage of my desire to have my own family? Normally calm under pressure, I cracked. My single loh on my forehead glowed green like my eyes, and the ones at my back ached. Without thought I reached up and grabbed hold of his right horn and yanked it to the side, forcing him to bend towards me and stare into my steely gaze.

I would not be told how *unsuitable* I was for mating.

"I will have my family, with or without your help, krelin," I hissed in his ear. "Do not presume what I am suitable for. My value isn't in whether I mate with anyone, least of all you." Shoving his head away with a flick of his horn, I pushed past him and slammed my hand on the scanner to open the door between the main shuttle and the private quarters of what was normally for the crew. This shuttle was unmanned, vacant, as it was only doing a simple transport between moons with only Gaven, Trent, and myself aboard.

When the door slid closed behind me, I locked it.

What did I just do? He was a diplomat for the krelins, we were already on strained terms with Krelis, and here I was, placing hands on him? I'd assaulted him...

Rubbing my face, I groaned. I wasn't a politician, and I'd probably screwed things up for Luan and the Almder's plans for some kind of peace. Fuck. Fuckity, fuck, fuck me.

The beep sounded at the door, informing me that one of them had attempted to come in after me. Probably Gaven. But I had locked the door. Gaven could override it, but he'd have to contact Hazel. The crew cabin was meant to have the ability to lock itself off from the passengers of the shuttle.

Slumping in one of the chairs, I folded my arms over my chest protectively. What was I going to do? I wanted Trent's kantos sack to see if that would help me carry an estreld offspring to term, but I also didn't like how I was put in this position. I would be forced to have my eggs removed, regardless of my decisions right now. It was for my safety, I knew that, but was Trent right? I wouldn't have my job as advisor anymore, I wouldn't be eligible for the mating ceremony anymore, and I wouldn't be able to have my own family if I didn't figure out my situation. Was my value solely in my ability to bring new life into the world?

Sure, I've always wanted a family, wanted offspring, but now that I might not be able to... Would I not be worthy of a mate?

I was going about things the same way all estrelds did. I would secure my family first, then worry about finding someone to share it with later. But that was normal for estrelds with offspring. They'd spawn with someone during the mating ceremony, they'd secure a mate who would like to be sired to them, they would send the offspring to the training center, or raise the offspring themselves. What about those that didn't spawn? They tried again next cycle...

My face fell into despair. I'd never once interviewed an estreld that was removed from consideration for the mating ceremony. Stories were not told of the estrelds that didn't spawn or couldn't try again. We focused on what worked, not what didn't. But, none of the elders could spawn. They were revered, honored, and contributed to the clan in significant ways. Elder Ezra was dedicated to the research of mating and reproduction; she didn't have any offspring. Letting out a sigh, I decided, I was obviously overreacting. I was not unsuitable to mate with just because I wouldn't be participating in the ceremony.

The beeping at the door repeated in a pattern like someone was playing with the lock by continually trying to open it. If I had paid more attention, I wondered if they were using some kind of code speak. I didn't bother waiting.

Annoyed, I released the lock and opened the door to say, "What?" I had expected Gaven to be at the door, trying to make sure I was okay. But it was Trent's imposing form standing there as it slid open. "Oh, it's you," I said with disappointment. I padded back to my seat and stared out the window into the palpable darkness of space.

He sat next to me in silence.

"Where's Gaven?" I asked with indifference.

"Asleep."

I snapped my head around to stare at him. He had to be joking. "Sleeping?"

"He would have tried stopping me from entering. It's good you opened the door, I would have disliked damaging it." Trent did not appear to be joking. He stated things in such a matter-of-fact manner, and his face did not fluctuate from the seriousness I saw.

"I guess engineering thanks you for not making their job more difficult?" I wasn't really sure what to say to that. The only thing on my mind was, why? I should have been afraid, maybe concerned, for Gaven in the other room, but I didn't feel like he was going to harm me. Being around him changed the air I breathed, and it took effort to stay upset with him.

He chuckled at what he thought was a joke, instead of my sarcasm. "I wanted to apologize."

"Apologize?"

"You have a habit of repeating what I've said. Yes. Apologize, for upsetting you. I will admit your reaction does not lend itself to preventing me from upsetting you in the future. I rather liked the feel of your grip on my kan, and would not be opposed, should you seek to do so again."

He spoke so formally, like a diplomat, I supposed. Even when he spoke of things like wanting me to yank on his kan. Color spread to my cheeks and heated the tips of my ears at knowing he'd enjoyed what I had recently considered assault.

Moments ago, I had been worrying about how my actions would affect future peace negotiations with Krelis. He had said I gripped his kan?

"Your horn?"

"Krelins call them kan. In our tongue, it means to feel or sense. That is their purpose, and your touch has confirmed things for me." He leaned in.

"What kinds of things?" I scooted back in my seat, though that didn't really separate us much. His hot breath on my skin gave me goosebumps.

"That glow thing you did with your loh, can you do it again?"

I cringed. That was not something I could do on command. His lips were hovering so close to my face, and his scent was in the air, a musk like that from the forest after a rain, fresh and alluring. My mouth opened as if in invitation, and I ruined it by saying, "No, I've never been able to do that before. I'm not even sure if I could do it again without being provoked."

"Is it a defensive mechanism of estrelds?" He spoke softly, and his hand reached up to trace the edge of my chin, almost as if he were trying to see if he could force it out of me in that moment. Just a little more teasing, and just a little more fear, but I wasn't afraid of him. My heart rate picked up, and my breathing quickened. My eyes widened at the realization that I wanted him in a way I'd never wanted anyone before. I guess I'd always knew in theory how I was supposed to have the family I always wanted to make, but this need growing between my... I'd never felt that, and I certainly hadn't thought I would feel it with a krelin.

I licked my lips and shook my head, speechless.

Chapter Four

Trent

From the time I saw her after my meeting with the Almder of Estreldez to having her appear on the transport shuttle, she was mesmerizing. From the deepest green emeralds of her eyes to the darkest of tarnpul hair, pulled back atop her head. She wore more clothing than most estrelds I'd seen. Her robes were made of a thicker material you couldn't see through, even if the moon's light was shining directly upon it. Why did I wish to see beneath her many layers? I found her more alluring than the females with their gauzy, light robes that left nothing to the imagination.

Krelins loved the humidity of Estreldez. The heat was nothing for us, but I understood why many of the estrelds wore very little fabric. Their bodies took in the atmosphere differently than a krelin. Yet, Mabel could wear such thick robes with not a single sign of perspiration like a hardened krelin warrior with no wind to soothe her skin?

She made me curious from the moment the Almder chose not to admonish her for interrupting a meeting with a delegate from another planet. Then to see that every inch of her was covered excepting her shoulders. Curiouser, I mused, but I couldn't shake her from my thoughts. Sitting across from me, questioning me about my mating habits, I swore to myself that my interest was nothing more than curiosity. Until she spoke of kantos sacks.

Was that all it took for me to let my mind wander?

I imagined my mouth plunging between her legs as she grabbed onto my kan. Her small hands stroking up and down the sensitive conductors, sending vibrations down to my core, stirring my cock to life. My cock hardened at the mere thought of making her moan as I plunged my fingers into her tight sheath, preparing it for what would be a strain on her if I were to enter her heat at full mast. With my imagination already thickening my cock, I didn't know whether an estreld her size would even be able to fit my girth. Grinning, I knew there was plenty else I could do that didn't involve my cock at all. She was such a small thing, even for her species.

My throat dried in anticipation of drinking her juices as her pleasure erupted from what my tongue would do to her clit. I've been told estrelds had them located beneath their pleasure centers and that they vibrated to stimulate their mate's release of their gland's secretions.

This tiny estreld did not understand what she was asking of me when she requested to create a kantos, which estrelds called larva. I could tell from the way her face stayed serious and lacked much in the way of seductive interest, she didn't know as much about krelins as she thought. That didn't stop me from imagining her giving me what I needed to create one for her. Would she still agree to have me make her one if she knew it would involve tasting the nectar between her thighs as I brought her pleasure?

She sought to have spawn, not to have a mate. That was the way of the estrelds, I reminded myself. My cock was already becoming attentive, preparing to fill her once I'd finished devouring her essence.

I had always wanted someone to share a kantos with, perhaps more than one, eventually. But if I wanted to seek peace with this planet I needed to mate with the Almder's daughter, Luan. Estrelds didn't need kantos sacks. I would contribute nothing but my secretion to my political engagement, but I had hoped for more. Knowing I mated with the future leader of this planet would solidify my hold over the fleet, and prevent my mother from waging war. If nothing else, my mother would not be able to sway the warriors under my control.

My mother... If it weren't for her, would I try to convince this slight estreld to be my queen? I blinked, clearing my vision with my second eyelids. What was it about her that was so fierce and attractive? Her own clan thought her unworthy to participate in the mating ceremony, and I'd said as much.

That was my mistake, but also possibly the only reason why she sought to touch me. Her grip was strong as she yanked my kan down to tug me at her eye level. I assessed her stance; it was grounded, and her knee was positioned to lift should it need to. Her other hand was ready to deflect me if I moved.

She was trained.

A thrum pulsed down my kan into my core as the electricity of her touch heated every nerve, even into my

46

fingertips. I suppressed a moan so as not to frighten her away. I liked the way her touch felt, and I wished to know what she sought from me. Would she demand I make a kantos for her this instant? I would gladly do so. The musk from my wings could have easily subdued her, but it wasn't every day that someone challenged me, and I didn't want it to end so quickly.

"My value isn't in whether I mate with anyone, least of all you," she hissed.

I couldn't help the grin forming on my lips because she all but confessed that there was nothing between her and my escort, Gaven. There was concern with the way he was possessively stalking her, and, as she pushed me aside, my grin broadened even more at the dejected expression on Gaven's face. He composed himself when he noticed I was observing him.

Politics aside, I wanted this Mabel to be my mate, though she was right earlier: I could not publicly claim her. For all outside observers, I had to mate with the princess of this planet, the Jewel of Estreldez. Because I was the Prince of Krelis, and it was expected of me if I sought peace against my mother's wishes. But she was wrong that she would be second to Luan.

Krelin males only have one mate.

Luan was the reason why I was even here to seek her as a mate. I had no intentions of being swayed by another alluring estreld, but there was something about her that drew me in. It was necessary to have a queen that sought for peace between our planets, a queen that would go the extra effort to do things others would find beneath them. Luan was that queen. She'd proved it to me over the last cycle winning over my Chief of Trade, and influencing the continued peace during exchanges on their small moon, Bina.

I suspected that the last misstep had everything to do with my mother's interference, Luan's absence at the exchange, and Ong's new-found comfort of thinking everything was solved. I couldn't dismiss the efforts Luan had made for our planets, and I would honor my original plan to make her my queen in name, for the sake of peace.

The reason why there were rumors of a Krelis harem were because our females did not keep a mate at all, but male warriors once bonded, only mated with one. If I made a kantos sack with Mabel, she would be my queen, whether or not the galaxy knew of it or not.

I'd released my wings before my escort began to speak. With a few flaps, I'd sent my musk spores for him to inhale. If he were attracted to me, that would have been an awkward situation, but his reaction to Mabel assured me that it was unlikely my spores would react with him in that manner.

Other than species with acute chemoreceptors, like the shol, who chuff and blow out the spores once smelled, my escort would not notice the spores until they were absorbed. There were only two reactions to the spores, either he had compatible chemistry that would make him want to mate with me... or, which I'd correctly suspected was more likely, he would fall asleep until the spores were attacked by his immune system.

Gaven's head lulled and snapped up straight as he slowly succumbed to the heavy sensation of sleep. He slapped his face to wake himself, but it would do no good. He would sleep. I wafted another spritz of spores his way for good measure.

"You seem tired," I said with mock concern while I approached to guide him down to one of the seats. There was no need to have him be uncomfortable when he passed out.

He mumbled, "Fucking krelin." I guessed he knew about

a warrior's musk, yet he'd made no attempt to protect himself from this possibility with a breathing apparatus. In his defense, there really wasn't anywhere I could go without his authorization that wouldn't be quickly secured. Perhaps he would have worn a mask if I'd stayed in the palace? I shrugged. It was better that he hadn't prepared well, this way was much more gentle than if I'd had to knock him out with force.

And I would have.

I wasn't going anywhere, but one thing was certain. When Mabel's loh glowed, I felt a warmth that triggered my mating instincts. It shouldn't have been possible with an estreld, or any species outside of a krelin queen.

For just a moment, I thought I heard her voice in my head, *"Why do I want you?"* I must have imagined it, but what if it were real? I had to know.

Only the hive queen, only a mate, could enter my mind with my mental blocks up, and I'd long since learned how to sense the intrusion before it gained a hold. It shouldn't be possible. It should have been impossible. And with an estreld, no less.

Trying to open the door between the main shuttle bay, and the crew quarters, all I received was an annoying beep that signaled my rejection. She had locked the door. Frustrated, I paced the shuttle bay once more. Gaven's eyes were rolled back, but his lids didn't close, making him look like he was staring at me with amusement that Mabel had sequestered herself away from me, rather than be in my presence. I had scared her away with my rash words; I knew that. Gaven's eyes still stared at me with a smugness.

"You mock me, even in sleep," I growled at him, closing his eyelids with my palm.

I wasn't good at this sort of thing. Any female in my hive

would have gladly mated with me, but my queen never pushed for me to pick any of them. For that, I was thankful, but in truth, I was afraid my queen would attempt to bless my union and her enzymes would not encourage my mate's fertility. I would have one shot at mating. If it failed, my mate would move on, and I would have nothing. Even the warriors I commanded would lose faith in my ability to bring prosperity to Krelis.

Mating outside of Krelis was different. Since an estreld had no need of a larva sack, there would be no need to solidify our union in that manner. But this estreld wanted to use krelin mating rituals to assist her own spawn. And on top of that, she may have spoken to me through a hive's bond... through a mate bond. Did the goddess of Lenkal see fit to gift me with a kansa mate?

I had to know if she could do it again, if she could speak to me once more.

Pressing my hand to the scanner once more, I heard the beep. Still locked. Lifting my hand, I replaced it several times on the scanner, creating a chiming effect that I hoped Mabel would hear on the other side of the door. The last time I replaced my hand, the door slid open to her pronounce snap, "What?"

When her green eyes met mine, she stilled, her pupils dilated with her approval at what she saw before she shook her head and turned back around with an irritated tone that seemed forced, "Oh, it's you."

I smiled, despite myself. The glands in my wings ached, wishing to spray her with my musk, but I held back. I didn't want her to agree to be my mate by force. If she truly was my kansa, then it was only a matter of time. I wanted more than simply a mate that was compatible with my biology. I wanted a mate that got to know who I was and chose to be with me anyways. Folding my wings back, their iridescent fibers reflected the light and camouflaged once more. I did not wish to scare her.

After apologizing, she seemed curious about my kan, scooting closer to me. I liked how she smelled, such a sweet and tangy scent that I could almost taste on my tongue. When I clucked against the roof of my mouth, my kan vibrated, and I closed my eyes, feeling the sensation of warmth pool in my gut enjoying her proximity. I leaned in closer, her words resonating, "What kind of things?"

I wished to feel her inside of my mind once more, hear her thoughts. "That glow thing you did with your loh. Can you do it again?"

Her mouth gaped open just slightly, like a delicious invitation I sought to dip my tongue into with a swipe, luring it to devour me. Most estreld females were a light coloring, but her skin was tan with just a hint of green, like she was meant to stand out from the rest. Males were flamboyant in so many jewel-toned colors, while the females' only coloring was around their loh. It was all part of their mating rituals to attract one another

I didn't have the lure of vibrant colors to seduce her. On Krelis, the size of our kan and the display of our wings would interest a mate enough to bring them within range to inhale our musk. Proximity was considered consent on Krelis, and we'd soothe a mate until we consumed enough of their juices to create a kantos sack to deposit our fertilized eggs into. It was a lengthy process that new mates were given a leave of Lenkal, two weeks of mating in the hive's underground oasis within the Kai Mountain Range. I didn't have two weeks of seclusion to convince Mabel to be my mate, nor would I be given authorization to take her with me to Kai Mountain's oasis.

I needed her to open her mind to the bond, if I wasn't imagining things.

"No, I've never been able to do that before. I'm not even sure if I could do it again without being provoked," she said with a pant. Her breathing was labored as I leaned in closer, taking in the intoxicating smell of her that had my cock swelling with need. The only word I heard her say was that she needed to be provoked to activate her loh. If that was how I could trigger the mate bond, then so be it.

"Is it a defensive mechanism of estrelds?" I asked, while my wings ached to flex behind me. Everything in me wanted to display myself to her, show her what I had to offer, but I needed more. I didn't just want her to want my body. I wanted her to want me. All of me. I needed her mind connected with mine. Mating would be so much easier if she could feel what I felt and get to know my essence in an instant of true mate bonding. If I was right, activating her loh would give us that connection.

She licked her lips, and all sense of restraint snapped. Mabel gasped as my nose rubbed up the side of her own, then over the top and down the other side, brushing our lips as I passed. The buzz of my wings hummed behind me as they tried to lift me from the seat, but I held on to the handles on the chair and the wall behind her head, where she'd pressed herself. My eyes closed as our lips hovered so close that her breath was my own, and then her hand grabbed my kan once more, pushing our mouths together. Such relief. Heat gathered within my kan, pulsing down into my chest.

Our lips worked against each other in a frenzied passion, as her other arm wrapped around my neck, pulling her closer. Her other hand still gripped my kan, rubbing up and down, driving me mad with sensations that had me roughly gathering her up into my arms and grunting as I pressed her against the window.

Yes, I thought, needing to taste more of her. My hands sought to move her robes to the side, thankful that though the fabric was thicker than what many of her peers wore, it was still designed the same way. Long, flowing skirts with high slits and plenty of access points to seek out their mating entrance. With little effort, my hand found its way to where she throbbed for me, and slick liquid greeted my fingers as I explored her folds. This was so different than my species, having it already be dripping with fluids that should be in my mouth, delighting my tongue and readying my gland production. My throat ached to taste it. I plunged a finger into her tight entrance, feeling her walls squeeze around me, begging to be filled.

Fuck, my cock's knotting kan were pulsing just from thinking about being inside of her. I removed my finger slowly, then pushed it back in to feel how she molded to me with perfect synchronization. Her whimpers of pleasure quickly turned to hungry need as she nipped at my lip and sought more pressure with our kiss. Happily, I complied. Her hips ground into my hand as my pinky rubbed against a hardened bundle of nerves at the base of her folds that vibrated with my touch.

Withdrawing my fingers, I brought them up to my mouth and released our kiss to have her watch me suck off the viscous juices before they dried on my skin from the circulated air. Closing my eyes, I moaned as her taste activated the glands at the back of my throat. As I swallowed her essence, she pulled on my kan to bring me back to her mouth. My cock hardened further.

Mabel's body clamped over mine, her leg lifting over my hip before I returned my fingers to feel more of her. The gap was closed and her skirts were pushed aside as her pussy soaked my pants. My glands ached at the loss of her juice, wasted on the leather barrier between us, but the sensation of her rubbing against my thick cock was something I didn't want her to stop.

She moaned, releasing her hold on my kan as she wrapped her arms around my neck instead. The thrum of her touch on my kan was gone, but, strangely, that warmth still gathered through my limbs and settled deep in my loins. My cock throbbed, and the more she rubbed herself against me the more the pressure built up inside.

"If you keep going, you're going to make me come," I warned her.

She moaned, "Don't stop."

A fire ignited in me, and I grabbed her ass to help her gain more pressure against my cock and heighten her stimulation. I adjusted my hold and slipped one hand under her to press my finger at her sheath from behind. Rubbing my middle finger in time with her own thrusts, I finally sank it into her flesh as she screamed her release.

"*Mine,*" I'd heard her in my mind. As the walls of her insides clamped around my finger, I imagined my own cock buried deep within. I pulsed, shooting a stream of my essence that warmed my skin as it dripped down my shaft. My knotting scales were locked, and quivering.

"Fuck," I moaned before kissing her fiercely once more. "*You can have me, Kansa,*" I thought through the bond.

This wasn't what I meant to do when I sought her out, but I'd heard her. I knew I heard her through the bond; she called me hers. She was claiming me, and yet, after I replied, there was nothing. The loh on her forehead were not glowing anymore, and her leg slowly retracted itself from my hip as she slid away from me, adjusting her skirts.

She flushed a gorgeous green hue in her cheeks as she

glanced away, not being able to look me in the eye. My stomach recoiled at the sight of her retreating within herself.

I did not want this, I thought. I wanted acceptance, not shame. Feeling the way her arms loosened around my neck, I released her, allowing her back on her feet. There was a chill on my skin from her absence. Was my mind messing with me? Did I imagine her in my mind, simply because I wished for it? A hollowness filled my chest where once there was warmth.

This was a trick, I thought. I was so sure she was my kansa, and was willing to create a kantos with her, despite the importance of needing to have a treaty with Estreldez. My excretions became sticky within my leather greaves, and it mimicked my discomfort both outside and inside the situation I'd put myself in.

What did I expect from an estreld? They weren't all that dissimilar from the female warriors of my hive. They would not stay with a mate unless they continued to be of use to them.

I had to refocus my efforts and make sure peace was secured for Krelis and Estreldez. The only way to do that was to replace my mother with a new queen. She was set on taking control of Estreldez the direct way... by force. Straining against my own instincts to spray Mabel with my musk, I backed away. Yet my hand remained on her waist, bringing her with me. A sudden guilt filled me, knowing that I had come to Estreldez for the mate who had won over my Chief of Trade, and had been drinking my own home-brewed nectar in preparation of my offer to be my queen.

An awkward smile lifted the corner of Mabel's mouth as she faked a chuckle. I cleared my throat, and removed my hand quickly, realizing she did not wish to have my touch any longer. I had served my purpose. The only thing I had left that I knew she wanted from me would not be accomplished easily, and I refused to make a kantos sack with someone that did not want more from me. More than this.

Luan had already proven our compatibility by accepting my nectar in trade for months now, and yet I couldn't stop myself from giving Mabel another chance to accept the sacred bond of being chosen by the Goddess Lenkal.

"Should you change your mind about my conditions, I will give you more than a sample of what I have to *trade*." A snarl escaped at the word trade. I hadn't meant to reveal my distaste for any transaction regarding what I could share with her, but if that was what it took to have her give me the time necessary to show her what it meant to be a kansa mate, I'd accept it.

Kansa mates were rare and given a chance to share that bond was worth swallowing my pride. Worth pretending Luan was my mate for the sake of both our planets. A selfless krelin would dismiss this bond, and fully commit to the queen that would free my planet. But I wanted more.

"How generous of you," she snarled back. It was obvious by her tone that she was being sarcastic. My jaw ticked as I gave her a strained smile.

I was saved from having to find a way to divert her attention away from the growing tension thickening the air when the shuttle entered the moon's atmosphere. Mabel lost her footing and stumbled forward, grabbing onto my armored vest for purchase. My wings created a gust behind us to counteract the jolt, and I then strapped her in the chair for landing, trying my best to avoid unnecessary touch.

This was for the best, I thought bitterly. I had become distracted from the one female that cared enough about krelins to get to know them, and support peace. Perhaps

Luan was on Bina this very moment assisting Ong with a smooth exchange.

"Where are you going?" Her voice squeaked and I could almost pretend she actually cared for my company.

"To secure my escort. He isn't strapped into his chair." Turning away, I dismissed myself from her presence to go make sure Gaven didn't get tossed around as we acclimated to the new gravity of the moon.

It was foolish to believe a kansa mate existed, and that a krelin born from someone like my mother should be considered blessed enough to have one. Time was better focused on what I came here for. I had to let go of the attraction I felt for this estreld female. I had thought I felt that same attraction to Luan before I even met her face-to-face and that's what I needed to go back to. Luan was kind to my Chief of Trade, she drank the nectar of my own making, and she would be the queen Krelis needed to survive what was coming.

Chapter Five

Mabel

Churning, buzzing, my whole body was on fire from where Trent had touched me. My clit still throbbed and vibrated like it was begging me to grab those deft fingers and return them to their previous workings. Fuck, I was so screwed.

I knew by the burn in my shoulders that I had dropped my eggs for him, meaning the only thing I could take from him were those deft fingers. Anything else would be too risky. Without a guarantee that he would create a kantos sack for me, I couldn't go anywhere near the hardened length I'd rubbed against for release. I flushed thinking about how large he was beneath his pants, and there was a flutter of movement that wasn't his fingers as I came on his hand and on the front of his pants. I blanched knowing that Gaven would see the evidence of what I'd done. He would report me to Almder in a heartbeat.

Was this it for me? I'd never convince Almder to let me keep my position as an M.R. advisor if this was how I behaved. It would be too dangerous, and it spoke of my lack of control around potential compatible mates. The shuttle rumbling from bouncing off the moon's atmosphere distracted me from my spinning thoughts. Trent had yet to return to the crew cabin, and I could hear the whirr of the airlocks decompressing as we docked at the station.

The moon was empty aside from the space station orbiting around it for trade transports. It was basically a large port to connect ships and facilitate loading and unloading of goods without ever having anyone unauthorized be granted access to Estreldez directly. It mitigated the risks of trading with species such as the krelin, who have been known to be aggressive in their negotiations and have been responsible for hostile invasions in the past.

Krelins have taken over planets, I reminded myself, and I was humping one of them like a rabid hergslat that hadn't eaten in weeks.

What was wrong with me?

Unbuckling myself from the seat, I got up only to stop at the door that was left open to the main transport of the shuttle. I rolled to my back, pressed against the wall when I saw another krelin at the airlock talking with Trent. Peeking around, I could see Gaven still passed out and strapped into his seat. The soft rise and fall of his chest assured me he was indeed sleeping, and nothing more serious.

The krelin bowed and slammed down on one knee, brown and tan wings fluttered behind the man dressed in warrior leathers before Trent's black wings flashed open blocking my view.

"Our queen had doubts about your commitments, but I

can see she had nothing to worry about," the man said with disbelief.

"You had your own doubts as well," Trent surmised from his tone.

"Every female warrior is being gathered to try to find a suitable queen for the hive. Forgive me for doubting you. We need to be strong for when King Sylve tries to claim this planet. Necias Delta Fal warships have been spotted in the sector, and we need to be ready."

"What have you done so far?" Trent was dismissive of the information and pivoted with a bored interest in whatever the warrior had to tell him. How was he not more concerned about outlaw warships coming our way? And what did the krelin mean about their commitments? What was a krelin doing greeting our shuttle and not one of the estrelds assigned to this station? An uneasy twist of my stomach was replacing any remaining sexual desires I had for Trent with a heavy anxiety.

But I did nothing. I listened with curiosity.

"The station has been secured, Commander. You were correct about all their resourcing being diverted to the mating ceremony. It's an honor to have you come to assure our success."

"I'm here to make sure your team doesn't screw up my plans for securing Estreldez through a mate contract."

"Commander?"

"You were there when I told my queen about needing time, were you not?"

There was a silence that I assumed meant the warrior was nodding instead of replying verbally.

"Then you are aware that what you are doing right now is counterproductive to my plans to secure the planet and open up the mating ceremony to our warriors."

"But there is no proof that—"

He was cut off by Trent, "I am the proof."

"Did you find a queen among the estrelds?" his voice was hushed, and awestruck.

"I've found that the radiation of the estreld's loh act similarly with our genetic mating markers as the queen's blessing. A mating contract with their future Almder will secure our spawnrates for many generations to come."

While Trent's wings were extended, and blocking the other krelin's view, I quietly padded around the doorway. Crouching behind a seat, I slowly peeked back to make sure I could still make my way to Gaven. I wasn't completely sure what was going on, but it didn't feel right.

"Mabel," Trent called over his shoulder, blowing my cover. Fuck. Well, there went my plan for being sneaky. I was sure I was being quiet. "This is Commander Li-aq," he introduced, and I could see as I popped my head up that Trent's wing was no longer hiding me.

"Who do we have here?" Commander Li-aq clucked his tongue and with a nod of greeting he asked, "Show me estreld, can you bestow one of your blessings on me?" The way he approached was predatory, and his question was more challenge than interest, like he didn't believe an estreld's loh could do what Trent implied. He could be telling the truth, but I'm not the one to prove or disprove this theory.

I haven't once released the light of the moon from my loh... until today. With only three loh to begin with, I even wore specialized gloves with amplifiers made to look like loh to help my body absorb more of the moon's radiation. Every specialist on estreld had said it was highly unlikely I would be able to release radiation due to my body needing all the radiation a few loh would grant me. There shouldn't have been any radiation to spare. Yet, when Trent kissed me. My thoughts wondered, and my lips tingled at the very recent memory.

"Don't be foolish," Trent chided. "You have your pick of the hive to mate with, and if you are to activate your glands, you'd be risking an end to your current exploits."

"Perhaps," the krelin agreed, though reluctantly it seemed. "So, you've mated with one then?" He quickly changed the subject on to Trent's business.

"My glands are active, but the estrelds have strange mating practices that I must adhere to before completing the Kloaph."

"So, you haven't taken the one that activated you? By our customs, it is your right to take her to the oasis to complete the claim. Display your prowess, and worthiness while you insure your seed fertilizes her eggs." He shrugged as if that information wasn't horrifying. "Even if she doesn't choose you, at least you know her future spawn will be yours."

My mouth hung open. Trent stood beside me and tapped my chin with a gentle finger to close it. "We aren't our ancestors, Li-aq, we do not steal our mates and trick them into continuing our genetics regardless of their interest. I have found my mate, but I will follow her customs, and make sure she is to stay by my side before I fill her so completely there is no other cock she'd wish for."

My skin buzzed at his words, ears burning as if he directed those intentions towards me, instead of Luan. I knew he intended to have an advantageous mate that would assist a peace treaty, and it certainly wasn't someone like me, but I couldn't help but imagine my folds stretching around him as he made sure not even his name was coherent in my thoughts, just the sensations of the deepest part of my heat being struck with his hard... my thoughts were interrupted.

"That is not the way of females," Li-aq chortled. I glared,

both irritated that he was so set in his opinions and because he reminded me such thoughts of Trent were making my folds slick with anticipation for something I couldn't have.

"You are not the choice of females," I clarified, disgusted with Li-aq's implications of both how he planned on mating with someone in the future, and his lack of respect for anyone that wasn't him. Who did he think he was, speaking of all females this way? I was sure there were some in any culture that were just as he described, but that didn't speak for the whole gender, across all species, including estrelds or krelins. That would be the same as me saying all men were chauvinist like he was choosing to be.

The smug smile of his snapped into one that made me think he'd charge me with his horns as his wings spread out in warning. "Hold your tongue estreld runt," he growled.

Widening my stance, liquid slipped down my thigh from my previous thoughts of Trent's cock finishing what we had started before, but I was prepared to fight Li-aq if I had to. I was more than ready to change gears and distract myself from a union that would never be mine. If anything, my frustration only amplified my irritation towards Commander Li-aq. My fists flexed at ready, and I gritted my teeth. I may not have been as large as the krelins, but I could certainly grab hold of the smaller joints of his wings and yank with all that I had. Concern about whether Trent would stop me didn't even cross my mind.

"Isn't your time better spent elsewhere?" Trent admonished. I was going to snap at him too, before I noticed his attention wasn't on me at all. Li-aq cracked his neck back and forth, calming himself while staring at Trent. Was he defending me? Or was he simply being the delegate he was, and directing us both towards more important things... like what the hell this krelin was doing without an estreld escort during a trade exchange?

Goosebumps traveled down my spine and into my toes.

"I'll resume the trade," Li-aq agreed, and pinpointed his gaze at me before turning to leave.

"Where is your escort?" I challenged. Something didn't add up.

He smiled ruefully. "Same as the escort on this ship, slumbering."

I couldn't keep my mouth shut. "You'll start a war..." If they were extorting us for more goods than what was agreed upon... this could be disastrous. The krelins had promised that was behind us, and Almder was willing to agree to a mating treaty. All of that would collapse if Li-aq was causing trouble. Where was Chief Ong?

"He will behave himself," Trent said more in warning towards Li-aq than actually addressing my worry.

Commander Li-aq squared off to stare Trent down. He was less reverent than when the conversation began, replaced with suspicion. "If you should succeed in your mating ploy, then I will happily hand over my command. Until then, know that if you fail, I will not hesitate to issue Rakin against you." His eyes darted to me, and I had no idea what kind of threat he was issuing. "No one wants a war. We only seek to have a thriving hive, as any estreld would seek for their clan. And time is running out for political negotiations for both our planets."

"I didn't take you for suicidal," Trent prodded, the only response was Li-aq's scoff before he exited. A hand squeezed my fist, that I hadn't noticed I was still clenching. "He will try to kill me before he attempts to undermine the treaty between our planets."

"He can't do this!" I wasn't a politician, but I had to get off this moon station and back to Estreldez immediately to warn the Almder. I tapped my comm to link up to the shuttle. Hazel would take control and secure the moon's transports at least. No one was leaving this trade satellite without her permission. Trent grabbed my shoulders to get my attention.

"You have no reason to trust me, but I promise you once I have Luan's commitment to Krelis, the hive will fall in line. The queen's influence is weakening, and I risk everything in telling you this. A krelin queen guides our warriors, calms their spirits, ignites their mating glands, blesses our spawn growth, and without a queen... we will die."

I stared at him for several minutes. Their whole species was dying, and he was pleading with me to not say anything to Hazel... to not say anything to my Almder. Could mating with estrelds really save their hive? Desperation for survival would make any species do unbelievable things, including invade. It was more important than ever that Almder knew about this, if she didn't already. Why was I even considering this? A tug within my chest ached watching the intensity of Trent's golden eyes, and that he needed an estreld that had control over their loh... like Luan.

"She won't agree to mate with you," I admitted, knowing how Luan felt about krelins.

"She doesn't have to," he said while straightening to his full height. Trent was like a large wall that I wanted to climb, but he didn't want me, he wanted Luan. "I need only prove to my hive that she is capable of doing the things we rely on our queen for. That a union between krelin and estreld will save both of our species. Krelins could freely mate without being reliant on the queen's blessing. This isn't simply about me. It's about the futures of generations to come."

He was right, this wasn't about either of us. And the way he said it so earnestly made me feel like a selfish hergslat to even think about my own needs versus those of my clan.

"So, what you're saying is you just want her to pick you for the ceremony?" That wouldn't prove anything, I thought. Sure, it could prove there was attraction, but I could prove that right now... if I wanted to. How would he prove anything before the rest of his hive decided to ignore him and invade Estreldez? The proof would be offspring, but the gleam in Commander Li-aq's eyes told me he wouldn't wait long enough for that, and Luan didn't deserve to be used as a vessel for offspring, she was more than that.

"I need her to become my mate," he said plainly. I shook my head, unconsciously portraying my doubt of this plan of his. "But, she need not follow through with her commitment," he amended and still it made no sense to me.

"How long did you think on this plan of yours?" There were logical conclusions he wasn't accounting for. She needs to mate with him, but not? It didn't make any sense. And the way my stomach flipped between flutters of hope and aching spasms of irritation didn't help the matter.

He groaned, but he was the one frustrating me. I needed more reason to not contact Almder right away than simply Luan would be his mate, and all would be well. My cheeks heated in aggravation towards the one friend that's always been kind to me. I'd never really been jealous of Luan before, she had a lot of responsibilities on her shoulders, but the steadfastness of how certain Trent wanted her as his mate was maddening.

"She just needs to come to Krelis and use her loh on my hive, standing beside me as her mate in name only, and then she may leave. The evidence would be clear enough when the hive is capable of spawning without the queen's assistance. They would stop following her mindlessly, and—"

"And they would follow you?" I saw where this was heading now, and all the pity I had for the krelins evaporated.

"I wouldn't put it that way, but—"

"This is all so that you can become the leader of your planet... and how am I supposed to trust that you'd be any better than the queen, or Commander Li-aq for that matter?" It wasn't my place to decide any of those things for Estreldez, or for Krelis. I had to talk with Almder.

His brows narrowed. "I am not my mother!" he roared, and I could hear Gaven stirring awake behind us.

His mother? My eyes widened. Trent was more than some delegate... I've listened to Loric's advisor briefings with Almder on Krelis. If the queen was his mother, there only one krelin that actually spawned from the queen's larva sacks. The Commander of the largest fleet of Krelis warships, and the one they called the Queen's Revenge because of his poisonous blood.

Stunned, I sat down in the closest seat and stared out the window.

Trent's tone was softer when he sat beside me. "I shouldn't have yelled."

I said nothing.

A heavy sigh expelled from him before he added, "I've been used by the queen my whole life. Warriors do not become more than an extension of her whims and desires. I cannot speak for my entire hive, but the queen's influence is strong, and the hostility between our species is as much of a manipulation as the peace I'm trying to secure. But like all things, consistency will form a new pattern for us to follow, whether it is me or your future Almder as leader of Krelis."

I couldn't believe what I was hearing. Was he saying he'd allow Luan to be the new "queen" and be Almder for both planets? He would step aside?

"This is not a play for 'power', Mabel, this is a stride

towards peace and 'survival'. And I am at the mercy of your decision to allow me the chance to prove it."

Proof... that word again. I shook my head in disbelief. There was no "proof" of intentions but his actions, and if I allowed him that chance that was also allowing for the chance to prove otherwise, and there was so much as stake. An entire planet. No, two planets, two species...

Yet, I had already made my decision when I sat down. I felt it in my bones.

I acquiesced, "Luan would make a wonderful queen." She was dedicated, understanding, and even with her distaste for krelins she would be fair. I dared to think that she'd even grow to love the krelins as much as estrelds with her big heart, if they proved to be as decent as Trent appeared to be.

It was possible I was making the one decision that damned my whole planet, but I trusted him. I didn't know why... but I did. Tapping my implant was all I needed to do for Trent's shoulders to relax, his reflection seen in the window to the vast darkness of space with only a few distant twinkles and the cusp of the largest moon seen at the frame. I had disconnected my comm from the shuttle, and the flight plan was already set to bring me back to the planet after dropping off Gaven and Trent. They wouldn't be exiting, but there was nothing I needed to do but wait.

Gaven made grunts occasionally, but didn't fully wake yet, the only noise on the shuttle until the compression valves sounded, and the whirring of engines engaged to bring us back to Estreldez. After the initial thrusters, the shuttle conserved energy to simply utilize inertia to get us the rest of the way, there was no need to hurry the transport unless I informed Hazel what was going on. An eerie silence unnerved me, making me question my decision.

Before I could think on it further, Trent spoke, "When you

68

are not interrogating prospective mates, what is it that you do?"

"I do data analysis, trying to find any correlations between subjects' answers and spawn rates. Then I take those theories and hone in my questionnaires, as well as propose different tests to disprove those theories."

He chuckled and I watched as he adjusted forward to lean on his knees from the window reflection. His wings shimmered from the light above us before he folded them behind, disappearing with their camouflaged iridescence. I was fixated on him, but thankfully he shouldn't know that since it was only his darkened mirrored self that I had to focus on to see amongst the viscous black thickness of space that at any other time would have been enough of a distraction to get lost in. "I shouldn't have assumed you might enjoy doing something for yourself in your off time."

"What is that supposed to mean?" I bristled. My job was very important and of course I did things other than work... sometimes. I hung out with Luan... though she's been distracted lately with researching different solutions to the food shortages. According to our last conversation about it, she was desperate enough to arrange a meeting with our most dangerous mining camps to see how we can increase Glorbin Flower extraction to feed people. It wasn't an especially tasty source of nutrition, and there was an abundance of it that would solve food shortages, but it wasn't safe to harvest.

"I like to make nectar when I am home," he maneuvered around my question, and I was too flummoxed by his candid conversation to keep being irritated. Imagining him brewing krell nectar was calming. A large warrior taking the time to hand measure his ingredients, delicately stirring the mulch over a fire, and ladling out the syrup brought a smile to my face. I buried my mouth into my elbow to hide my enjoyment of such a thought. There were automated facilities for krell nectar, but the process was a painstakingly delicate process that took patience and care when making it at home. I even thought for a moment, perhaps he was bad at making nectar and just enjoyed the process like a meditation.

My guard lowered, I turned to face him. "I keep a secret stash of nectar in my quarters. Different brews, but I always have to wait a long time for one with my favorite flavor."

"They all taste fairly similar, don't they?" he joked. Krell nectar wasn't popular on Estreldez. I always had to bribe one of the advisors on trade duty to negotiate for some of the more rare kinds, before I met Chief Ong. Krelis included a few batches with every trade as part of their customs, and Almder never really negotiated for more. What was brought was what we got.

"You have got to be kidding," I balked in jest, but a bit of seriousness as well, "Sure they all 'taste' the same, but each brew has a different kind of afterflavor on your tongue depending on what was used in the brew." That was because the main ingredient in nectar was so strong that it overpowered all other flavors that might have happened, so most brews don't even try to do much different, but each facility did something different that caused a different aftertaste that I noticed right away.

"Not many know this. So, then what is this afterflavor you like best?"

"It tastes sweet, like candy but with a heated kick. I like the headiness of it, but I have no idea what it is, because I haven't really tasted anything else like it, and off brand nectar doesn't label its ingredients."

"Ah, so you've been importing some of the home brews that circulate then?"

70

"I guess I have." The momentary distraction from what was happening was welcomed but didn't last long. Home. It simply reminded me that mine was not guaranteed, nor was my future. It was a sobering thought.

Sensing my unease he said, "It's unusual for someone not krelin to care for more than what nectar can do for a person. It eases the mind, and the soul, but there is an ingredient within each batch not discussed on any label." I leaned in eager to know what secrets were held in the nectar. It had always soothed me when I drank it at the end of the light cycle. "There is a reason why they call it Krelis Nectar, one of its key ingredients is from our blood."

I gasped, covering my mouth with my own hands as if that would put the words he said back into his lungs where they would never be uttered again.

He continued, "It's why the factory nectar has a different aftertaste, as you call it, the factory uses many krelins to develop and brew the nectar... so the aftertaste is so diverse and yet somehow bland because of it. It isn't what gives the nectar it's calming effects, it is merely that our blood nullifies the poisonous effect of the toxin that is the main ingredient, and so happens to also give it the aftertaste you describe."

"I've been," I stammered, "drinking krelin blood..."

"That isn't as bad as the hewve lard Estreldez begs us to export...for consumption." He wrinkled his nose in disgust, "Absolutely repulsive."

I lifted a hand to stop him from continuing. "I don't want to know... I only tried it once and never ate it again..." Though, he was right... most estrelds thought the hewve lard was tastier than the jewels they ate regularly. The lard was added into most meals for flavor and extra fat stores to make the food hardier. I avoided it at all costs... it gave everything a gross gritty feel. The way he said the word consumption had me thinking even though the hewve lard was an export for them, it was never intended as food. Squinting through my own scrunched up face, I dared to ask, "What is hewve lard's actual purpose for krelins?"

"We use it to fortify our hive. It's an affective means of preserving stone and adding insolation against the mountain winds."

"But, I don't want to know where it comes from..."

He smiled. "No, it's best that you don't. Though, I will say this was explained to Estreldez several times during negotiations, and if you're ever curious... the records are probably held somewhere as to what hewve lard is and how it's produced."

"No," I quickly snapped, mostly to tell myself not to become curious. I was always one to ask questions, and even now, repeating the word, no, in my mind didn't sway my unruly brain from thoughts of obtaining those records for later. "No, some things are best kept a mystery. All I need to know is the compound was scanned by scientists to show it is not harmful, and in fact, has many healthy, and desperately needed, nutrients to help sustain estrelds." Again, I repeated this to myself, hoping that would stop me from researching the file on hewve lard.

My brows furrowed in concentration to distract myself, which only led me back to thinking about devastation and war... I slumped in my chair, defeated. I'd been drinking the blood of a species bent on forcing their way into the lives of estrelds, whether that was by mating... or spilling our blood for something other than Krelin Nectar.

And the worst of it was that I was comforted every time.

Trent's tone became serious to match my mood. "I aim for the same, sustaining estrelds and krelins. As much as I want to reassure you there won't be hardships to come, I can't."

"What are you saying?"

"There is a bigger war brewing, and the reason why my queen is so desperate to speed along uniting our planets. Estreldez will have to defend itself, whether it's with Krelis or not. Warships are coming, and they aren't ours."

I believed him.

"How much time?"

"Before the trill come, or before other planets start making moves?"

A long silence filled the air, and I braced myself for the crushing reality I feared would come with an answer.

"Either?"

Trent stared out the window and sighed. "None. Both of those are already happening. I must unite our planets, and then lead my warships to battle, defending our homes."

"Together," I added.

"Together," he agreed.

I didn't know why I trusted what he was saying, but there was no reason for him to lie about war. If anything, he had every reason to lie to me about any danger at all. Any sane person hearing about such things would believe the only war would be coming from Krelis, and him telling me about this should make me run in the opposite direction. Which was exactly why I didn't, and why I believed him.

"Then for the sake of both our planets," I paused, my chest tight with what I was agreeing to, "I hope you can convince Luan to work with you." Politics weren't up to me, and he had the approval of Almder to seek Luan as a mate, but my throat became coarse speaking of such things. I couldn't even bring myself to say mate with him. Was it possible that they could simply work together, prove to the krelins and estrelds alike that they could bring peace with their mutual efforts... without mating? I didn't like the idea and it had nothing to do with him being a krelin.

And everything to do with how he made me feel, being this close. My skin tingled with the slight breeze his wings made, and our kiss was still fresh on my mind.

Chapter Six

Trent

The trip back to Estreldez was thick with an uncomfortable silence after Mabel told me she accepted what I had to do for our planets. Mating with the Jewel of Estreldez, future Almder, and Queen of Krelis, was what I knew needed to happen. But my face had turned to stone, unsatisfied with the ease with which she dismissed the issue. I should have been pleased that she wasn't upset with me, but I was seething inside that she was not more chagrined by the prospect of another female having claim to me.

I was already thinking of ways that I could fool my hive into accepting Luan as queen without actually mating with her. Groaning, I knew that would only be temporary. If she wasn't mated with me the hive would seek another queen as soon as one presented itself. All our efforts of merging Krelis and Estreldez would fizzle.

It was for the best, when I had probably imagined the connection I felt with Mabel, but everything in me didn't want to give up on that briefest of feelings when our lips touched, and I tasted her nectar. I would have to find a way to forget about her, to move on, for the sake of our planets. Rid her from my mind and refocus on why I was here. Luan. I needed to mate with the Almder's daughter.

Further rising my ire, I watched as Mabel left the shuttle as soon as we docked, without so much as a goodbye, she disappeared down the corridors in the direction of the palace. Leaving me to return and pace my arranged living quarters, unable to refocus on anything except for her. The only image in my mind was her black hair scattered about my bed cushions, and her legs spread for me, offering the feast of her delicious juices as she called out my name. It was fantasy, I knew, but it didn't stop me from imagining how it would feel to plunge my hard cock within her welcoming heat, and knot inside of her until every nerve of her body felt only me.

Only me, I repeated, as my hand reached down to adjust my length within my pants, just in time for my doors to slide open to an angry estreld. I couldn't blame him; I did leave him snoozing on the shuttle. He had a double dose of my musk, and even though he stirred on the trip back, he stayed knocked out for longer than I had anticipated. This time he was prepared with an air filtration mask, with two tiny cylinders following the line of his jaw that processed and analyzed the oxygen as he breathed in. It would surely make for speaking with him entertaining, as often times people sounded muffled when wearing them.

"What did you do with Mabel?" he asked with venom as the door slid closed behind him, his shoulders heaving.

I lifted a brow, my hand sliding over to my side from

where I had fixed my cock's positioning, his eyes followed my movement. If I had done anything with Mabel, I wouldn't be so unsatisfied at the moment, but I doubted his question had anything to do with my own spiraling thoughts of ravaging her.

"She was headed towards the main palace from the transport deck last I saw her," I replied in a bored tone.

He groaned his frustration, having not received the answer he was looking for. "That isn't what I was asking. I know where she is. I want to know what you did."

This piqued my interest. Did he know that I licked her juices from my fingers? I grinned over at him, pleased with the idea. Bringing my fingers up to my lips, I could still smell her on me. By estreld standards, Gaven was an attractive mate prospect. He was well fed, muscles toned, and he displayed many loh jewels along his arms. His green skin would even be considered alluring to even a krelin warrior, being much more vibrant than what a krelin would have.

His green skin reminded me of Mabel's eyes, and I grew increasingly irritated that this male shared anything with her at all, even if only in coloring. Though, I suspected there was more between them than the jeweled pigment with his current reaction to my interest.

"You'll have to be a bit more specific," I replied, not feeling in the mood to be generous with any information towards this male. Gaven was showing too much involvement for my taste.

"She won't speak with me," he reluctantly ground out. "I don't know what you've done, but I know you have no intention of giving her what she deserves. I will warn you only once, you will keep your distance."

My wings whipped out, the tips fluttering in their own kind of warning. His words rattled me, and my body reacted before I could think clearly. Who was he to Mabel to know what she deserves? Who was he to decide I could not give her everything a mate could desire? Both of my hearts pounded in my chest like I was standing before my queen, the obvious disdain and disappointment clear in her eyes that I was not a female heir.

I've trained my expressions to remain neutral, cold, and I looked down my nose at him with practiced boredom.

"For the sake of peace between our planets, I should hope you'll have a change of attitude towards my efforts of claiming a mate."

"I've already taken care of that. You'll have your mate, and you can be on your way."

I lifted a brow. "Is that so? And how did you manage this?" With the way Mabel rushed off, I hardly thought persuading her to give me more time to prove our compatibility would be as easy as having some guard play match maker. And he had clearly said she wasn't speaking to him, so his claim was not convincing.

"Mabel will inform Luan that she's to give you a tarnpul offering at the ceremony's mate matching. You will be given one-on-one time with Luan to secure your political mating. Seduce her, and then leave. It shouldn't be difficult for you. I'm well aware that if you and Luan are compatible that your spray will induce mating, instead of a nap."

I laughed. "You think I'd risk making Luan faint in front of the whole mating assembly?"

Gaven didn't know that I had already confirmed Luan's compatibility before I even set foot on this planet. My musk would induce mating pheromones. There were no doubts about that. She had consumed my nectar many times, and Chief Ong had assured me that she preferred my nectar to all others, even going so far as to request it often during trades.

We were compatible.

"It isn't a risk if Luan's loh are activated," he countered with a determination which made me bristle. His efforts were not self-less, he was purposefully shoving an opportunity I couldn't refuse within my grasp to keep me from Mabel. He knew I'd have to make the attempt, for the sake of avoiding a war not even the Almder realized was already waiting impatiently upon her own moon, where I'd left Commander Li-aq. I had to gain Luan's cooperation, regardless of my obsession with the delicious Mabel.

I grunted my temporary agreement with this plan, but only because, if Gaven was to be believed, it relied on Mabel telling Luan to gift me a piece of tarnpul jewelry at the opening ceremony. Would Mabel stake her claim, keeping this information to herself? Grinning, the smile reached my eyes as I watched the scheming Gaven. Perhaps, I would make my final decision at the ceremony. If Luan gifts me with her tarnpul, I'll know whether Mabel harbors any feelings for me, or not. If she is truly my kansa, then giving another female permission to claim me would require great effort.

I would have to accept her decision.

"You need a mate that will provide spawn, Luan is who you need," he said, trying to convince me further. Was he suggesting that Mabel was incapable? That was not what I gathered from our previous discussion. She merely needed a different method of carrying her spawn to term, from her interest in kantos sacks this was normal for any krelin mate.

She was not krelin, I reminded myself, estrelds didn't need such things. What I didn't need was some other male telling me what I needed, or didn't, for that matter.

"And what is it that Mabel needs?" I stepped forward, my wings still extended. Gaven was a strong warrior not to flinch at my approach. If I wasn't at odds with him, I'd have considered him the kind of warrior I'd like at my side come war, or otherwise.

"Someone to care about her best interests. I'll find another way of getting her the larva sack she wanted from you, but her life is more important than being a brood-herglat for the clan. She is smart and will bring great achievements to the clan regardless of her mating status."

"For someone trying to dissuade me from mating with her, you are doing a remarkably abysmal job. Sounds to me like you're not listening to what she wants from a mate."

"She wants a family, and it doesn't matter to me how we achieve that as long as she's alive. We could both transfer to the offspring training facility, where there are plenty of spawn who grew up just like she did. She could give them the same experience Almder and Luan provided for her. Family doesn't start and end with blood."

Gaven's impassioned speech was moving, but not in the way he probably hoped for. Most would hear his words as they were intended, a declaration of his affections, and an obvious sign that most would not measure up to such claims of commitment and back off. For me, all he did was affirm the compassion of the woman we both held esteem for, and highlighted a need for some kind of change in the way the estrelds currently conducted their spawn training if she was denied this basic need of familial bonding.

I understood the ache of rejection, of never measuring up, and the absence of what my queen could never give me. My only saving grace was in the warriors that followed my command. There, I had respect, and though not entirely the same, a bond like no other. And I could give her a bond that would surpass even that.

It was something I've always craved but held no real hope of obtaining. A kansa mate bond. I swear, I could hear her thoughts in my head. That she was inside of my very soul, but it was so quick, so fleeting, that I could have imagined it. Perhaps, it was simply that I wished for it to be real, and dreamed it to be, if only for a moment.

There was a job to be done. A duty to be fulfilled. Even if she was my kansa mate... I was required to mate with Luan, for the sake of both our species.

I nodded to Gaven. "I will approach Luan for her tarnpul offering, you may guard me from outside of my accommodations, unless you'd like to stay while I relieve myself?"

Given the mask over his face it was hard to tell, but Gaven wasn't amiable to the idea of being audience to such things. He quickly turned his back, and reminded me, with his voice echoing off the sliding door as he approached to leave, "I've already submitted my request to be sired with Mabel prior to your involvement, and it was accepted. Our bonding ceremony will take place after the off-worlders are dismissed."

"Not during the mating ceremony then, when your moons are most auspicious?" I questioned, knowing full well that most estrelds would prefer to mate while conditions were optimal, and radiation was plentiful. It was my way of stabbing a bit of uncertainty into his claims, because she certainly didn't act engaged with another while I massaged her inner most walls as they clamped down around my fingers.

My cock grew hard once more at the thought, and I was thankful Gaven was facing the opened exit as to not instigate him into attacking me. I would not back down from a Kloaph Rite, if he challenged, and I had no doubts I would win, even if it meant dislodging his gasmask to spray him with my musk once more. By Krelis law, I would have every claim to take Mabel to the Kai Mountain Oasis to convince her to accept me as my mate. In ancient times, kidnapping our mates after a Kloaph Rite was part of the mating ceremony, and a warrior would not return until every egg was fertilized by our victorious seed.

I was not so barbaric as to expect I'd be able to kidnap Mabel to Krelis to claim her, but the idea that she'd come willingly was making my cock swell with need. Perhaps she'd even be excited to run and hide within the cave's tunnels so I could chase her down by our bond alone. Gripping my length, I closed my eyes, and imagined her smile, as she glanced over her shoulder with a wink before her hips swayed with her excitement to see how fast I could find her and claim her as mine.

She'd call out my name, then leave a trail of her garments on the stone floor, until all there was left was our bond to follow. It didn't matter if it was all concocted in my mind, the affection I saw in those seductive green eyes of hers was enough to undo me. My seed wasted at my feet was evidence enough that if nothing else, my trip to estreldez had indeed triggered my mating glands, and if it could be done for me, perhaps not all was lost for the hive.

Chapter Seven

Mabel

When I closed my eyes to sleep, all I could see was the inside of a cave carved from yellow-orange stone that had a faint glow to it. I was running through the corridors, getting lost in the maze, glancing over my shoulder as I went. It should have been terrifying, not knowing where I was, and this intense knowledge that I was being chased, but I was smiling. Like the whole thing was part of a game of some sort. Then I'd wake up.

The opening ceremony to the mating cycle would begin today. All the off-worlders would be shuttled in from the largest moon, after they completed their exams and security checks. There was a buzz in the air, the radiation of the moons could always be felt more intensely during this time, even if I wasn't outside, I could feel my loh hum in approval.

It was like being wrapped in a warm embrace that settled and spread out from the two loh on my back, and the small jewel above my brow. I chuckled, not even my loh listened to convention of centering itself perfectly upon my forehead.

With a groan I forced myself to leave my bed, even without having slept much, this was an important day, and I had to support Luan. This was her first official mating ceremony where she would actually participate, and I was required to tell her that the Almder insisted that she bestow the Krelis diplomat, Trent, an offering of her tarnpul. I understood why Amlder would wish for someone else to ask Luan, and it would have been between Loric or myself that would make the information more digestible. Loric was participating, and would be among the rest of the eligible mates. It was left to me.

I understood all of that, but I didn't have to like that I would have to put being her friend behind the duty of advising her of what Almder thought was best for the future of Estreldez. It wasn't entirely self-less, I secretly hoped Luan's distaste for krelins would continue, at least in the sense of attraction for the mating ceremony. The idea of her mating with Trent, after I'd tasted him on my lips felt wrong.

I cringed. Somehow, I would have to find the time to tell her what I'd done. She would know how to fix things, if I screwed up the future diplomacy between our planets by getting involved. Tugging a few strands of my black hair forward, I covered my forehead, but stilled. My fingers rested at my temples, pulling my hair back to see my loh had darkened to a deep green. And the freckle on the other side was bigger... was I growing another loh? Quickly, I covered it up and braided the rest of my hair back, dismissing the thought as a trick of the mind.

Then I tugged on my gloves that were warm from the

extra radiation in the atmosphere. They were designed to simulate having more loh on my arms, while also helping my skin absorb more of the moon's rays due to only having three loh... or four now? I shouldn't have tried to cover the one on my forehead at all, but it felt less awkward to hide than to be reminded I had one small jewel, on the right side of my temple, rather than a crown of perfect ones like Luan. It was even more embarrassing to know that I might have a tiny loh growing at the age of twenty cycles like I was still an offspring coming into my own.

Luan was normally in the library at this time, but when I checked, her books were scattered around, and she was gone. The halls were crowded with much more off-worlders along with their escorts than I'd ever seen before. Many were male, but even some females from different planets were here. The mating ceremony usually only had a select few brought in every cycle, but this cycle there were so many mates that I was worried this was a result of the desperation for more offspring.

The palace was bustling with potential mates every which way that I looked, I feared I'd never find Luan, and the opening ceremony would begin soon. That's when I spotted her, hunkered over a tablet, among the excited throes of eager estrelds on the viewing deck. She wasn't even scanning the mates, or concerned with many of the males that had already taken notice of her from the lounge below. That was to be expected, she was never interested in mating. There was an odd bit of comfort in that knowledge.

I took a seat next to her, and noticed a list of the mating candidates, with a male's image displayed. A breath I hadn't known I was holding exhaled, as I didn't recognize the muscled off-worlder. Grinning to myself, I thought about how I was wrong about whether Luan was interested in finding a mate this cycle or not.

"He's handsome," I remarked.

"He's one of those pleasure seekers," she explained, dismissing him, while quickly swiping to the next image, which stilled my heart.

Would she swipe past him as well? Her finger hovered, but stopped. A 3-D image of Trent took up the tablet's screen, and I stared at his yellow eyes, reminded of the caves I had dreamed about. She didn't pass by his data, instead keeping it open for both of us to read over.

It was astonishing to see that the scans and exams gave the krelin a higher compatibility rating than I had ever seen with an off-worlder. Our biological chemistry was so similar, and yet that one percent was so vastly different. For one, we did not have horns like they did, scales, or those wings. I wondered if his wings were capable of flying, or if they were just like the virxup's skin flaps that were colorful and expanded out from their throats to attract mates, but otherwise were superficial. Then my gaze wandered to more personal statistics, my eyes widening.

Would something that size even fit inside of me?

Not that Trent would ever be inside of me, I thought with a blush, he was set on having Luan as his mate.

I tempered down my racing heart, and forced myself to do what was required of me. Gaven told me of the Almder's request, and I had a duty to inform Luan, whether or not she acted on it or not. Did I hope she wouldn't? I couldn't think like that, I saw the determination in Commander Li-aq's stoney features. If Trent didn't negotiate some kind of mating treaty with Luan, we'd be at war sooner than we could prepare for. It would be my fault for keeping my mouth shut, but I trusted that Trent wanted peace.

Why did I trust him so much? When we shared what we

did, and he still chose Luan?

Biting down on my lip, I then sucked in a breath to finally try to tell Luan about Trent, but she spoke first, "Mabel," she paused, then continued, "You've been on the M.R. team, and advisor to Almder for a few years now..."

Luan seemed to be nervous, and that was unlike her. I agreed, prompting her to continue. Whatever it was, she didn't want to ask, but similar to what I was going through, she forced herself to push on, she was stronger than me, "I need your help to search for new technology and treaties that could help us save our clan."

I hadn't expected her to divert from our conversation about the mates staring at us from below the tiered viewing deck. She swiped back to the bounty hunter with tattoos on his shoulders as black as his eyes, his stats said they were blue, but similar to midnight, as if looking at blue in the depths of darkness. Not anything like the eyes of Trent, which were closer to the light of the sun, than that of when the moons rotated beyond the reach of the closest star. I was torn between relief that Luan was focused on another male and disappointment that this was probably the closest I would be to Trent ever again. Seeing him through a viewing tablet.

"Of course, anything I can do to help," I assured her. Anything for her... even ignore the pang in my chest preventing me from telling her about giving Trent a tarnpul offering, knowing what that would mean for both of them being alone, under the moon's influence...

Luan rambled about her impending rise to Almder one day, her desire to find solutions to our clan's offspring rates, food resources, and things we'd already discussed previously. Nothing new, and she wouldn't look me in the eye, even her fingers fidgeted with her skirts at her thighs,

87

before she finally got to what she wanted to have my support for, quickly sputtering the last part of how she would need to see to these diplomatic dealings, personally.

My eyes widened when I realized what she was saying. She wanted to leave Estreldez. It wasn't simply leaving the planet, but me. This was not a request for me to join her. She would leave me here to help smooth over her escape, because that was what it would be considered. She would be running away, delaying the transfer of leadership. No, not simply delaying... would she ever return?

"Luan..." I tried to tread carefully. I wanted to be supportive of her ambitions, but I couldn't remove the part of me that had always tried to advise, and guide under the orders of our Almder. "You are forgetting, you would be putting our whole planet's future in jeopardy by leaving the safety of Estreldez. You *are* the future Almder, the Jewel of Estreldez, and easily a target by those that wish to control our resources, or worse enslave us." I left out the very real threat of the krelins not commanded by Trent directly, invading our planet.

This would have been an ideal time to say something, anything, to see if Luan would agree with me about keeping this from Almder, but I didn't want it to be a wedge between negotiations they could both have during the one-on-one later this evening.

"We are not cowards," she bit out, her shoulders squaring off. I had offended her... and it was not the response she needed from me as a friend. I had to switch gears, she was my family, not some random estreld that I was relaying information to on Almder's orders.

"No." I agreed with her, I didn't mean for it come across like I didn't think estrelds could hold our own. "All of our warriors have proven themselves against the krelins before our treaty. We are not cowards. If you think this will show our strength to have you part of the mission." Yet another secret I had to keep from Almder. "I won't tell your mom what you are up to, but that's the best I can do."

When I said 'we', I didn't mean myself. It was the estrelds that were strong, and brave. Me, I was a coward, who couldn't even bring myself to help Luan leave Estreldez on a diplomatic mission.

She would leave.

After the cycles we had been together, it was clear this was like every other time she set her mind to something. Nothing would get in her way. The urge within me rose up to do what I always did when she had a plan in motion. Follow. Protect.

But this time, something was different. We were both different. I required her to ask me to join, to want me to be with her. And I knew she'd never ask that of me. I bit my lip, stopping myself from saying more, from inserting myself into her plans. *Take me with you,* my mind roared while equally shouting, *don't go.*

So I said nothing.

Her resolve and thoughtfulness was what made her such a promising leader, and because I believed in her, I reasoned that she would one day be Almder. So, who was I to prevent her from doing what she thought was best for the clan, for Estreldez, and perhaps even for herself. Her shoulders relaxed, knowing that I wouldn't go to Almder and interfere with her plan to leave. Though, she should have known that I wouldn't, that she could trust me.

But, could she?

Guilt made me turn my attention away from her. I was keeping vital information to myself.

"That will have to be enough then," she said with

determination, like a true leader, she would not impose on me, but she would press forward with her plan, whatever that entailed.

I stood up, unable to keep still, knowing I had disappointed her. Knowing I had disappointed myself. I should be going with her, to protect her. "The games will begin soon," I diverted.

"Mabel," she approached, cautiously, "We are friends?"

There should be no doubt about that, but I had failed her. My eyes watered with emotion, and launched my arms around her while she sat, bringing her into a hug, uncaring of who was watching.

"We are," I said, near to sobbing into her beautiful silver hair. I sniffed and sucked in a breath to steady myself before I pulled away to smile at her. "I will see what I can do to help, but right now," I tried to lighten the mood with a joke, "we must see if any of the mates can make your shoulders tingle."

The tears in my eyes stung all the more, thinking of who she'd choose as a mate.

She laughed heartily, and stood up from her seat, enveloping me back into the hug once more. Luan was much taller than me, and she had to stoop to press her cheek against the top of my head. "I have my doubts," she said with humor, but there was a grain of truth in her voice.

My best friend was uncertain of finding a match this cycle. She was the Jewel of Estreldez, envy of many, and there would be no shortage of matches that would vie for her attention. She had to know this, even if I had to remind her. Squeezing her arms in reassurance, I knew she'd find a mate... even if it was with someone I wanted for myself. "It is different when they display their talents to you personally."

In the heat of the moment, she would see what I saw in Trent. I had to tell her what the Almder wanted of her. Now was the time, wasn't it?

"I don't understand," she said skeptically.

I blushed thinking of how I had dropped my own eggs as Trent's fingers explored my heat, my pants and moans echoing in the shuttle chamber. Looking away, I explained, "As a scientist of behavioral analysis…" I paused, this was an excuse. It had nothing to do with being an analyst for the M.R. team, but I knew if someone like me could be triggered to mate, so could she. "I've interviewed many that have successfully mated. Some knew as soon as they saw them, and others needed to be in close proximity. You've been far from attentive during the previous ceremonies, participating may change things for you."

The ceremony opening would start soon, and both the viewing deck, and the arena below were filled with mates from all across Estreldez, and planets from all over. The moons were up above, radiating in the open-air training arena, which was only used by our warriors when not hosting the mating ceremony. Even the floors were stamped with tarnpul slabs to help amplify the radiation, which was to assist warriors with tapping into their loh, but served dual purpose for increasing fertility.

My eyes locked on a pair of golden ones within the crowd of off-worlders. Others gave him ample space, creating a bubble that made spotting him easier than if I had tried to spot where Loric was within the group. He did not remove his armor, though that didn't hide much of the muscle along his torso. Only his arms were covered with scale-like leather, and bracers. Krelins were confident in their abilities to protect themselves, wearing armor that would assist with blocking, and then attacking their opponents. Part of my training, when I stood in this very arena to be certified as any other warrior among the estrelds, was to learn about krelins and using their hubris against them.

They had two hearts, I remembered, and my eyes landed on his pectorals molded with leather. My head had leaned against his firm frame as he touched me where my heat pooled with pulsing need. A shriek thankfully drew my attention back into focus. Flauna fidgeted in front of us before she turned in her seat distracting me from my thoughts.

"Him!" she was pointing to the image of the bounty hunter on Luan's tablet.

I absentmindedly read his name out loud, "Vareo." As I processed what Flauna was saying, I also noted how Luan was biting her lip... did she have interest in him? "A bounty hunter passing through the star system," I explained, hoping to hint towards his unsuitability for Flauna while adding my approval to Luan, "He seems like a fine mate, even if his motives may be credit-inspired rather than diplomatic."

It didn't seem to help as Flauna ignored my words of warning, "Doesn't matter what got him here, all that matters is that he's here now. He's looking this way!" Flauna's blue skin turned purple with a blush. Her back loh were pulsing with interest, signaling her readiness to mate. I tried to distract them both with nudging Luan to pay attention to the arena. There was plenty to look at, and Flauna wouldn't think too much on us anticipating the ceremony instead of chatting about her interest in the bounty hunter.

Trent was staring in our direction, and I could swear he wasn't looking at Luan. His double-lidded golden eyes cleared his vision, and my stomach fluttered. As he took steps towards the center, the space between him and others followed, not a single off-worlder, nor estreld, would dare approach him. He had a presence about him, and my feet itched to move. Unlike everyone else, not to give him space, but to remove it. My blood pumped, and I felt my heart hammering in my ribcage, not once did his gaze leave mine. I gulped. "That's unusual," I said breathless. I've never felt like this before, simply by being seen.

Luan gasped when her eyes followed mine, I quickly explained my interest in him, dismissing it as professional, "He's an ambassador from Krelis."

"But, he's... participating?" she scoffed her disapproval.

Resisting a smile, I shouldn't have been pleased by her reaction to him, but I was. Salph's voice resonated through the arena to begin the ceremony, she was an elder advisor, and helped coordinate the mating ceremony. With her introduction, she initiated the first offering of tarnpul for females, regardless of if they were from Estreldez or not, would gift a piece of tarnpul to mates they were interested in. Any mate with tarnpul would participate in the ceremony, getting to know their mates, and copulating under the moon's blessing. Those with no offerings would return to their ships, dismissed from the ceremony.

Luan's tablet flashed, and I read the note from Almder with both relief and defeat. I hadn't accepted that I was avoiding my duty to tell Luan about needing to give Trent a tarnpul offering, but the message was clear: You'll offer the ambassador of Krelis some tarnpul, My Jewel.

There, it was done.

Almder had beat me to it.

"What is it?" Luan questioned my shocked expression.

"One piece of tarnpul doesn't mean you'll mate with him," I tried to reason more to myself than to her. She didn't have to mate with him. She wouldn't mate with him. Was I going to hyperventilate?

It was out of my hands, Almder wasn't saying she *had* to mate with Trent, but I knew what happened on one-on-ones during the peak of the moon ceremony. After all the

93

interviews I'd conducted, I knew more than most that mates hardly stuck to talking points. They would be alone, the radiation would increase their mating hormones, and with the added boost of the Almder's blessing... it was rare for couples not to copulate. A clamminess slicked my palms, and I wrung my robes to dry them, only to remain gripping the fabric as if my life depended on it.

I was upset... I hardly ever became upset. Even my eyes watered, close to brimming over. I didn't even register that Luan was talking to me, when she sucked in a breath, and gave me a soft doe-eyed expression of pity.

"Might as well get this over with then," Luan pivoted the conversation, and I was thankful that she wouldn't force me to talk about my new status as infertile, nor why I was so affected by a message that had nothing to do with me. But didn't it?

She headed down the benched seating towards the arena of mates, towards Trent, I knew that was her destination. My feet moved without thought, following close behind her. *Mine*, my mind repeated like a chant. Fingers clenched and unclenched at my side, an irrational anger unfurling within me towards my best friend the closer she got. Trent quickly moved through the mass of off-worlders, they parted like a sea in a perfect storm to make way for him.

My back loh burned, and throbbed, like they would melt if his strong arms didn't wrap themselves around me. With every step he took, his shoulders heaved, and his nostrils flared as his golden eyes locked on me. No, not on me... Luan, I corrected. I stilled as his wings snapped open, murmurs buzzed through the crowd as they watched, curious as to what was happening. He was magnificent, the iridescent black with a sheen of yellow glinting in the moon's light reminded me of the universe and the twinkling stars of countless planets I'd never see.

I'd stay on Estreldez, become an elder like Salph and Ezra, unmated, but respected. I would find my place in the clan once more, even if it wasn't with him. With him? What was I even thinking? When did I start including him in my plans for anything? He certainly wasn't going to stay on Estreldez, he was the Prince of Krelis, and...

A small gasp escaped Luan's lips, as her mating loh burst from her back into diamond wings so beautiful, they captured the awe of everyone as Trent stood before her. I was but an insignificant being hidden behind the future leader of Estreldez. It was rare for mating loh to extend so far and grow so much... so quickly. She was truly compatible with him, and it wasn't my place to destroy my clan's chance at peace.

I knew her mating loh would emerge, but there was a large part of me that had hoped it would be with someone else. It was obvious with his proximity, and her silver eyes homed in that Trent would be her mate... her loh would emit a pheromone encouraging them to be together. Though my own mating loh hummed and I felt them grow from my shoulders... it would never compare with Luan. And if Ezra had known I was even here, she would scold me for putting my life in danger by tempting fate.

Letting him go was the right thing to do, I assured myself, and I turned to leave them. I would only get in the way.

A voice entered my head, "*My mate...*"

My lip quivered at how cruel my imagination was to hear his voice calling me his. I ran through the crowd as fast as I could before I humiliated myself further.

Chapter Eight

Trent

When Mabel descended the viewing deck, I had assumed she made a choice to be here, to see me. It was obvious by the wide breadth everyone gave they knew I was a krelin, and feared I may harm them. That was the reputation estrelds have marked my species with, and it wasn't earned without reason. My queen had made many decisions that prioritized krelins over any other, and it wasn't how I wished to continue. Without a queen at my side, overthrowing my mother's rule would require great sacrifice I didn't wish to put my warriors through when there was a path avoiding death.

I had to sway the opinions of her most zealous followers, and that would only happen if I had another queen to place their trust in. Luan, the future Almder would be the ideal figurehead to rule and guide our planets, but the one I wanted was hiding behind her.

Outstretching my hand in offering, Luan's loh glowed like the moons, making my second eye lid close to protect my sight on instinct. From her back diamond-like daggers sprung forth shaped like wings. The uncanny similarities to a warrior, and queen, of Krelis was difficult to ignore. A single display of her fierce loh would convince many warriors to switch loyalties, especially if the radiation blessed them with active mating glands in the process. But, it was the back of another that I watched running away from the arena which froze both my hearts in an instant.

Mabel had made her choice, and I was not among them.

Luan's wings flexed behind her, a glow enveloping the arena in a warmth when I heard a mate's call in my head, "*Mine.*"

Was this Luan? Had I been wrong to assume this connection was with Mabel?

I closed my eyes, and sent my response through the bond, "*My mate?*"

Luan's cheeks blushed fiercely when I reopened my eyes. Had she heard me? Her hand laced into mine, I had forgotten that my hand was still extended in offering. She took a cuff from her arm, pulling it down and passing it over her slim wrist and on to mine. The black jewelry which fit snuggly on her arm, was a perfect fit for my wrist.

Tarnpul.

This was an offering, and I had to wonder if she was giving this to me because Mabel had told her to, at Gaven's insistence, or she was my kansa, and this was genuine interest? Only time would tell.

Another large male approached, an off-worlder with the mark of a slave on his neck. And the Pride of Acatalec, Loric, an estreld known as a great warrior, and an agreeable politician. I had trouble focusing on either of them too closely, continuing to stare at Luan for signs that we were forming a bond. Already, I could feel my mating glands react, seeking to spray her with my musk and take her back to Kia Mountain to begin our mating.

It was auspicious that Luan should be a prime candidate for queen, and my kansa mate. The goddess had truly blessed this peace treaty's success.

"I have not made any final decisions on anything," Luan snapped at Loric, bringing my attention back to the task at hand. Being the Almder's daughter, it was natural for there to be competition for her affections, and I was unsure how our kansa bond would be felt by her, being as our bond wasn't complete and she was not a krelin. It was possible the reason why she was unable to communicate through the bond was a side effect of her being estreld, and we would have to consummate fully to solidify the mental link.

Kansa bonds were rare, but there was never a recorded instance of the bond not being reciprocated, even with the few mates that were found outside of Krelis. My second believed his own mother was kansa bonded, but she sent him away. If he was correct, then rejecting the bond was possible. There was a male found from a planet called Rewrth, a species called hoomon. Gho-ran was half-hoomon, and had told me he wants to visit Rewrth someday.

"My apologies for assuming," the off-worlder replied with mischief in his tone. There was obviously some kind of pissing contest between Loric and this male that I needed no part in. I wished to leave. Nothing about this situation was comfortable for me, and I struggled with whether it was due to Mabel running away, or the way Luan's eyes kept darting over to the other males.

Some would be agitated with such displays over a mate that was clearly mine to earn approval from, but there was no contest when a kansa bond was involved. I was unconcerned with their petty bickering, and surprisingly, I was also unaffected with the blue estreld warrior leaning into whisper, "When you're ready," to Luan. He intended to court her, and he was an honorable mate, *for someone else*, I added internally with a smirk on my face.

My hearing was impeccable, whispering would not deter me, but Loric knew that. It was a challenge.

Well played, I thought, but it didn't matter.

Luan dismissed herself with a curt bow of her head. "I'll be in the library for the meeting phase of the games."

Her hips swayed in her exit, but my eyes stayed on her wings that looked like ice and deadly daggers. She lived up to her reputation of beauty and power, the Jewel of Estreldez. I would have no trouble convincing my mother's sycophants to follow a new queen, especially if her loh could activate the mating glands of my warriors. It was a true blessing of the Goddess Lenkal for peace to have Luan be both the future leader of Estreldez, and my kansa mate.

In a daze, I left the arena filled with the potential mates of the ceremony. There was no point in remaining there when I had already been gifted with a tarnpul offering from my future queen, Luan. My thoughts wandered back to Mabel, and how wrong I'd been about what there was between us. Was it Luan the whole time, or my imagination?

Once I was out of the arena, wandering down the now empty corridors since everyone was at the ceremony, I rubbed my face with frustration. I could still remember the taste of her; the urge to claim Mabel with my swelling cock did not fade. In the tongue of the hive, bel meant warrior's cry. To be a Ma-bel was to be a warrior's rallying song, a song that spoke to a krelin's hearts and led them into great victories. It was one of the reasons why I found her so intriguing to be named in a way unlike an estreld at all, but that of a krelin warrior.

I could see myself crying out Mabel's name with her legs wrapped around me, and my cock buried deep inside her heat, but I had to give my kansa mate the chance to solidify our bond. For the sake of our planets, and in respect of krelin traditions, a kansa bond was not meant to be dismissed. Only should Luan reject me could I try to repair what I'd lost with Mabel. My opinions had not changed, even with seeing how Luan could shine, I could not rid Mabel from my mind.

Dark black hair, and bright green eyes that seemed to see right through me. My glands in my throat ached, and a hunger grew to taste her once more. I lifted my hand up to my mouth, and a string of both of our essence solidified. Forming the gel into the shape of a wing, I smiled to myself. This would be the first gift to our spawn, placed at the bottom of a kantos in offering. I should destroy it, crush the newly hardened trinket knowing that it would never be used, but I couldn't. Instead, I placed the start of a kantos I would never finish between my breast plate, and where my heart's beat.

Had I ruined my chance to have a true kansa bond by being too hasty with my need to taste Mabel on the shuttle? I didn't think there would be any harm, and in my defense, I had hoped she was my true mate. With her juices inside of me, the proof of my glands preparing to create a kantos sack was sitting within my armor. How would I explain this to Luan?

Perhaps, I'd never have to?

Luan should have no need of a kantos.

Luan should have no need of me, I thought with annoyance.

This kansa bond was not off to a good start, I was already feeling the distance my mind was putting between the bond and myself. It was faint and growing weaker. Just a small warmth at the back of my mind. I clucked my tongue, and the echo worked its way through the hall, bringing attention to a moving figure behind me. When I turned, I couldn't see anyone, but I knew they were there, my kan horns did not lie. It was obvious who it would be.

"I know you're there, you can join me," I called out.

Gaven, my escort, and apparently a well apt spy, moved away from the wall, and it was like he appeared out of thin air. Estrelds were remarkable when trained properly. Like my wings could reflect the light, and appear invisible, the estrelds could use their radiation to blur the surrounding space around themselves, like a heatwave. A large change in temperature over a small distance bends the light rays around the object like a mirage. Gaven was quite gifted with his loh to accomplish this so seamlessly, but my kan did not rely on my eyes to detect things. There was only one warrior with such a prominent stealth skill like this from Estreldez, my hive called him the Sky Bender, and he was known to have killed quite a few of my warriors, though it was unproven.

"They didn't exaggerate your skills, Black Prince."

So, he was using nicknames then? He must still be upset with me over Mabel. Since I was still craving her, I couldn't blame him, but that didn't mean I had to accept it. If he truly was Sky Bender, he would have some explaining to do, or I would be forced to apprehend him for trial by hive verdict. He'd discover why they called me the Black Prince, or even the Queen's Revenge.

"Did you want me to act like the Black Prince, Sky Bender?" I baited. He need only confirm my suspicions.

101

"You know, if the Sky Bender was more than a mythological redirect for your own hive's cleanup, then I'd say you should be thanking him."

"Should I, now?" I waited for him to explain. It'd been proven more information was always gained from one's enemies by playing along for a bit. So, I remained patient, while I seethed internally at the loss of any warrior at his hands.

"We couldn't very well take your word for the loss of your warriors, and the circumstances of their deaths, well, upon investigation, those warriors were undermining our peace treaty. You are lucky this Sky Bender decided to stop them from their pursuits, or our planets would have been at war many cycles ago."

"And I'm supposed to take your word for it?"

"Of course not," Gaven scoffed at the idea that either of us should trust the other. Despite the distasteful delivery of this fact, I respected him more for the temporary honesty of the matter. If he was Sky Bender, and I was to take him at his word, then he was supporting a continued peace between our species. It wasn't difficult to believe that the warriors killed were my queen's zealots, bent on invading and claiming what they believed was rightfully theirs and owed to them.

Nothing was owed to anyone, I thought ruefully. Least of all, the very life we were given in this universe. It was a gift, and though I had gained a reputation as the Black Prince for poisoning my enemies, I did not take death lightly. I have killed more krelins than the Sky Bender has, and that did not include the spies from King Sylve of the outlaw planet Necias Delta Fal. It wearied my soul, but I reasoned that these small deaths saved many lives. Small deaths become many over time. Each one more easy to dispose of than the last.

A sign of the degradation of my soul.

Perhaps, that was why my kansa bond was so weak. I was not worthy to accept it with the many wrongs I'd committed over the cycles.

Forever branded the Black Prince.

"You have a way to prove your words, I take it," I prompted. Otherwise, why tell me at all? If he were krelin, all I would have to do is force myself into his mind to see if he was lying, but without any hive bond, that was impossible. There were other tells to look for to gauge deceit, yet Gaven was displaying no sign of foul play. Even so, I couldn't trust my eyes when it came to someone of his skill level. My double eyelids cleared my vision hoping for new data to display itself. He was not one to give away his secrets so easily. His face a mask of disinterest, similar to my own.

"I don't like you," he stated matter of fact, a pointed scowl wrinkling the bridge of his nose. "My dislike of you and your hive doesn't change the reality that a war between planets as close as ours would be devastating to both our species. I want you to mate with Luan. I don't even care that you would be second in command to the future Almder, and one day be someone I take orders from. Not if it means the clan is safe.

"You may be the Black Prince, your reputation of death precedes you, but so does your reputation among the krelins for protecting your warriors, having the respect of the ones that follow you, and even now you show restraint, though I know you wish to harm me for speaking so blatantly about the death of your hive. Your power rivals that of the queen herself, and I know you seek to take control of Krelis with a new queen at your side."

Brazen, and so confident in his assessments, he wasn't wrong, but he'd given me more reason to believe he was the Sky Bender, or at the very least someone who had read reports by the spy. No one should know my plans to overthrow my mother, except my closest warriors, and apparently the Spy of Estreldez, Sky Bender. Was that why Almder was so amiable about allowing me to seek her only daughter as a mate? She knew I wished to replace Queen Kai.

Or this was Gaven's own attempt at confirming his own suspicions. Did it matter?

Smiling at him, I teased, "I will happily give you orders, if you'd follow them."

A crinkle around his eyes told me he suppressed his own grin. "I wouldn't have expected anything less from a prince. Sliding around the accusation while also being affable. It only proves my point. You can bring peace to our planets for many cycles to come, and Luan is who you will do it with." He punctuated Luan's name to emphasize that I would keep my distance from Mabel. Even now, he did not trust I would let well enough alone. Mabel had made her decision, and my foolishness had created a wedge between me and my kansa bond.

I would respect this male's claim to court her.

For now, I couldn't help but add. Luan needed my full attention and yet I couldn't fully give up on Mabel. Gaven may be wrong about my worthiness to bond with either of them. My mind kept battling within itself. Luan soothed my warriors during trade negotiations, which I assumed had something to do with her loh's allure reflecting her own calm state of mind on the krelins she's in contact with. And yet Mabel occupies my every desire, pushing me to think of new ways to help my hive. To let me keep her, but I never had her to begin with.

Chapter Nine

Mabel

Luan buried her face in her hands as she collapsed beside me in the spot we normally both retreated to for privacy. A secluded place within the palace garden with plants that grew thick enough to hide behind. Most estrelds didn't approach close enough to realize they were Retreating Wops from the AsunGor planet, brought in as a diplomatic gift many cycles ago. Upon contact with heat they retracted, making a path to enter into a little area of the garden away from prying eyes.

I didn't say anything as she groaned beside me. This was a place of safety, and I would let her have her meditation until it was obvious she would like my support. Staring at the small pond of water at our feet, I watched my reflection ripple as the light of the moons bounced around its surface.

My thoughts kept returning to Trent, and how he watched Luan's loh expand into magnificent wings that displayed both her beauty and her power. She would make a wonderful Almder one day, and not just because the clan would respect her newly activated loh, which even I could feel heightening my urge to mate, but because I knew her. Knew she'd do everything within her ability to guide Estreldez... and Krelis through the coming war with King Sylve.

But, she was also planning on leaving…

"Fuck me," Luan huffed out.

I sighed. She had to know I believed in her. "It wasn't that bad..." If anything, she had done nothing but show Estreldez she was worthy of ascending to Almder, and her loh would secure the peace with Krelis. If I hadn't left when I did, I would have ruined everything for her. A burning sensation ached through my back loh, even now, and it made me want to claw at my own skin. The gardens were closer than my living quarters, and this little hideaway had a small pool that I hoped would ease my loh if it got too much to handle.

"How is this possible?" she bemoaned, rubbing at her face in disbelief. Her wings were still on full display, and I assumed she was talking about her activated mating loh. I tried to explain that her wings were a strong mating response, and in most instances of an estreld's back loh growing a successful offspring was born. This was great news for the clan, though I knew Luan had no current desire to have any offspring.

She even said as much once more. Luan groaned.

"He's quite handsome," I commented, trying to keep my emotions in check. Trying to help her accept her response to Trent was making my stomach churn like I would vomit. "His file says he's a warrior, and one of the leaders that help protect our system from outlaws."

Pressing my lips together, I stopped myself from adding that he was the Prince of Krelis. Why did I do that? I knew the answer. Secretly, I hoped she would think he was some mere krelis diplomat, and perhaps she would simply find another way to bridge peace with him that didn't involve mating with him at all. I didn't want to give her any incentive to think mating with Trent was the best option for both of our planets. Luan was practical, and she would mate with him for the sake of the clan, while still running off planet to do her diplomatic galactic quest. If anything, that was perfect for her plans. She could mate with him, bring peace to our planets, then keep herself occupied off-world finding treaties that would free her from her obligations to Krelis.

"He's practically an outlaw himself with how the krelin have been extorting us for our minerals and rock deposits." Her exasperation on the topic of krelins made me smile, like that little bit of indignation was a kernel of hope for her to find another way to help Estreldez. If there was another way, she would find it.

"And the bounty hunter isn't?" I blurted out with a laugh, wanting to change the subject away from krelins. As much as I liked that she still didn't like having a connection to Trent, I still didn't enjoy hearing how she lumped all krelins in with outlaws. A small part of me wanted her approval of Trent, while still not wanting her to like him herself. It was messed up, but I couldn't stop my mind from spiraling. "Don't think I didn't see how you responded to him. Maybe you're just into strong outlaw types."

Luan's face blushed a light purple upon her white-blue skin. It warmed my heart to see she liked another male. Then she gripped my hand as we sat. A silence between us as she squeezed, and then her brows narrowed in concentration. Something was wrong. I shook out the numbness from my fingers as she released me.

"Luan?"

She snapped, "Why do I feel so possessive?"

I could ask the same thing of myself. It seemed both of us were experiencing the chaos of the mating cycle. I explained more for myself than for Luan, "It's common for the mating loh to want potential mates to choose them over others."

Reminding myself that what I was feeling was normal, was all I needed. This would go away, based on my interviews, I told her, "The feeling passes after you've copulated. Biologically, we seek mating to replicate ourselves."

It was all very clinical, I assured. This was all body chemistry, nothing more. I continued, "And once seed is inside us," or our egg sacks are removed, I thought with gloom at my own circumstances, "we feel more free to choose. Many have found they've enjoyed the ceremony much more after the first mating of the evening and go to find other compatible mates while the moon is still at its brightest."

Luan sighed in the same relief I felt after saying it out loud.

Closing my eyes, I could see Trent spreading his black iridescent wings behind him as he undid the straps holding his scaled pants together. Wetting my lips as his hands lowered the fabric down the v-shaped creases that led to the apex of where his cock bulged. A slickness dripped from my folds, and I squeezed my thighs together. My mouth went dry, and my own possessiveness took over.

"You don't have to mate with any of them," I spoke softly, not wishing to give away how much my body yearned to be touched. It was not entirely self-less to support her decision to mate or not, but I also needed her to know that just because she was to be future Almder, she still had agency. She still had choices.

Luan would sacrifice her own happiness to help Estreldez, and as her friend I couldn't allow her to do anything without knowing that not everything would be on her shoulders. We were a clan, not a planet of one. "The mating loh is a powerful feeling, but just like you had the strength to walk away from them earlier, you can walk away from them again, even at the peak of the ceremony.

"You are a strong estreld." I meant every word. I believed in her. "It is by your choice, and grace alone that one of them may mate with you, if any. And whomever you choose, whenever you decide will be a lucky mate." Even if it ended up being Trent, I would accept her choice. Fingers dug into the dirt beside my hip and I felt like my back loh would explode. Moisture prickled at my eyes, threatening to escape.

"Thank you, I needed that." Luan pulled me in for a hug, and I buried my face into her silvery-white hair to hide my emotions. All I wanted to do was stay in this getaway within the palace gardens, waiting until the ceremony was over before I emerged once more. If Luan needed me to give her my strength, whatever I had left in me was hers.

"Do you need me to stay and supervise your ceremonial greetings?" I gulped, praying that she would say, 'no'. I didn't know if I could bear to see her embrace whatever connection she had with Trent, not when my own mating loh were so affected. I had to see Elder Ezra, and have my eggs removed immediately. This was too much.

Thankfully, Luan assured me she would be fine on her own, but the way she dismissed our conversation as yet another interview disheartened me. I pulled away from our embrace, and my training to remain neutral no matter what any mate prospect said kicked in. Many times I doubted whether Luan truly believed we were friends, and a pain throbbed through my chest. If that's all she wanted from me, then I would gladly give that to her.

"What did you feel when your mating loh came out?" The question would never be added to the interview records, not when Almder had already removed me from my advisor duties to the M.R. team, but I needed to know.

"My nerves were on fire, and my shoulders burned. The thought repeated in my head, 'mine'."

I nodded, my heart breaking into shards of irreparable slivers. A mask of indifference plastered on my face as Luan stood to leave. Not daring to meet her eyes once more, I stared into the water, turning my attention away from her as her feet padded away. The rustling of the Retreating Wop plant indicating that she was gone. A sob croaked from my throat.

She would mate with him, I thought with dread.

I'd heard this description before, and it always resulted in a successful pairing. My back seared with pain, and I lunged forward to potentially fall into the water. The dirt crumbled in my fisted hands as I sought some kind of purchase to alleviate my firing nerves. I bit my lip as I ground out a muffled cry. Eyes squeezed shut, I eased them open as I felt a pull at my shoulders that felt less like frying flesh, and more like I'd stretched out the kink that had been hurting me to begin with.

What stared back at me had my jaw dropping.

I flexed, and watched in awe as green veined wings flapped. They sparkled in the water, and I didn't know if that was merely the reflection of the moon's rays or a hallucination brought on by the heat and pain. I didn't dare reach behind me to reassure myself of my sanity. They weren't anything like Luan's jeweled-looking loh, they were

110

leathery... iridescent... with sharp claw-like spikes on the ends.

Slapping my hands to my mouth to cover a gasp, I sucked in air to hold my breath.

One of my parents was... a krelin?

No one could see me like this, I panicked. Blinking my eyes, I willed them to go back inside of my back loh, from which they emerged. Any estreld could retract their back loh on command, but I wasn't any estreld, and these weren't traditional mating loh either. Squinting from one eye, I saw that did nothing. Panting, or more like hyperventilating, I tried to relax my shoulders, and they folded against each other like I'd seen Trent do. Turning to my side, I saw a ripple in the water where my wings were and I shifted to see the wings again. They were just like his... disappearing with the reflection of light when they were closed, but it was merely an illusion of the eyes. If I couldn't control myself, then I'd reveal what I was.

Tears trickled down my cheeks. Luan would look at me differently. I had to see Elder Ezra, immediately. Or I could convince Luan to take me with her on her journey off world. I stayed in my little oasis away from the problems I would have to face from this new realization, building up the courage to confront them.

Chapter Ten

Trent

The connection with my kansa mate buzzed in my blood, a sharp jolt in my mind told me she was under some kind of distress that made me pace the garden waiting for her. Luan would meet here soon, and I worried that this distress she felt would affect her acceptance of wishing to mate with me. I tried to distract myself with the flora, taking a knee to smell the sweet aroma that reminded me of Mabel's juices on my fingers. Quickly, I shook my head to rid myself of the thought. I was here for Luan, and I didn't wish to create more barriers to my kansa bond. Everything in me wanted to feel her in my mind and have her trust me with her thoughts.

"You like the blackpul rose algae?" Luan's voice asked cautiously from behind.

Not wishing to frighten her, I kept my wings folded. For

other krelin warriors it was a display of power, and a way of attracting our mates, but Luan wasn't krelin. I had to keep that fact in mind and respect our differences, if she was going to accept me. I turned at a lazy pace. "It's sweeter than Krel Nectar. I like it very much."

But it wasn't sweeter than Mabel, I closed my eyes to the thought.

Luan rambled on about the bitterness of the algae before it flowered, but quickly added that regardless they smelled nice. An anxious energy consumed me that muddled my mind and I pushed past it to show Luan how compatible we were. I smiled, and tried to charm her with seduction, "I can only think of a few things sweeter." Mabel flashed within my mind once again, and I felt my cock harden from the memory of her taste. Was this my fate? Constantly pushing against my mate bond with Luan because I was foolish enough to touch, to taste another.

She shifted uncomfortably, and a distasteful tang bittered my mouth, making me think I should switch into a more diplomatic approach. The flirtation didn't sit right with me when all I thought of was Mabel. There was still a very real possibility that Luan only gave me her tarnpul offering because Mabel asked it of her.

With a curt nod, she gripped her skirts and took a strong step forward. It was nice to see she wasn't afraid of me, but that was to be expected from a future leader of her clan. "Have you been sent here to discuss trade?" Luan beat me to the conversation switch, confirming she didn't feel comfortable with our arrangement.

I kept my tone pleasant, on the edge of teasing, since it was well known one-on-ones during the mating ceremony were notorious for fooling around to see how the couple responded to one another. I hoped it would disarm this

113

coldness I felt from her. "I've been sent to assess other assets that might be agreeable to Krelis."

I grinned at her hesitation after the mention of assets, we both knew it had to do with mates. Many of my warriors would gladly see if estrelds would form bonds with them, and I was proof it was possible.

No, I corrected, we were proof.

The muscle in my cheek twitched from smiling, it was forced, and though I'd been told my smile was hard to resist, I hadn't been in need of this tactic for many cycles. I could only hope it was still as charming as it once was, though I doubted my own assurances with the way she flinched.

"You wish for more krelins to participate in our mating ceremonies?"

Ah, her hesitancy was about logistics then. Was she testing to see if krelins were amenable to coming to Estreldez for mating, instead of our traditional abduction rituals? Or perhaps, was she concerned about whether krelins actually found estrelds attractive without having wings to speak of, or scales? I nodded, her concern was valid, but I've seen the strength of estrelds, and she was a perfect queen they would follow given she had wings, ones of magnificent fierceness.

"Your females are strong, and our males are fertile when their glands are activated by your radiation. With more men than there are fertile females. Our female warriors are without wings, a sign of carrying fertile eggs for spawning," I explained. These were all facts we both should know. The hive was strong, but we would not be for long if we do not find a new queen, one who is not bent on sending more of our warriors into war when we cannot possibly recoup from the loss.

Her body leaned back, instinctively showing her intentions to flee, or at least the need she felt to extricate herself from my presence. The krelin's and estreld's mating facts were not enough so I continued, keeping my tone soft, "Our warriors are harsh," I admitted with agreement, "they spend their time defending our trade, our planet, and fighting outlaws without the comforts of a clan to soften them."

It was possible Luan did not know of how much Krelis defended Estreldez as much as we did our own planet. Countless times we've stopped King Sylve from coming too close to this sector, and enslaving our hive, or that of estreld's clans. It was natural for my warriors to feel used, and unappreciated when they are treated so abrasively by estrelds during trades. Some of them became disgruntled and sought to receive their own reparations for their efforts by increasing their own take before handing over agreed upon goods. It wasn't ideal, and there was a way to mitigate these circumstances.

I explained this to Luan, "Entitlement has them rebelling, causing tension between our treaties. Something must change, and that change could be the Estreldez clan that soothes the souls of our krelin warriors."

She snapped, "Are you not a warrior yourself? You seem soothed enough to control yourself."

A true warrior, I thought happily of my kansa mate, she would confront me, challenge me, and my warrior horde to be better. Stronger. I smiled broadly, showing off my teeth, she would not be fearful of them. My thoughts went back to how she wasn't the only estreld to confront me, to not be fearful of me, to accept me... No, Mabel didn't truly accept me, though her body complied it was not the same.

It took training to make sure my smiles were pleasant, but keeping my lips closed to cover the carnivorous nature of krelins. The teeth ran down along my throat, but they only

115

came out when triggered by food. Many species were wise to be frightened of how our teeth were strong enough to eat a beast whole, bones and all. Though that fear would ease when they realized krelins mostly consumed nectar... not meat. The teeth were equally good at grinding plants into pulp used to create the nectar our hive needed to survive.

"I am as possessive, and greedy as my hive," I took a step forward, closing the distance between us, "I feel the restlessness within them even now, but I have something to focus on that they do not." A summons tingled up my horns, and one thing I kept to myself was how influenced my hive was by my queen. The queen's bond with the hive was toxic, addictive, and many sought out her affections even at the cost of harming others. Very few rejected this connection with the queen, and if her sights were set on someone... many would not be able to resist her pull.

I had my suspicions that the warriors I'd lost to the Sky Bender were simply puppets at the queen's behest, and I couldn't blame the spy entirely for their deaths. This was on the queen's soul to bear, and soon there would be a new queen. One who respected the hive, respected her clan, and valued life.

Luan. I approached her with a renewed vigor, needing her to distract me from my queen's warmth tingling at my skull, prying her way into my mind.

Knowing I had a kansa bond, and the distance between my planet and Estreldez, made it easier to reject the insistent summons my queen sought out from me. She probably wanted to know how my reconnaissance was going, or perhaps she wanted reassurances that her invasion plan she'd concocted behind my back was in progress. It didn't matter, all that mattered was solidifying my bond with Luan, and knocking my mother from her throne to save my hive.

If she was not afraid of my teeth, then she would not be afraid of my wings. I flared them out to impress her, to show her that I was capable, and confident in my abilities to please her.

"What do you focus on," she rasped out, feeling the effects of my musk in the air. I hadn't sprayed her, but it was impossible for a compatible mate not to be affected when my wings were displayed, and a kansa bond would make the urge to consummate our bond even more difficult to resist. I needed her to see we were made for each other, that the goddess had made me for her. That we would complement each other perfectly.

"You," I replied with restrained eagerness, while wrapping my arm around her waist to bring her against my chest. Trailing fingers up her exposed flesh I sought to show her that her mating loh would respond to me, to my touch.

"You only just met me," she whispered. I pressed my forehead to her to bridge the distance between us, hoping that the contact between my kan horns and her crown of loh would help ignite our kansa bond further. I needed to hear her voice in my mind, I needed her to let me inside.

"You are the Jewel of Estreldez, and the only way my mother will accept a union between our species." My queen would never guess that an estreld would have wings, and even still that one would be able to challenge her hold on the hive.

"Who are you?" She asked with seriousness. I realized my mistake, she didn't know I was the Prince of Krelis, and I had called the queen my mother. *Foolish*, I thought, but she would have had to accept my past eventually.

"I'm the warrior who found a solution to both our problems that doesn't involve bloodshed," I avoided direct acceptance of what she already knew to be true about me. I

117

was more than simply a Krelis delegate. She shivered in my arms.

"You mean to take me," she said with a scowl, though her body still melded to mine in contradiction to her harsh words. She was about to retreat as she snapped at me, "Do you even have the queen's permission to be here? To make this treaty?"

Desperation entered my voice as I begged her to understand that she could change everything, lead our people to peace. Indecision still in her silver eyes, I cupped her chin in my hand, gently tugging her to me as I whispered into her ear, "I will cherish you beyond all else. Not merely a mate, but a partner, a queen. Will you accept me?"

My words felt like ash on my tongue, like I already knew the answer before she spoke. She would not have me.

Luan huffed out my name and at the same time I heard my name echo in my mind... *"Trent."* she was reaching out to me through our bond. It had to be. Though, it still held so much doubt, like she was searching for something to grasp onto between us. Trust that needed time to form. I had to give that to her. I owed her that much, but we were running out of time. I needed her to stop the buzz of my mother seeking purchase within me. Seeking to control me.

"I like my name on your lips," I confessed. Would she say my name again? Wings beat fast behind me, as I wished to take flight, taking her with me. We needed time to bond, and if she'd let me, we could have that time in the Kai Mountain's oasis, just as my ancestors before me.

She groaned, and I took the momentary acceptance to trail kisses down her neck, taking care to be gentle around her sensitive loh. Her wings expanded behind her, and I grinned into her shoulder, satisfied that there was proof of her interest, of our bond.

Mind buzzing, I sought out the connection between us. Followed it while I nibbled down her arms, and sucked on her inner wrist before seeking out her lips to see if she tasted as sweet as the blackpul algae in bloom. Luan trembled in my arms, and I pulled her closer, grabbing her ass, and letting her feel the hard length of my cock, eager to show her the pleasure I could give. "I feel you," I said breathless, closing my eyes to grab hold of our mating bond.

I lifted her into my arms, her legs wrapping around my waist as she ground her fragrant folds against my thickening cock. But my nose twitched at the smell, and the glands of my throat did not respond to her despite our bond. What have I done?

"Not yet," she rasped, but again her words contradicted the way her hands pawed at me to be closer. Her loh brightened the more I explored her flesh. Only my pants prevented our bodies from completing our union. She clung to me, breathy, and eyes hooded with lust as she tried once more to end things, "Too fast."

And I had to agree. Everything felt different, not as it should.

If she truly did not wish for us to bond yet, then I would respect that, but I needed her to say it, because her fingers still laced through my blond hair, tugging at my braid, pulling my lips to hers. Before we could kiss I gave her the exit she sought, "Tell me to stop, and I will."

Though, even as my lips hovered over hers, feeling the heat of her breath, I was already easing my hold on her. A flash of Mabel crying penetrated my mind, and any thoughts of pleasuring Luan vanished.

"I need time," she took my offer of ending this tryst. Her feet already hitting the ground as I eased her from me before she finished her words. "To think," she added.

I nodded, not wishing to prolong this encounter when an urgent need came over me to find Mabel and make sure she was okay. My cock was already disinterested in fooling around, and I folded my wings back allowing them to disappear from sight. I took a step back from her, and glanced around, already seeking out Mabel as if she were just beyond the bushes. Clucking my tongue, I sought to follow the echo with my kan just to be sure she wasn't. That she hadn't witnessed what I'd done with Luan.

Why did that matter? Why did this make me feel so guilty?

"Come to me during the ceremony when you've decided on things." My offer felt flat, and dismissive even to my own ears. Simply a throw away gesture to end this meeting so I could focus on what I truly wished to do. Find Mabel. I sniffed the air, my nostrils flaring... I hadn't paid much attention before, but I'd smelled this before at the greeting arena. A shol? That was impossible, wasn't it?

"There's no guarantee your plans will work. You'd still be mated with me... why?" Luan's voice sounded distant, though she was still within reach. She was concerned about committing to me, to us. With a kansa bond, she would not be able to give of herself to another male as many estrelds are wont to do. Her hesitancy at being faithful to our bond disgruntled me further, and the immediacy to leave her intensified.

I forced myself to remind myself why I chose Luan to begin with. Aside from her birthright to lead her planet.

"I'm fully aware of what your mating loh means, Luan." I couldn't keep the bite of venom from my tone, and I tried my best to calm myself and be soft when I added, "We would succeed." Kansa bonds were rare and respected amongst the hive. "Why you?" I repeated her question out loud before

120

answering her, "Because only a queen will do, and you're the only estreld who dared to research ways to destroy us should negotiations not play in your favor. You are kind, but you are also a warrior at heart. Even your mating loh are beautifully deadly in their pursuit of a mate. You are perfect." *Perfect for the hive*, I thought bitterly, knowing that this perfection wasn't what I wanted, and there was another estreld whose imperfections begged for my attention.

That was all I had to say on the matter, and she could decide at the ceremony later. I turned to leave, sniffing the air, and clucking my tongue to find whoever was spying on us. Luan's feet padded away from the garden, leaving me to my pursuit.

Lifting up into the sky, I flew above the stones and overgrowth to find the male marked as a slave from before, Vareo was his name, and his pointed ears were more pronounced from this angle. He was definitely a shol, spying on me. Whether he was here to seek revenge for his planet was unknown, but I could hardly blame him for whatever reason he had to watch me from the shadows. Revenge, my queen certainly deserved it, but killing her only heir would hardly upset her.

She'd killed most of her spawn already.

Being the only one of the queen's eggs to develop her black veins, she considered me her only spawn. I only knew I had brothers by rumor alone, and not one of them ever stepped forward to confirm or deny relation. If I had the choice, I would have preferred to keep my distance from her as well. She ordered every other offspring to be disposed of, but it's possible some of my siblings were still alive.

I landed before the shol, his growl predatory as he prepared to fight me. At least he wasn't afraid, they trained that out of the slaves early on, and his mark appeared old, faded with time. Shols were sensitive to a krelin's smell, and he wrinkled his nose in response to my nearness. If he was unruly, and bent on revenge on krelins that had nothing to do with his lost planet then I would have to dispose of him. My ki horns extended from my wrists, poison pumped through my veins towards the stingers, ready should he choose violence over discussion.

"You're Prince Trenton," he snarled, recognizing the black veins for what they were.

"You're a shol," I replied flippant, as if we were merely playing a game of let's state the obvious. "My mother still hunts for your kind, obsessed that too many were bound to seek revenge."

Pacing around each other, we stalked cautiously, seeing what the other would do. Did he intend to kill me? Or perhaps something else?

"Is Estreldez your next target?" He spat out as if his very words were as deadly as the venom in my arms.

"Not in the way you assume," I explained protection was my only motive, for both of our species, estrelds and krelins. He didn't believe me and he questioned my intentions to form peace.

His shoulders sagged when he whispered to himself about taking Luan to Krelis as my mate, before he reasserted himself. "She will not choose you," he growled.

"What can you offer her?" That I cannot, I added internally. My wings spread out, and I sprayed him with my musk, wishing to have him sleep so I wouldn't be delayed finding Mabel any longer.

He gagged, and snorted out, possibly preventing the musk from being absorbed into his nasal cavity. Shols had such sensitive receptors that made targeting them with our pheromones difficult. I had no intention of harming him, but he was the last person I wished to be spending time dealing with at the moment. Either I had to kill him if he was feral or allow him time to cool off if he was reasonable.

Testing him I baited, "Your species are nothing but barbarians."

"Right," he scoffed, "that's why the krelins have taken it upon themselves to eradicate all shols."

So, he remains to be a talker. That's good. I smiled at him, keeping my ki stingers at my sides, pointed down.

He began negotiations, "If you're here for diplomacy, you won't kill me here." He believed I wanted him dead... and yes, my ki was an indicator of intention, but also one of reasonable preparation given many would not blame him for seeking to kill me for my hive's past crimes. I needed to know he would not harm krelins that had nothing to do with his planet's destruction. He continued, "And if you're worth being chosen by Luan, then you'll wait to inform your ship about the shol you found on Estreldez until after the ceremony."

Reasonable. It was true, all it would take was a communication to my ship, and we could make sure no ship left here without confirmation they were without a shol passenger. He'd never make it out of the sector, if I were inclined to remove what was possibly the last shol around.

Retracting my ki, my venom receded back down my forearms, and I warned him, "If I see you at the dance, then I'll assume you've changed your mind about our deal. I'm not a monster, shol. Your species has been through enough, and I only seek to make sure my own doesn't find itself in a similar fate, nor the estrelds." I stepped to the side for him to leave, giving him the chance to put in a cheap shot to harm me, if he wished.

The shol glared at me but made no move other than to

watch me closely. I remained still, not even allowing my second lids to lubricate my eyes. Then I heard Mabel's voice from the direction I just came from. I crouched where the shol had spied on me before, and there was a clear view of her, and Gaven. I had wondered why he didn't follow me. And it was clear now that the reason was a beautiful estreld we both had eyes for.

Chapter Eleven

Mabel

Running into couples in the garden was normal during the mating ceremony. Many of them never even noticed they had an audience if someone passed them by. That was what I was betting on to even attempt to leave the hideaway beyond the Retreating Wop. But it wasn't long before I passed by the one couple I never wanted to see.

Trent... I thought, broken hearted in my mind. Luan's legs wrapped around his waist. I didn't have to see past her wings to see her hips grinding on him amongst the blackpul algea. Moans echoed through the air, and I gasped, covering my mouth with both hands. Legs turning to jelly, I couldn't even move away to stop watching them until my body was tugged backward, and I spun to see Gaven holding me in his arms. His loh pulsed brightly and everything blurred around us like we were underwater.

He whispered, "What are you doing here?"

"I was heading to Elder Ezra," I admitted, but it didn't stop me from thinking about what Trent was doing with Luan this very moment. Closing my eyes, I could almost feel like his hands were on me, even though it was Gaven that pulled me in close. My breathing hitched when it felt like there were nibbles tingling down my neck, along my arm, and landing at a sensitive spot on the inside of my wrist. I bit my lip, my new wings ached to move, and I had no idea if I could stop them.

A moan escaped, and I snapped my eyes open in embarrassment. Gaven's eyes were glowing a pastel green, hooded with a desire I hadn't noticed from him before.

"Gaven...?" I tried to snap him from his trance, concern laced in my voice. Was Luan's loh affecting him?

He blinked back the haze, and pulled away, but kept hold of my shoulders. "I'm glad to know you're heading to Elder Ezra. Your life is more important than," he stopped himself from finishing that thought, short of saying, more important than having my own offspring, "than anything. This may not be the appropriate time to ask this of you, but I've requested leave of my position within the palace to be sired."

Sired... he found someone he wished to be bonded with, care for their offspring, and essentially retire from his role as Chief Tactician of Estreldez. He was the best warrior we had, alongside Loric. Of course, he'd wish to settle down one day. This was natural. I nodded my understanding. He was telling me that he would no longer be around the palace. How did Loric feel about his best friend stepping down from his position?

I smiled. "You're not really around the palace much

anyways, are you?" I joked. He was usually off doing whatever it was that was top secret about his job. There were many times he was gone even when Loric returned from diplomatic excursions.

"I wish to change that," he said while leaning in. "I wish to see more of that smile of yours."

My breath caught, and I didn't know how to respond. So, I didn't.

"Mabel, I wish to be sired to you."

I blurted out more loudly than I intended, and feared I'd be heard by Luan and Trent, "You could have anyone!" The question unasked was, why me?

"I know you've done more than simply advise on your findings from mating interviews. I speak with Loric, you know."

"What's that supposed to mean?" I didn't know what he found out about me, but it could be anything.

"It means, I know you're the one that gave Luan information on how to act against the krelin if they kept extorting us during trade. It means I know that I have you to thank for saving my own life during particularly dangerous negotiations."

"Gaven?" Luan swore she wouldn't tell anyone how she came across the information. I would be reprimanded severely if Almder found out that I had relationships with the krelins who came by for deliveries. There was no other way to bribe for the different brands of nectar.

"You are resourceful, and though your heart is open to krelins, you also know the practicality to protect yourself and our clan." He turned his gaze away as he added, "I'm required to tell you before you make a decision about accepting my offer as your sired that I've been mated before. Almder has respected my privacy, and as long as I stayed in a

127

position that all estrelds knew I was not allowed to participate in mating rituals, and never tried to mate with someone potentially fertile, my secret would stay hidden."

It was shocking to know that he'd been bonded with a mate before, but that was no reason for me to reject his offer. It was generous of him to risk even asking Almder permission to be a sire to someone like me. There would be little for him to do being sired to someone with no future of a family to care for.

"I don't understand... we are in a population crisis. Why would Almder keep someone fertile away from other mates? That doesn't make any sense," I reasoned, and the only thing I could think of was that he was being punished for some crime. I narrowed my eyes at him, suspicious of the answer he may give, "What have you done?" Voice wavering, I felt my wings buzz behind me.

Not now, I thought, *not now. Keep it together*, this wasn't the time to see if he still felt like being sired to me after revealing who one of my parents was. There was no love lost for krelins on Estreldez. I tensed up my shoulder blades just in time for him to capture my eyes with his. That's right, keep those pale green eyes focused here. Anywhere was better than noticing the distortion of space behind my back from the camouflage of my wings.

"It's how my mate died," he admitted, startling me. "I may be fertile, but it was my spawn that took my mate from me, and I won't have it happen again," he said the last part with resolve.

Gaven swooped to bring me into his arms, and I shrieked. A quick glance around showed that Luan and Trent were no longer in the clearing near the algae plants, and I panicked. If he picked me up, he might smack right into my wings, so I used my training before he could finish his attempt. Blocking one of his hands with my forearm, I slid my feet between his open legs, and kicked to ground him. He saw immediately what I was doing, and why shouldn't he, he was our best warrior. Gaven parried, ducked before my other hand could connect with his jaw to guide him away from his task of lifting me into his arms like a newborn.

"I won't have you die on me," Gaven insisted. "Please come with me to see Elder Ezra." He grunted, while we sparred on fairly equal footing. I knew he was holding back, but so was I. It took extra care to maneuver, knowing I had to account for wings that though they weren't seen... they were very much physically there, and I didn't need Gaven colliding with them.

Sticking out a hand to stop him from continuing this game, a low buzz came from the bushes that set the hair of my arms on end. My attention pivoted in time to see Trent flying out from behind the foliage. I gasped, turning to Gaven only to see him lifting the mask he had dangling from his neck. He expected Trent to spray him with whatever knocked him out on the shuttle, and I couldn't blame him. Using the distraction to my advantage, I knocked Gaven's feet off balance, and my elbow blew to his chest finishing the trajectory of falling on his ass at my feet.

Trent landed behind me to say, "I see my concern was unwarranted. My apologies for interrupting."

"I had everything perfectly handled, thank you," I clipped back, preening from winning the duel, even if I did cheat a bit. Neither of us were really fighting each other fully, and Trent had actually stopped Gaven's next move which would have been much more difficult to avoid without revealing my wings. So, I guess I should have been thanking him for the interruption. "Shouldn't you be off doing what mates do, alone in the gardens," I pointedly glared at him with a hand on my hip. I didn't have to add, with Luan, not me. My irritation was enough of an indication that I knew what he had been doing. Though I had to accept it, I didn't have to like it.

Gaven dusted himself off and made sure his mask was secured.

"I allowed you some privacy to copulate... are you finished, already?" Gaven's voice echoed a bit through the filters of his mask, but it was clear enough that he'd just made sport of Trent's mating abilities. I couldn't help a chuckle from escaping, though Trent didn't seem ruffled by the pointed mockery. His expression was still regal, and amusement crinkled his golden eyes that made me think Gaven would be getting a taste of his own punches soon enough.

That wasn't all my own eyes took in as I watched, trailing up his chiseled jaw line I stared at his horns peeking out from his hairline. It was almost as if they vibrated the more I stared. Krelins called them kan, I recalled, and I clucked my tongue. A buzz surrounded me as if the air was filled with a heavy energy, and I could feel exactly where Gaven stood beside me, and Trent in front.

"So beautiful," I heard Trent whisper, and I couldn't believe he was talking about me.

"What did you say?" I directed at him.

Gaven replied in his stead, "He didn't say anything. We need to get you checked out by Elder Ezra, immediately. No more games."

I could have sworn he said something, but perhaps that was what I wished he'd think about me. Wanting someone to think you're beautiful was natural, wasn't it? Wanting Trent to think I was beautiful... was foolish. He needed to secure a politically advantageous mating with Luan... not a rejected advisor. Given that I was part krelin myself, it was even less advantageous for the future of our planets to choose me. I didn't even know who my parents were. Why did I even consider myself an option for him? I needed to stop thinking of him like we even stood a chance outside of that shared moment in the shuttle.

"As it is Gaven's duty to escort me around Estreldez, and you are in need of this Elder Ezra, then I shall accompany you. If that is acceptable?" He didn't even glance at Gaven, his golden eyes fixed on me, making my stomach flutter.

I nodded, unable to untie my tongue. Why did I accept him coming along? He just had Luan's legs wrapped around him as she ground against his cock, and here I was a puddle at his feet. As if he could tell my hesitancy he addressed the large hergslat in the room, "And regarding your previous question, I couldn't continue my seduction of Luan while my mind was filled with another."

My cheeks heated at his words. I dared to ask, "And who might that be?"

Gaven scoffed, an odd sound when wearing his mask. "Do you honestly think Mabel is some brainless glorbin that would think you are not going to mate with Luan simply because she isn't wrapped around your cock this moment? If I'd known you were such a claw of male, digging into whatever hole you are presented with, then I'd have protested any match with you directly to the Almder herself."

I didn't need Gaven to stick up for me, and I certainly didn't appreciate being compared to a glorbin. According to him I'd have to be brainless to desire Trent, and that would mean I was exactly like a glorbin flighter attracted to the shiny jewel that was Trent. Just a flitting fancy before finding a new bauble to admire and consume at whim. Was that so bad? To want him?

Before either of them could say another word I snapped, "If he were a claw, then this conversation wouldn't even be happening!"

Pausing, Gaven stared at him, hurt in his eyes. "What are you saying?" He spoke softly, trying to make our conversation private once more. It was too late, we had already opened this can of rocks, and krelin's hearing was known to be impressive. I doubted our whispers would go unheard.

"She's saying I wouldn't have stopped at a taste when we were on the shuttle," Trent completed the thought that made the back of my neck color from my pounding heart. I had to tense up my shoulders to keep my wings from fluttering. This was not the time to go from one uncomfortable topic to another equally uncomfortable topic. Why did he have to bring that up? I guess I was the one that actually brought it up, but the way Trent was watching me made my insides squirm with anticipation like he was offering a do over.

"Why did you?" I ignored Gaven, and blurted out my thoughts.

"You know why." I heard a gruffness to his voice as he took a step forward, challenging me. "Are you accepting my conditions?" His wings snapped out in what should have been threatening, but something in me melted at the display. All it did was bring attention to the way the black wings glittered in the moon's light making them look like the universe sucking me into a trance. They were beautiful. They were deadly. And I wanted to touch them.

Clearing my head, I tried to make my brain work through what conditions he was talking about? The one where he basically wanted me to be his second mate, I recalled with irritation.

"I am nobody's second!" I screamed out loud... and

hushed as soon as I realized what I had just said in front of Gaven.

The green pallor of Gaven's skin paled, the veins in his neck bulged like he was clenching his jaw, which I couldn't see fully with his mask on. I didn't need to see his mouth to know I had offended him.

It was insensitive to say such a thing when he had just revealed to me that he'd lost his first mate. I felt sick to my stomach, and with myself. Any mate would be blessed to be chosen by Gaven, and it was wrong of him to think he was to blame for his mate's death. Knowing him for as long as I had, he was a bit reserved, and sometimes stiff with his approach, but he was kind, and attentive.

"I didn't mean..." I tried to unbury myself, but instead groaned in frustration with both of them.

Gaven grabbed my bicep, and bit out, "You don't have to accept me to prioritize yourself... your life."

Trent's wings created this threatening buzzing noise that made my skin tingle, and my stomach flip. Why was his warning making my own wings twitch to respond back in kind? Gritting my teeth, I had to chew the inside of my cheek to distract myself so I didn't flash my wings, destroying the camouflage that made the light bend around them when folded back.

Yanking my arm from Gaven's hand, his grip fell away gently as I nodded my agreement. "Fine," I clipped. "But I don't need a chaperone. I was already heading there."

"What is threatening your life?" Trent demanded, the intensity in his golden eyes told me that he wouldn't take no for an answer.

It wouldn't be a secret forever, and if I truly wanted him... he'd have to know the full truth eventually, didn't he?

"None of your business," Gaven came to my defense,

despite my rash outburst from moments before.

"It's fine," I dismissed. Looking Trent in the eyes, not blinking I said, "I'm having my eggs removed."

I expected him to object, or say there must be another way, because I knew that he needed a mate that could give him offspring, and without my eggs that wouldn't be possible with me. He did none of that. His eyes softened, and his arms lifted for a moment as if he wanted to hold me, wrap me up into his arms to protect me, but he stilled to stop himself.

He merely nodded his understanding and then said, "One should never be alone when they lie their spawn to rest with the Goddess Lenkal. I shall join you, if you will have me." He bowed his head.

I blinked in astonishment. This was not the response I had imagined, and I definitely didn't prepare my heart for how much his words and his offer of support made my insides break. I shouldn't want him there, but just having him next to me fed me a strength I never knew I was capable of. Half of me believed I'd get to Elder Ezra and try to convince her to find a way to save my eggs, or escape off planet and try my luck with the outlaws on the chance I could find technology to help me. But, with him standing there, stooped in mourning for the offspring I was losing, for the future I would never have because it was what was best for my survival made the threat of tears sting my eyes.

What was he doing to me?

My lips quivered, and I sucked in a sob.

He lifted his eyes to see me nod with my chin then I squeezed my eyes shut. Next thing I knew, a hand grabbed my fisted one and gently stroked with his thumb. He was there for me. I didn't have to look to know it was Trent. His smell was unmistakable, and I collapsed forward into his chest.

He whispered into my hair, "Even a queen must have her hive to carry on in difficult times. I am here, Mabel..." His arms were wrapped around me, and suddenly he faltered, his voice catching. Oh fuck... my wings...

Chapter Twelve

Trent

Both of my hearts stopped when Mabel proclaimed she would be nobody's second. I hadn't realized until that moment she thought I had made her a lower priority than that of my efforts to secure a future for my hive with Luan. My political union with Estreldez was important, but when I offered myself to Mabel on that shuttle, it was as my only true mate. My kansa... nothing less than the only one my hearts would beat for.

But then... it was Luan who spoke to my mind, wasn't it?

Was I rejecting my kansa bond for Mabel? When I thought she was in pain, I dropped everything to find her. Luan wrapped around me brought a tangy bitterness to my tongue. The very idea of thinking Mabel was distressed harmed my very soul. I'd do anything to take that pain for myself, and I was the one that caused her that pain with my words. I was not clear enough with my intentions.

She had to know, that I would sacrifice whatever there was with Luan for her... I would find a way to have our peace treaty without mate bonding if need be. Luan could still be the queen of the hive without making her my mate. *I'd find a way*, I repeated to myself, feeling this ache building within my gut at watching Mabel look at me with such venom in those beautiful green eyes. It was unthinkable to turn down a kansa bond, but I would do it for her.

Gaven spoke of her life being in danger, and my wings buzzed to protect her, to fly into battle, and destroy whatever it was that would harm her. As his fist gripped her slim arm, the only danger I saw was him. My vision blurred to red, and his only saving grace was that Mabel had wretched from his hold and he did not attempt to subdue her once more.

Sadness in Mabel's eyes tore through my chest and squeezed my hearts as she spoke of having the family she longed for be removed and lost from her future. I bowed my head in sorrow and respect for her own mourning. "I will join you, if you will have me."

When I lifted my eyes, tears brimmed and dripped down her cheeks before both of us. As if magnetized, we came together in a heap. I pulled her into my arms, and pressed her to my chest. Only then did my hearts ease. Allowing me to lend her my strength was not a weakness, but a show of truth to accept support when it was needed. The Krelis hive was strong because it was not one warrior but many working together. We are weakest when we work against each other, and with my mother as queen... the cracks in our unity were growing.

A soft flutter of air wafted on my face as I nuzzled into Mabel's silky black hair. My arms slid around to hold her closer, and I stilled at the solid barrier that prevented my attempt. I moved up, following the obstruction that was soft, and firm with just a bit of give, but I stayed close to her back, and then moved under to fully hold her. The pressure of the bottom of what I knew to be impossible touched my forearms, the protrusion of wings from where her loh resided. Yet they were as imperceptible as my own. Now that I thought to look for it, I could see the distortion of light rippling, and with me so close to her... it wouldn't be long before Gaven could see the change in how I appeared behind her form, so I pivoted and extended my own wings to distract him.

I whispered, "Does he know?"

With her cheek pressed into my chest I could feel her gnaw at her lip with uncertainty. She shook her head instead of speaking. So, he didn't know what she was...

"Who is your—" I stopped myself, remembering what she had said before about being raised by the Almder, and what Gaven had said of being raised by the offspring training facilities. She didn't know who her spawn makers were. "This shouldn't be possible." But it was... She was a krelin, raised with estrelds. I should have seen the signs, but with her estreld markers... I dismissed them. She wasn't just any krelin...

My hearts beat rapidly, and my mind whirled just as swift. What did this mean? How was this possible? I shook my head into her hair, closing my eyes to think, hoping that Gaven wouldn't interrupt me before I had a moment to process.

I knew how. I merely needed proof.

If I was correct, then I could save my hive, and convince this hidden treasure that she was who my hearts belonged to, regardless of any kansa blessing or not. But first, we had to make sure she was safe from harm. We would see this Elder Ezra first, and perhaps gain more proof of my suspicions if an elder knew more about Mabel's heritage.

"It seems I've received a better offer, Gaven. Mabel will be taking over your escort duties for now," I informed him before bending my knees and launching into the air, my hands swooped down to lift her by her firm ass, and her legs instinctively clung to my waist. I grunted my appreciation, and her own arms pulled close to my neck.

She whispered against my skin, sending chills down my spine, "Thank you."

"I wouldn't thank me yet, I require payment for my services," I joked, though I didn't know how much my own body believed I was teasing about wanting her. With her small frame cocooned in my arms, and her warmth pressed against my hardening cock, my interest was obvious. A different kind of instinct built within me, seeking to steal her away from here, and sequester us away for me to seduce her.

Instead of being frightened she purred, "Don't make promises you can't keep." She nibbled at my neck, and it nearly undid me, before her hand trailed down my torso, and latched onto my bulging length through my pants. My flight faltered and we dipped in the sky before I righted my balance.

My voice vibrated as I warned her, "If you don't stop, we will be taking a detour before we visit your elder. This is a promise I intend to keep." The palm of her hand rubbed firmly against my shaft, and I sucked in a heady breath.

Her green eyes were hooded with lust, and I suspended our flight out of the gardens. My wings buzzed behind me, keeping us afloat, I adjusted my fingers around her ass to slide along the crease of her cloak, wishing that I had thought to grab her beneath the layers instead of atop them. She bit her lip and closed the distance to explore and seek out more pressure from the colliding of our eager mouths. Her lips worked against mine, plundering for purchase with teeth tugging and delicate swipes of her tongue meeting with my own. I wished to lace my hand through her hair to intensify our kiss, but I would not stop the timed motion of my fingers rubbing in time with her own strokes of my cock, like we were one.

But it was not enough, and she did not stop as I had warned her to. This time I would not deny the nectar she offered, and I would accept the consequences of that. Needing to feel more of her without the constraints of her robes in the way, I rushed through the gardens to find a secluded spot away from prying eyes. When my feet touched ground, her wings burst out showing me the gorgeous green and yellow iridescent colors that swirled like stars in the midnight sky. They were exactly as I remembered the images of the last queen to be born to the hive beside my mother.

Queen *Leahme*...

Between heavy breaths Mabel asked, "Who's Leahme?"

Had I said her name out loud? I must have.

"I'm sorry for the distraction. Your wings remind me of her." I tucked some of her black hair behind her ears, and kissed her once more.

"Who was she?" she insisted, and I could have sworn I detected a bit of jealousy that made me grin.

"No one to be concerned about. She died when I was still a spawn." Her shoulders slumped and I feared I had ruined the mood so I tried to explain a bit more about her so she would not dwell on her death. "Queen Leahme, was the reason why I exist today. My mother's larva sacks were fertilized, but not growing... her care over the hive's last batch of warriors brought fresh life to Krelis, without her I probably

140

wouldn't be here, and neither would many of the warriors that follow me."

I didn't finish the story of Queen Leahme, not wishing to frighten her. Many of the hive were in discussions of marking Leahme the new queen of Krelis when she died giving her last blessing to her only spawn. Some believe her spawn never grew, and others believe someone stole her only heir. Many of my hive believe there was a missing queen in the universe that would perhaps look surprisingly close to Mabel, if she weren't half estreld.

Imagine, Queen Leahme mating with a male estreld all those years ago. It seemed impossible, but my eyes did not deceive me. Mabel was in my arms and had wings just like who I believed to be her spawn maker. I needed proof to convince the hive, but I didn't need proof of anything to confirm how I felt about her. Regardless of if she wished to claim her rightful place as queen of Krelis... I would make her mine.

"And I remind you of her?"

"Very much so. You are strong, kind, and without you I'd be less of the male I want to be."

"And what kind of male is that?" she teased, while her hand squeezed my cock.

"The kind buried inside of you, while my name echoes from your lungs." Now that we were on the ground, I could swiftly tug her cloak's fabric away from her, but she eased herself down and unlatched my coverings to sink her hand down my pants. Feeling her skin on my strained cock sent shockwaves through my nerves, and I growled.

"Not until I taste you," she said, while releasing her hold to slip both hands along my hips, over my ass, and tug the pants down to unburden me from my leathers. My cock stood eagerly awaiting her appraisal. Would she be frightened to see my sex so freely exposed, unlike that of an estreld male locked inside his sheath? Her eyes widened at the sight of me, and I worried before the side of her lips lifted in a grin and her tongue swiped across them in anticipation for what she had planned for me. My wings hummed behind me, and I listened to her command to taste what she wished.

The glands at the back of my throat pulsed with a clucking noise that was involuntary with my species to lure in our mates. If she had horns, she would feel me inside of her and be drawn towards fulfilling more. And for me, with each pulse my body prepared to drink her juices once they were offered... preparing the proteins I would use to make our kantos, I preferred this term to the estreld title of larva sack. It spoke more about the bond needed to create the space our young would grow from.

The trinket I had made from the last time I tasted her molded to my chest beneath my chest plates. Tradition would be to gift it to Mabel and she would wear it as a sign of us starting a family together. Krelins would congratulate us upon seeing it, and we would celebrate.

Our young... I thought sadly before Mabel brought me back to her beauty with a drop of her robes. My goddess, she was perfect. Her skin had a green sheen tinting at her contours that before I had dismissed as purely estreld, but the patches of scale along her thighs hidden by her robes spoke of a different heritage. My own scales along my cock fluttered and flexed at the sight of her. A low growl rumbling in my throat echoing with my mating glands call.

Her hand lifted to her chest, and gripped there as if she were stunned. "You haven't even touched me... and I can feel you inside my veins," she said with a gasp. "How is this possible?"

She felt my call, and I brimmed with happiness that both

my hearts and body were in sync with their need. That she would both stir my hearts and connect as if she had kan of her own was a blessing. I paused in my thoughts, perhaps she did have kan of her own. Her wings sprouted from her loh, and I recalled seeing two small jewels on her temples, above her brows, now hidden by her hair. I risked closing the distance she created between us and brushed her strands aside. My fingers caressed the small black nubs protruding from where there was once green loh to match her eyes. That's where they were hiding. She shivered at my touch.

"These are kan," I fondled them, knowing how sensitive they were, and wished for her to feel me more inside of her. She moaned deliciously. "When you are done tasting what you desire, I will show the pleasures of having them."

"These?" Mabel lifted her hands to touch her forehead, feeling for them until she discovered the two horns, her kan. "Why now?"

"It's common for queens to take time to sprout their kan as well as their wings. Triggered when they are ready to mate." I glanced down at my hardened length bringing attention back to what she wished to do with me.

She smiled mischievously as she slinked forward, her breasts pressed into me as her hand slid down to grip and squeeze. "Tell me why you want me. Tell me why there can't be peace without a mating treaty. Tell me," she growled out. I closed my eyes feeling my skin heat with her touch.

"I can't stop thinking of you. I lie awake dreaming you. During the day, every female merely reminds me of you."

"Even Luan?"

I realized where this was going. I had to make up for what I'd done earlier. Guilt filled me, but I would take it. "The moment I thought of you in distress there was no interest, and there would be no mating even if I willed for it." My cock

143

was as flaccid as gelatin when I thought of Mabel in pain. But as she holds it firm in her grip, it throbbed for more of her. My scales fluttered in her hold, flexing with my blood flow. She tried to stroke her hand down my shaft, only for my scales to fold back and stop her attempt. Quirking a brow, she expected me to explain, and my mind was electrified with even the slightest of movements.

"They are meant to do that inside of you with ample lubricant," I said, but she grinned, lowering her head.

She brought the tip of my shaft to her lips and her tongue swiped out with a flick, then another. The saliva from her tongue helped her slip from one scale to the next as they expanded at her hot touch until her mouth devoured me.

"Fuck—" I gritted, sucking in a breath. My wings beat behind me with a buzz, and my glands continued to pulse more quickly. It was unheard of to have a mate do such things to a warrior, the way her tongue played with my scales, and fluttered around was making my toes curl in my boots, I had yet to remove.

I huffed and assured her, "You don't have to do that."

She glanced up with those bright green eyes hooded, her hand squeezing the bottom of my length, my precum dribbling across her cheek as she rubbed it. "Do you not like it?"

"It's not that, it's just—"

Her tongue dipped out to lap up my excitement in a slow tantalizingly torturous lick. "I don't care what I'm supposed to do, if I did then neither of us would be here." She was right. We both had reasons not to be together that went beyond whether we were attracted to each other or not. For the sake of our planets, the clan, and the hive... we had obligations to something greater than ourselves.

"That's not what I meant. I want you, all of you." Mates

didn't play with a male's cock because our scales were meant to knot, making this kind of foreplay difficult with unruly scales that didn't listen to whether they were inside a mouth or a throat... it was highly likely for a mate to become stuck... or even suffocate if I wasn't careful and came in her mouth.

Pressure built up as she suctioned, using her tongue to swirl around, expertly flowing with the scales as they fluttered. During sex, the scales would add more pleasure, filling, and touching her inner walls, until the scales became hard as I ejaculated, locking us both in place. I couldn't let that happen yet. Biting down on my lip, I moaned, regaining control as the sensations rippled through me.

"You're going to make me come," I warned her, but she didn't stop. Did she not know what was going to happen? "Mabel, I'll swell, and—" My own groan interrupting my warning. Her hips moved in time with her head movements, and I noticed her other hand was between her thighs, sending me over the edge. Just as I came her hand clamped down on my scales like she was catching a fish. She smiled up at me like she had everything handled from the beginning, and perhaps she did.

Swallowing, she licked her lips, and said, "I had access to your mating file."

"And you read it." Thoroughly, I thought with satisfaction.

She shrugged coyly. As soon as she released my cock my scales sprung out rippling taut.

"Then you know I'll have to use other methods to please you now." I didn't allow her the time to reply, a gleeful squeal erupted from her as I lifted her and devoured her lips with mine. Her precious smile making my lips meet her teeth a few times, and I couldn't help but chuckle myself. She was perfect, and I would show her what my kan were capable of.

Chapter Thirteen

Mabel

My body buzzed from tasting him. His cum tasted better than my favorite nectar at the end of a long day... like the blackpul algae's crushed petals. I didn't think I'd enjoy that as much as I did, but now that I'd done it, I wanted to do more of it again. I should have felt guilty for doing this behind Luan's back, against what the Almder's wishes were to bring our planet's together through political mate bonding. But I didn't. I wanted him. I wanted this.

I knew I couldn't have sex with him, not without risking my life, so I did the next best thing, and according to his file krelins weren't able to use their cocks again while their knotting spines were hardened. My intentions were to explore him without the risk of fertilizing eggs that I would soon have removed, knowing that it would be too difficult to go through with removing them if there was a chance I'd created spawn. Even if the chance was small, I'd find a way for them to live at any cost.

I'd hoped that tasting him, and feeling my own fingers between my thighs would be a memory I could keep with me. That it would be enough to sustain me as he once more chose a queen like Luan, but a possessiveness was coming over me. Trent's lips crashed into mine, and the hunger didn't fade, it grew. I reached up and gripped his horns, and a surge of energy rushed through my fingers and down to my core.

"Can you feel me inside of you?"

All I could do was moan, and wished his cock wasn't unable to ease the ache of my throbbing walls, needing to feel him deeply seated within me. I could feel my nerves firing off, but it made me crave pressure, a fullness to stretch and relieve the pulsing need of my heat.

I need to feel more of you, I thought as he moved to nibble down my neck, pulling my body in by the dip of my lower back.

"It would be my pleasure," he replied like he could read my thoughts. His nose nuzzled into my shoulder, and he trailed kisses along my skin. Heat pooled in my chest, and my head felt light and tingly.

Breathing ragged, his palm cupped my folds, a finger slipping between to explore. When he hit the tip of my clit I squirmed, but he held me firm against him. Stroking down then up, I bit my lip against the pressure that could only be satisfied with more touch, more of him.

"That's not where I had expected your pleasure nerves to be," he said between kisses along my neck.

"I'm not a normal estreld," I joked, but my words were more true than I knew only yesterday. Most estrelds had their clits at the bottom of their folds to give the male more

147

stimulus for fertilizing their eggs, mine was similar to the human female I'd interviewed before the ceremony, she was brought here through the exchange program to stay with Estreldez for a few cycles to learn of our planet, and I was fascinated to see our similarities.

"I can see that," he paused. I could feel the grin on his mouth against my shoulder. "Mabel, being estreld or krelin isn't what makes you remarkable."

"Stop talking," I begged, wanting him to continue what his fingers had started.

He cupped my heat, and stilled, making me squirm. My hips lifted trying to find purchase once more, but he held me still with him, then forced my chin his direction to look at him. His golden eyes were serious, narrowing at me. "You are remarkable," he repeated. I tried to look away, but he growled, and I reluctantly returned to see the fire in his eyes. "It has nothing to do with what you are, but who you are, and I will say it as many times as I need to, and more, for you to hear this truth."

A single finger slid back between my folds, and I shivered, my eyes closing.

"Open your eyes," he demanded.

With a moan, I complied.

"You were the one that gave Luan the intelligence on how to defend against krelins," he said with a silky voice that almost made me gloss over the weight of what he was saying. Did he overhear what Gaven and me were discussing? He must have. Was this why he was now suddenly okay with seducing me? For confirmation, counterintelligence? My muscled tensed up, then his finger plunged inside of my heat, making my eyes roll back in pleasure. Distracting me with his touch, he continued, "You told me you enjoy home-brewed nectar, and if you somehow created a deal to receive some, then that means you were close enough to one of my warriors to glean information about krelins." He nipped at my ear.

There was nothing to deny. He already eavesdropped on my conversation with Gaven.

A second finger pushed beside the other, as his thumb rubbed in circles around my clit. His breath hot on my skin he grunted in time with my own moans as he pumped in and out of me, the intensity increasing with each thrust. My heart pounded in my ribcage, and I clung to his shoulders as his tongue licked up my earlobe.

"I was going to put a stop to what my warriors were doing unattended at the trade routes, but when I arrived—" He grunted, pulling me closer, his fingers working faster, harder, and I gasped. He whispered, "I saw a hooded figure, completely obscured, chatting with my Chief of Trade... making him smile."

Fuck, did he know it as me? I knew the aggression coming from him was about finding out I had somehow become a spy for estreld through my love of nectar, but I didn't want him to stop. My walls clamped around his fingers, filling me and thrusting in and out so adeptly that I couldn't tell they were fingers anymore, but a magical instrument about to make me come undone.

"I thought it was Luan, who had made efforts to uncover ways to infiltrate and use her knowledge to protect, make peace, or destroy krelins from the inside out, but it was you, wasn't it." He bit down on my shoulder, and I moaned as my orgasm built. My head flung back, and he took a nipple into his mouth, licking and suckling.

He stopped, making me whimper, and a third finger slipped between my folds. "Tell me Mabel, tell me it was you charming my warriors, while buying your nectar."

"You already know," I rasped.

"I had my suspicions when you talked about liking different nectars before, but Gaven confirmed it for me. I gave Luan all the credit for your efforts. You were the reason why I thought there was another way to join our planets. You were the one I wished to have as my mate before I even met you. The queen willing to risk herself to help her clan. The queen willing to open her heart and make another krelin smile, though she did not have to. Kind but capable of doing what had to be done to protect her people."

Trent's forehead rested against mine, his horns tapped against my own, a wave of lighting sparked through my body at the contact. He moaned along with me.

"*You are mine, Kansa. Come for me.*" His words echoed in my mind, and a liquid heat spilled down my thigh as I screamed. "Say it," he growled.

"You are mine," I said, reeling forward and clinging to him as my wings fluttered behind me. My hips grinding on his fingers as I repeated the words in my mind over and over again.

"I hear you," he whispered, and I could swear I felt his words in my very bones. When I opened my eyes, we weren't even touching the ground. Both of our wings buzzed, keeping us afloat, making the bushes sway with our wing's movement. "My queen," he kissed my temple, then my cheek, and searched out for my lips before hungrily devouring my moans.

His fingers slipped from my folds, and with a smile on his face he lifted them to his mouth to lick my juices.

"You taste fucking amazing, My Kansa," he said before lowering us into the hidden pool of water. Our wings folded back disappearing, but I could feel them soaking up the cool relief, my nerves still firing off from his touch.

As my mind unspun itself from the throbbing between

my legs, I clung to him, wrapping my legs around his torso as we waded within the buoyant pool, cleaning off our sweat from the humidity of Estreldez, and the delicious things he just did with only a few fingers.

I bit my lip before asking him, "You aren't angry?"

"Angry? For saving me the trouble of reprimanding my warriors for causing trouble?"

"For spying, and uncovering a krelin weakness?" I clarified. His eyes softened, and he pulled me against his chest.

"You think my own warriors wouldn't tell me what they had revealed once I interrogated them? The Chief of Trade Operations told me about the woman that bartered for nectar and told me of her questions as soon as I confronted him. I wish you hadn't been so good about hiding who you were. It would have saved me the trouble of seeking out the wrong mate."

"I don't understand..." I whispered, muffled into his firm pectorals, tracing the sensitive skin around his nipples with my lips. An indent of a wing was marked just above, and I smiled at it, wondering if it was an emblem from inside his armor.

He moaned, and then chuckled. "I thought Luan was you in more ways than one. First, I thought she was the one that uncovered a krelin weakness. It wasn't like the chief stated it outright, but you were clever in your deductions, weren't you." It wasn't a question, he sounded proud, and I grinned with embarrassment. This was not how I expected him to react to this information. I had betrayed him, and the chief, by telling Luan about the reason Krelis needed our Glorbin Flower deposits. They only requested small amounts, but it was the only thing they wanted from the trades.

"Why hide that you don't use any of the supplies we

trade for except for the Glorbin Flower? Luan was convinced that you requested more and more of our resources for the food we need because Krelis wants to weaken the planet for takeover. Take enough resources, no matter what they are, to increase the demand for hard labor, and give less and less food in return until Estreldez is dependent on only what Krelis can provide."

"Is that what you think?"

I shook my head. "I think you're hording the Glorbin Flower so that no other trader can access it, and perhaps the outlaws may believe there isn't enough of the resource on our planet to risk trying to attack us for it."

"You didn't tell this to Luan, did you," he remarked with a lilt that suggested he was amused.

"No, I only told her that krelins don't have any need for the jewels they trade for. You don't eat them, and there's been no reports of increased exports of jewels outside of Krelis for any trade agreements with other planets. Other trade agreements we have in place haven't reduced their demands on the jewels we offer, so Krelis hasn't offloaded what we've given. If you truly wanted to fuck with Estreldez, all you'd have to do was flood the market with the trade you've already accumulated."

"Luan still believes we intend to use our stockpiles to threaten Estreldez," he reasoned, and nuzzled into my wet hair.

"Are you the spy now, Prince of Krelis?" I teased, though it wouldn't be unreasonable to think he could have both. Feelings for me, and a desire to seek out information that would benefit his hive.

"I've bedded the enemy, have I? That is what a spy is, is it not? No, My Kansa, we are not enemies, we are leaders seeking out truth to save lives. She isn't wrong, my mother

152

fully intends to use those stockpiles to ruin your trade if her plans to secure the planet do not succeed."

"Why is Glorbin Flower so important?" I didn't know everything about what was going on, but I needed to if I was going to try to help.

He smiled. "There is a scientist from Trillume—"

I interrupted him, "On the other side of the galaxy?"

His mouth flattened. What he was about to say was serious, and he lifted me on the edge of the watering hole. "The scientist found uses for Glorbin Flower, one of which is how to break it down into its components. Its high concentration of a substance they call Ordin is a highly efficient fuel source for ships to travel greater distances without needing to recharge or stop at waystations. With Ordin, the Trillume warships are capable of crossing from one end of the galaxy to the other without delay. And they will. The Ordin will allow them to have oversight on more than this galaxy. More planets will submit to their control, and Krelis and Estreldez will be next."

I shivered. From talking with Loric on occasion, I knew what Trillume was capable of. They policed the galaxy and we appreciated that they would not allow planets to go unchecked if they crossed any galactic laws, but even he was skeptical about how the laws came to be. They were set by Trillume themselves and the stories of how they gained the armies at their disposal were horrifying.

To some the story of how the trill went to Necias Prime, challenged their tribal leader, and won the 'respect' of the planet to become their new overlord, was an act of true benevolence. They didn't war to gain control of the warriors that serve as their sword and enforcement of laws across the galaxy.

But I'd always wondered, what would have happened if

the trill lost? And how exactly did they win? The details were never revealed in the stories. What if the trill were just as vicious as the outlaw planet Necias Delta Fal? They simply saw an easier way to get what they wanted and it worked... but if it didn't... would they have taken the planet by force? I had my suspicions, and I was glad we were too far away from the planet Trillume for them to have any particular interest in reaching this sector. But now... that wasn't the case.

And I was frightened. Trent could see the horror on my face, and he rubbed my thighs with his hands as he waded between my legs. His cheek rested on my leg, and he squeezed my thigh in a hug with his face.

"The trill can't find out how much Glorbin Flower is actually available on Estreldez. I'm aware that the only reason why you can't trade more is that it's considered a food source for estrelds... and the stone is dangerous to mine. You have to stop Estreldez from exporting anymore Glorbin Flower, it has to cease to exist outside of this planet."

I agreed with him, but what was I supposed to do about it. I could talk with the Almder, but it wasn't my decision.

He saw the uncertainty in my eyes. "Mabel, do you not understand who you are now? You are the future Queen of Krelis. You aren't simply an advisor to the Almder of Estreldez, you are a leader speaking with another leader."

I stammered, "You are the Prince of Krelis, that is—"

"A queen's duty to implore the Almder to listen to reason," he finished for me. I gnawed on my lip uncomfortable with his certainty that I would be a queen of any planet. Being his mate didn't make me a queen, and I doubted his mother would be stepping down willingly. His tongue licked up my leg, and I arched back to stare at the stars above us. His arms wrapped around the back of my knees and pulled my ass forward to expose myself to him.

His mouth buried between my slick folds, distracting me from the future he described. Trent moaned into my heat, and I hung onto his horns to pull him closer. His tongue dipped and plunged into my core, as he sucked up my juices like he wasn't surrounded by water and to drink from me was the only way to slake his thirst.

Chapter Fourteen

Trent

The craving for my mate's nectar was overwhelming after accepting that my instincts were correct all along. Mabel was the queen I had searched for since that day I saw her mysterious form on the satellite transfer station of Bina exchanging pleasantries with my chief, then found out to what extent my chief divulged information to her. I waited to see how the information would be used, and prepared for the worst, only to find her return once more and nothing but a successful transfer of goods with no incident. I thought it was Luan, but this whole time it was Mabel.

From the moment I met her, I didn't know who she was, but she was the key to merging our planets. I didn't know how true that was until now. She'll make a wonderful Queen of Krelis, rule fairly, but not be pushed over. And I understood, as I drank in my mate's wet heat, the need to please her, the need to be connected with her more than any other. Her smell overwhelmed my senses, and it was so obvious now what she was.... who she was. She had the musk of a krelin. It was no wonder that my chief was compelled to share so much.

I still needed proof that she was Queen Leahme's heir, and the whole hive would be hers. Even without proof, they would follow her eventually, but I wished for her to have an easy transition, and there was no telling how much time we had before King Sylve tried to gain access to Estreldez before Trillume warships arrived.

My mating glands throbbed, and I knew my body was preparing a kantos sack for our family. Pain surged through my chest knowing where she was headed to after our momentary escape from reality. Perhaps I could convince the elder to put her eggs in stasis, so I had time to build a kantos and attempt to spawn without harm to Mabel. I let the thoughts itch at the back of my mind, pushing them to the background so I could enjoy the feast before me.

Mabel stroked my horns as she bucked into my mouth, and I greedily accepted every drop her body gifted me. Insatiable, I wanted more, needed more. I played with her clit as it pulsed, and hummed its pleasure, licking up and down her slit before pushing my finger up, petting the inside of her clenching walls. Feeling the stretch and give as I added another finger had my cock begging to fill her, but with my scales locked up, I could do nothing to ease that ache. Even the cooler water sloshing against it did nothing but remind me that I was not inside of my mate, giving everything I had.

She deserved nothing less than all of me, and our kansa bond was yet to be fully accepted until we were one.

Pumping within her heat, I sought to be deeper, but I

only had the length of my fingers, and the only way I feel more of her was to use all of them. Teasing the entrance with a third finger, she moaned and wiggled to open for me. I had feared estrelds would be much too small to take a krelin at all, but exploring how perfect my kansa mate was proved otherwise. The craving to bury my cock within her grew, and I needed to know beyond doubt that I'd fit. Pushing my three fingers together, I twisted and massaged my pinky at the base of her folds while I sucked on her clit. This would be impossible to do if she had her clit on the bottom like other estreld females, and that only further excited me that she was mine, and she was perfect for me.

"Let me fill you," I begged. She lifted her ass slightly to adjust, and her thighs spread wider to accommodate. I grinned as my fourth finger slipped inside, knowing that my thumb could tuck between them all, and I'd have her sitting on my fist until I felt every part of her. My hearts thrummed as her moans grew louder the deeper I got. I let her drive the pace, her hips grinding my hand. She lifted on her arms to guide the angle, and I felt the pressure of her walls at my fingertips before she stopped at the hilt with tiny taps at the nub that brought her pleasure the more I touched it.

"*There it is,*" I told her through our bond, satisfied that she'd come for me again.

"I can't," she pulled away, and I placed my other hand on her abdomen to guide my hand inside of her.

"You can," I encouraged, feeling her inner walls thrum and quake.

She grabbed onto my horns and began to rock back and forth.

"That's it," I said grinning against her clit. "Come for me mate."

And a rush of heat pooled in my chest when I heard her

158

in my mind, "*Trent!*" My name echoed over and over for every time my middle finger tapped the back of her core, and her juice leaked down my forearm as I felt her rocking intensify. She pulled my horns closer, and I held her hips down to help keep my fingers where she needed them most.

"Yes, yes... yes!" she panted as her thighs clamped around the back of my head.

My mouth filled with nectar made just for me, and I drank with greed. It tasted sweeter than any flower, and my whole body warmed from the inside out. My mate was magnificent, and she was mine.

Her walls flexed around my hand, and I waited for the waves of pleasure to ebb before I slowly eased out of her folds. My cock strained, and I saw that my scales had collapsed. I knew I could fill her once more, but the sigh that came from her throat had double meaning. I had satisfied her, but life beyond this hidden section of the garden called to be answered. She was right, and I preferred to complete our bond in the oasis of the Kai Mountains following our bond through the caverns. So, I would wait for a proper Kloaph Rite that she deserved.

Mabel cupped my chin in her hands and I lifted myself from the water to meet her lips.

"There is more that I wish to give you kansa, but I wish to take you to Krelis to mate with you properly," I said, and kissed her before she could think on it right now. I did not need her answer this moment, and I feared she'd reject any idea of leaving her planet, so I quickly added, "Let's go visit your elder, together."

"Together," she agreed with a smile.

Chapter Fifteen

Mabel

Still reeling from being so thoroughly fucked like this night was the last I had to live, I thought for sure I wouldn't even be able to walk. Not wanting to show up at the research center on shaking legs, I decided it was best to see Elder Ezra tomorrow morning, and it didn't hurt that I would get to spend a bit more time with Trent before the final mating ceremony after everyone's one-on-ones were complete. The moon would be at it's peak radiation in the evening, but I didn't think I'd feel up to going if Elder Ezra believed it was necessary to have surgery immediately due to my negligence.

I was going to show Trent where my rooms were, but I rested my head on the ground, thinking I could have a few more moments of reveling in the afterglow. My eyes were heavy, and sleep consumed me. The last thing I heard was

Trent chuckling softly and assuring me, "Get some rest, Kansa, I'll get you to bed."

His heartbeats lulled me deeper to sleep, and I smiled at the rhythm that two hearts could make.

Dreaming of the strange glowing mountain was what I expected, since I'd dreamed of that for the last few days, but this time it was different. I saw offspring running around my legs, nearly toppling me over, and I turned to see Luan smiling as she corralled them to behave. My heart warmed at the sight, because the boy appeared so much like her with pale blue skin, and beautiful loh even for someone so young. The girl turned back to me with golden eyes that blinked with a second lid that should have shocked me, but I didn't have to guess who's offspring it was, she had his smile... Trent.

It wouldn't be mine, I knew that, but it was such a nice dream to see that even when he didn't choose me, I could still be part of their offspring's lives. Both the kids ran around, and then tried to climb up my leg, begging to be picked up. I laughed and hefted the boy up on one hip with one arm, and the girl with the other. They squirmed and tried to push each other off of me, claiming that I was theirs alone, and I laughed some more before I told them both if they didn't stop squirming, I'd have to put them down.

I snorted, and sucked in breath that woke me. When my eyes opened again, limbs were sprawled out everywhere. I was drooling on Trent's chest, with a leg flung across his stomach, and my hand was gripping his horn. Even in my sleep I feared he'd leave and had to cling to him. Groaning, I stretched and slowly extracted myself, but he pulled me back and smiled into my hair, sniffing deeply.

"My kansa, your dreams are beautiful," he said with a sleepy yawn.

161

I blinked up at him. "Uh, thanks?" He couldn't have seen my dreams, so I'm assuming he just believed I had a good dream since I was so relaxed, all my saliva ended up on his chest.

"I will speak with your elder about preserving your eggs for our kantos," he said, then kissed my forehead.

Kantos was what he called larva sacks... for offspring. Had he seen my dream? No, I assure myself, because if he had, then he'd know that both the offspring were not mine, but I would treat any of Luan's spawn as my own. And since one looked just like him... it was obvious that I believed he'd still choose her to be his first mate, while I would be the mate on the side that couldn't give him that future.

I had to stop daydreaming, my reality was set, and I had to accept it.

"Right, well, Elder Ezra will be wondering why I've been avoiding her for the last few days," I changed the subject. "I should get going."

"Together," he reminded me.

"You don't need to," I tried to give him an out, and he frowned.

"Mate," he growled. "Are you playing hard to get? I'm all for a bit of games when we finish our Kloaph Rites on Kai Mountain, but until then, I do not like feeling the ebb of our bond straining when you push away from me. It's like an emptiness fills my soul, and a vacuum consumes the space of my mind that belongs to you. I will wait for you to trust me, but I will not leave your side until our bond is accepted," he said with a determined resolve that I didn't think even a hergslat could smash.

His brows furrowed and he asked, "Why are you imagining those beastly rodents with heads harder than steel, and claws that cut through stone?"

"Hergslats..." I watched him curiously, and my mouth fell open. "How are you seeing my thoughts?"

He grinned and leaned over in bed to kiss me again. I melted into the kiss and moaned. What was this hold he had on me? Trent pulled away, and he turned to swing his legs from the bed, the covers sliding off of him to reveal he hadn't worn a shred of clothing. I blushed, and glanced away, but not before getting a clear picture of his cock hardened, and at attention.

He was gorgeous, and I didn't know how I had the willpower to resist riding him the other day. I turned an even deeper shade of green thinking about his fingers so deep inside of me, and I squirmed, thankful that he was facing the other direction now.

"I thought you would have figured that out by now," he said with a husky tone, almost as if he knew what I was thinking about. According to him... he did, and it was becoming unsettling how accurate he was in guessing. Then a voice echoed in my head, "*You are my mate, and if you need me to take care of you again before we leave, I will always be thirsty for you.*"

It was all in my mind, I thought. He can't read minds... that would be crazy.

"Mabel," his tone dark was filled with promises, "I can feel your need, and if you don't get a hold of yourself, I will dismiss traditions and fuck you where you are."

I shivered and contemplated teasing him to make him follow through with his word, but I didn't think either of us would stop at foreplay this time, and I couldn't risk what would happen if I found out my eggs were fertilized with the scanners.

"Right," I said while slapping my face to distract myself from how hot he was standing there with so much confidence, and a cock thicker than his fingers combined. My goddess... I would take it all, but I didn't know if I could accommodate more than what we'd already done. I blushed profusely, and his wings burst out, the buzz of warning about him that he would fuck me if I didn't get a hold of myself. Scrambling to my feet, I turned so I didn't see him. "Put some clothes on!"

He laughed, and I heard the hum of his wings fade as he walked to pick up his pants. My own wings folded back, and I stepped into my robes while peeking over at his sculpted ass. What was wrong with me? Yesterday wasn't our future, I knew that. I wouldn't let him throw away the chance at building peace with Estreldez. Could I keep my feelings locked away so Luan could lead our clan and the hive? I had to.

"I know this day will not be easy, but I'm not going anywhere," Trent said, sensing my unease. He didn't realize how deep that unsettling feeling went. It wasn't just about losing my eggs, it was about losing him.

When the door slid open on Trent's room, Gaven stood in the hallway, his face devoid of any sign of what he was thinking.

"What are you doing here?" I asked, and there was a tick in his jaw before the blank stare returned.

"Trent, your services, are no longer required. Elder Ezra is expecting us."

"You spoke with her?" I narrowed my eyes and didn't know why I felt so defensive about that. Was I having second thoughts about what needed to be done?

Gaven stayed very still, if I didn't know better I'd say he was a garden decoration. But we weren't in the garden, and there were much more attractive things to look at than the hard lines of his stern face. "She needed to know that you

164

were risking your life for a male that will not stay on Estreldez, and will not choose you when he is required to mate for the sake of the clan, for the sake of his hive."

Fingers dug into the palms of my hands as I fisted them at my sides. Before I could say anything, Trent dismissed the accusations, "There is more than one way to save our planets. Mabel is my queen, and I will have her discuss a new treaty needed for the coming threats to our sector after she has recovered."

Thunderous bootsteps marched in time through the halls, and it seemed much too rhythmic to be the milling about of our off-worlder guests preparing for the final day of the ceremony.

"What's going on?" I asked Gaven.

"I'm escorting you to Elder Ezra," he replied simply.

"She means the commotion through the palace," Trent pressed, and took a step forward. It was almost like we were in whatever this was together, backing me up when needed, but allowing me to take the lead. I liked it too much and knew it would sting when it was over.

"Loric is leading a search of the palace to find where Luan disappeared to. She's not in her usual places, and she's missed her one-on-one in the grotto. But I wouldn't call it a commotion, they won't reach this side of the palace for a while yet, they must search every section thoroughly."

"On the other side?" I repeated in a hushed whisper. How was I hearing the loud thumps of their feet? They had to be closer than that.

Trent got my attention, and I watched him point to his horns. I quickly made sure my hair was covering my forehead, and sighed in relief that everything was hidden adequately enough. He frowned while folding his arms over his chest in annoyance. Was he annoyed with me? For

165

covering my horns... my kan, as he called them? He wasn't pointing his horns to warn me about my own in front of Gaven, I realized. It was a gesture to say the kan was why I could hear the footsteps on the other side of the palace.

Trent grumbled, "Vibrations of such a large number of warriors searching the grounds is easily detected by my kan."

"They don't care about your sensitivities," Gaven snapped, the only sign he had any emotions at all. "They care about finding Luan, and so should you." He turned his back to us and walked down the hall towards the palace exit closest to the research facilities. Walking there would take some time unless we rode a few of the muffals. A few were waiting for us mewling with snorts, and shuffling their claws that allowed them greater traction on smooth stone surfaces such as the plains we were about to cross.

Staring out over the vanishing point of green mayluck stone, veined with black tarnpul. My namesake, I thought, reminded of how Almder once told me the story of how these plains used to be nothing but sand until a great storm threaded lightning through the ground, bringing the tarnpul deposits closer to the surface that attracted the moon's radiation. The mayluck sands heated up and adapted, turning to stone. Where the tarnpul is harvested, the mayluck turns to dust.

I was like the mayluck, hardened when supported by the stronger tarnpul that feeds it energy, and nothing but dust by myself. Sighing, I bowed to the muffal to show my respect, its boney snout nudged me with approval. This one knew me well enough by now, part of his jaw was missing from some predator it encountered on the plains, but it still returned to seek what the strange estrelds were doing at the great palace made of tarnpul. A few muffals were trained out of every litter to know we provided food and entertainment for allowing us to ride them, but they were still very much wild creatures.

Trent opted to fly beside us. My wings itched to spread out and join him, but I didn't know how to fly, and I certainly didn't want to learn in front of Gaven. I kept them folded back, hidden by the way light refracted around them. I guess I could be thankful I didn't have to have that conversation just yet about being krelin.

Riding across the stone, pockets of dust from the scuffling of the muffals's claws billowing around like a soft green fog, was usually a welcomed break from reality. There was a suddenness of feeling alone, despite Gaven riding beside me, and Trent flying above. An emptiness ate away at my stomach the closer we got to the glinting walls of the Mating Research Facility. The muffal snapped and gnashed its teeth before it sat down, making me slide from its back. It rushed off into the plains again without staying for a treat, probably sensing my dismal attitude.

The large domed building awaited, and neither Trent or Gaven said a word. They waited for me to choose when I was ready to approach, and they didn't dare push me to speed things along.

Bhedre guarded the door, and she nodded for me to enter. My footsteps echoed, clacking against the brown stone floors. Even the walls were beige, like the skies with a bit of pink in them. I went straight to the labs, not wanting to wait for Elder Ezra like a guest. I'd worked here long enough, and she hadn't officially fired me from my role as advisor yet. The closer we got the more I could just make out her voice talking to someone possibly on a video communication.

"It'll be taken care of. She's already arrived. Removing her eggs should prevent full maturation. We won't have to worry about revealing who her mother was. She'll be safe, I assure you. Her mother would rather she lived than risk the queen killing her. This is what is best, Almder. Yes, I've secured a few larva sacks, and have created a few synthetic versions to test viability. I can test compatible fertilization samples from our off-worlders, and see how Mabel feels about transferring to care for the newest batch of offspring from the current mating cycle. She will have the family she always wanted... we simply cannot tell her they are hers."

I fell to my knees in the hallway.

"Mabel?" Gaven reached to assist me.

"Stay back," Trent growled at him. A darkness vibrated in his voice, and I stared blankly at the ground, unable to process what I wasn't supposed to hear. My heart was shattering in my chest, and I heaved as if the very air around me was too thin to fill my lungs.

Images of me caring for offspring that had my eyes, or my nose, or even a few mannerisms that I would dismiss as simply a byproduct of my proximity flooded my mind. Mine in body, but disconnected from my spirit as I'm constantly reminded they are someone else's spawn, not my own. Too many differences with an off-world donor, I would never know. But they would have been my own, and they would have grown up the same as me... thinking they were abandoned to be raised by the sad estreld in the offspring training center, who looked at them with longing in her dull eyes.

My wings spread out, making Gaven gasp when I whirled on him, glaring up from the stone floor. "Did you know?" I sobbed out with venom.

He shook his head. "You're krelin..."

"Not that," I screamed, not caring if Elder Ezra realized she had company, that her private conversation with Almder was not so private anymore. "Did you know there was nothing wrong with me?"

"What are you talking about?" Gaven's brows pinched, and he tried to soften his tone like he was speaking with a particularly dumb diplomat that needed hand holding. It was how he sounded when he was placating a dignitary from off-world.

Shaking my head, I felt my whole universe collapsing around me. I trusted Elder Ezra... she was just as much like a mother to me as Almder, or even Elmon, my caretaker at the offspring training facility, and... she was speaking with Almder on the vid comm. They both betrayed me.

Elder Ezra heard my scream and walked calmly into the hallway. She was always a scientist first, assess the situation before you jump in sort. Her grey eyes took in my teary-eyed appearance and my position on the floor, then back up to the two males facing each other off.

"Good Morning, Prince Trent," she spoke sharply, like he was to blame for whatever was going on, then she shook her head at me with pity, "Mabel, do not waste your sorrows on either of them."

"Elder Ezra," Gaven questioned her intentions, and I wasn't the only one. How could she act like she was looking out for my best interests like she didn't just betray me moments before?

She waved her hand at him, "I do not care if she chooses to waste her life with a sire or not, she is much too precious for either of you. Mabel, come inside and let's discuss the next steps for your recovery."

I scrambled to my feet and took a step back. Only then did Elder Ezra actually pay attention to the wings spread from my back, her eyes widened. "Mabel, you need to come inside," she insisted.

Shaking my head, I narrowed my eyes at her. "You," my

voice quivered with anger. "You know who my mother is, and you never told me. You knew nothing was wrong with me, yet you lied to my face. No," I rejected that, it wasn't accurate enough, "You've been lying to me my whole life." I took another step backwards, everything in me needed to get out of there immediately before someone decided it was best to detain me for the rage brewing in my gut.

Wings wafted, and a dust cloud blurred my vision, making everything hazy. Elder Ezra coughed, and fell against the wall, sliding to the floor. "Mabel, you must understand," she tried to clear her throat to explain.

I cut her off, "I think you've explained enough. You don't care about me at all... I trusted you. You would have me raise my offspring without ever knowing they are mine—" My breath hitched, and I clutched at my heart beating rapidly. Wings beat swiftly, and my toes hovered, barely touching the ground.

Elder Ezra's eyes became glassy, and her chest slowed, rising and falling softly. She blinked and whispered, "It's too late, you must protect her."

"I will always serve my queen," Trent said with derision towards the woman I thought was family.

Chapter Sixteen

Trent

"What is she talking about?" Gaven glanced between Mabel and the elder. Neither of them was listening to him, he was irrelevant to what was happening, and the pain throbbing through the bond I shared with my mate. So many coiled emotions wrapped up around finding out she wasn't losing her future family, but she was losing the one she already had from betrayal.

I heard everything.

And I broke for her.

The Almder, and the elder knew she was half krelin, and the possibility that she would inherit her mother's traits, the mark of a queen. Her mother had to be Queen Leahme. Why else would they go to such lengths to keep Mabel's heritage a secret? My mother wouldn't have any need of killing a krelin unless they posed a threat to her, and our clan needed a new queen. All respect from the hive would be lost if a queen was murdered.

Mabel sprayed the elder with her musk, but a queen's musk worked differently than a krelin warrior. While mine would knock out my opponent... the elder would get past the stun stage and feel compelled to do whatever Mabel wished of her. It was a highly toxic brain stimulant that could kill with a high enough dose. I already felt my skin tingle where the spray settled on my arms. Sweeping my wings, I circulated the musk away, so I didn't inhale it.

"Who is my mother? Is she alive?" Her voice cracked, already knowing the answer to her second question.

The elder smiled sadly. "She was a kind soul. Queen Kai kept her close at all times, until she demanded to be shown proof that our Glorbin Flower was so difficult to extract. Scans of our planet showed an abundance of veins, and our yield was low. Your mother was always at her side. Steam from the mountain caused the tunnels to collapse, and your mother was caught inside. Even Queen Kai thought she'd died that day, but your father worked in those mines..."

"Where are they?" Mabel's patience was wearing thin. The story was one I only knew half of. I was a boy at the time, and my mother came back to Krelis before informing the hive of the loss. That was the day many believed Queen Leahme died, but rumors spread months later from the warriors that worked the trade routes between Krelis and Estreldez. That she lived, and months later... more rumors that she spawned, before my mother had her very last visit to Estreldez, never to return to this planet again.

I didn't think my queen capable of putting the whole hive's future at risk by killing another queen when our numbers dwindled, but I remembered the dark look in her eyes as she left, and there was no warmth in my mother even then. Would she ruin our hive to stay queen... even if it meant the end of Krelis?

"Nobody knows, they disappeared shortly after you were spawned, and you resembled an estreld so much more than a krelin that when Queen Kai came to inspect our offspring, there was no need to hide you. If they are alive, they would not return here, and they certainly couldn't take an offspring with so few loh away from the moon's radiation. It would have been a death sentence," the elder explained, and though I knew her heart was in the right place... the information would be painful for Mabel to reconcile with no matter which was true.

Her parents are alive, it meant they left her.

Her parents are dead, then that meant my mother was responsible, and her life would be in danger.

Whatever the truth I would be here to support her, however she decided to handle things. Even if that meant storming the city and removing my mother by force. I had expected to have the hive follow Mabel by choice and the bond to the warriors be transferred to the new Queen of Krelis without ever approaching my mother at all. She would have little choice in the matter once Mabel was accepted by the hive. The transfer was already happening to Queen Leahme before she left...

Just then the noise from the entrance reached my horns, and I turned to Mabel. "We have to leave."

She glanced over her shoulder down the hallway we came from, hearing the same thing. The chorus of an army of warriors. She didn't run. I admired that in her. Squaring her shoulders, her wings buzzed in preparation for what we would face. I let my ki stingers drop from my wrists. Mabel frowned, shaking her head with disapproval.

173

"Showing them how deadly you are will not warn them away from attacking us, it will mark us as threats to be neutralized."

"She's right," Gaven agreed. "She's gone through the same training as any warrior of Estreldez. You'll only increase the odds of a fight."

Reluctantly, I retracted my ki, but I didn't like the idea of being unprepared. My black venom was not instantaneous, it had to be pumped from my glands to reach my stingers. Only residue would be left, and that was hardly enough to disable a trained warrior from harming Mabel. She folded back her wings, and they disappeared, the light refracting around them only visible by a discerning eye. I followed her lead and folded my own as well.

The warriors came around the bend of the hall, and a blue male estreld was at the lead, the Pride of Estreldez, Loric, wearing full protective uniform, including a clear mask that would prevent my musk from reaching him. I could take him on, if I thought Gaven would keep to himself, but he was a wild card that I couldn't afford to risk my mate's wellbeing with. If he was the Sky Bender, then he was capable of protecting her, but also equally capable of killing her if he thought she was a threat to Estreldez.

"Mabel..." Loric sounded shocked to see her. His shoulders sagged in a kind of defeat. She was not who he was expecting to see. "Almder was concerned with the abrupt manner Elder Ezra ended their conversation, I came straight away. Have you seen Luan?"

"Not since the ceremonial greetings..." she replied, gnawing her lip with renewed anxiety for yet again someone else besides herself. Would she not think on her own safety? I didn't trust any of them. Her own Almder tried to steal her eggs so she wouldn't become a krelin queen, and I couldn't trust my own mother would see reason. We had to get to my warship, where I could trust my warriors with defending her, with doing what was necessary to lift her to her rightful place as Queen of Krelis before King Sylve was prepared to take this sector.

Tugging at our bond, her green eyes lifted to meet mine with a quirked brow. Did she feel it? I hoped she'd hear me, know that we had to leave, prepare, and then return to negotiate peace.

"My Kansa, I can't protect you here..."

"I don't need you to," she said, smiling at me with a sadness that wrenched at my hearts. She heard me, but she had yet to reach back through the bond. It stung to think she didn't wish to accept me as her mate, but she had a lot to process and I understood wanting to take on life's burdens alone, not wanting to weigh on another person's shoulders. But she would realize one day that I carried whatever troubled her regardless of if she wanted to share the hardship. She wasn't alone.

Loric observed us both skeptically, but then nodded. "Her radiation signature's being picked up by Hazel... she's either injured, lost in the mountains, or--" he couldn't finish his thought.

"Not on Estreldez," Mabel sucked in a breath, "It's all my fault..."

Why would Luan's disappearance be her fault?

She continued, while sniffling, "I should have said something sooner. I'm so sorry..."

"Say what sooner?" Loric demanded, and I clicked deep in my throat in warning for him to check his tone with my mate. "Stay out of this, prince." The way he said my title was purposeful, ignoring that I led a great fleet of warships as a commander of the Krelis Horde, but that I was a prince and

175

should maintain a dignitary's stance on this situation.

I waited to see what Mabel would say. This was her choice to answer him or not. I only hoped whatever she had to say did not mean we would have to fight our way back to my ship, because every one of the warriors before us were protected against my musk, and our only chance would be for her to stun them with the queen's bliss, it didn't need to be absorbed by breath... it merely needed time to sit on their skin, which was still exposed due to their reliance on their loh for battle and defense.

"She wanted to leave to be an off-world diplomat," Mabel blurted, and then quickly added, "I think she intended to use the bounty hunter's ship to meet with our closest trade partners and negotiate new deals."

"How can you take blame for her choice to risk her safety by leaving Estreldez?" I tried to assure her that this was not her fault if Luan did choose to abandon her clan by leaving secretly.

Imploring Loric, she shed fresh tears. "Please, we need to find her. I thought I had time to tell her about King Sylve... it isn't safe."

"How do you know about King Sylve?" Loric's blue eyes hardened, and his loh glowed as if preparing for battle, and I stepped between them defensively.

"You will not speak with the Queen of Krelis like this," I warned. The glands in my throat clucked, and my wings flared out.

"Queen," Loric's voice trailed off, and he stared around me. Mabel's hand gripped the bottom of my wing, and her soft fingers stroked making me shiver. "Mab... is this true?" Not liking the way he had a sweet nickname for her, my face became blank and just a tad unsettled. I folded my wings back, and she chewed on her lip. She didn't feel comfortable with the title, I knew that, but Krelis needed her. Would she deny her place among the hive?

"Not officially," she shrugged, trying to act unaffected, but I felt her unease. What could I do to help her? Did she even need me? I backed away, feeling foolish for thinking that a queen would require a warrior such as myself for anything but to help fertilize her eggs.

I had snapped at her for being estreld when I told her of my desire to have a mate that wanted to stay with me, but krelin queens were no different. More certain now than ever that she was the daughter of Queen Leahme, and she was the next Queen of Krelis, but what did that mean for us? Was there even an us to have? Queens were different than warriors, not any different than what I'd learned of the mating habits of estrelds. I had accepted the queen of our hive had obligations to the many, not the one, but when I met Mabel... I had hoped my kansa mate was only for me.

As queen, she would have her pick of any warrior she chose, and there was no obligation to bond with any of them, as she would be bonded with the hive. I was selfish to want her for myself... she would bring the next generation of warriors... and one of her offspring would be the next queen. An overwhelming need to throw her over my shoulder, bring her to Kai Mountain, and make sure every last egg of hers was fertilized by my seed consumed me. If every egg was mine, then she would have no need for another mate.

The genetics of our hive would be screwed, I thought disgruntled with either option. I couldn't ruin the hive, but I couldn't reason with myself to allow another male to touch her. She had already made up her mind anyways, there was no need to think on it further. She did not want to officially be my mate, and my hearts tore a bit at the thought. I folded my arms over my chest to hide the ache and took a step back

177

to give her the space she needed.

Loric tapped behind his ear, and I could hear on the other end of the communication that they had news about Luan. "A transport tech admitted that they let Luan use a carry pod to board a ship registered to an off-worlder."

"She can't be too far, that our own ships can't follow," Mabel insisted, but there was doubt in her assertions. The way Loric's face fell only added to the affect.

He shook his head. "The ship's logs were falsified, somehow they had a scrambler from the black market that as long as the ship was docked at the moon's waystation's computers it was constantly replacing the accurate ship data with the falsified data as long as it was connected to our network."

"How did we not catch it?" Mabel fumed at him, as if he were the technician behind the problem. I shouldn't have been even partially relieved to see her upset with him, but aside from the worry that Luan's disappearance caused, I had no issues with her disliking a male that otherwise had developed a relationship close to her enough to have a nickname.

He had nothing but the face of a trained diplomat, I should know, I was trained from a young age to have the same neutrally pleasant expression, no matter my feelings. "It's new technology," he said firmly before explaining, "the virus was attached to its original data logs, and preyed on the fact that we scan everything, using it to its advantage that it wouldn't be the only ship being scanned within a short amount of time. The delay allowed it to burrow and replace its own data with the falsified information. The original files are too corrupted to have any other lead except the virus was built by a well-known outlaw hiding out on Necias Delta Fal, called Xel.

"He's never been caught, and he's too cocky to hide his signature. After a job is completed, he has extra code in his programs to shove that fact in people's faces, while not revealing who the client is."

"So, we have nothing..." Mabel heaved in dismay.

"Not necessarily," I added, not able to stand the way seeing her upset made me feel. They all turned their attention to me. "Xel's work is expensive, and there are very few who can afford it. Given the warships that I passed on the way to Estreldez, we can reasonably assume King Sylve was one step ahead of us, and the ships were not his first action."

What I had to say wasn't comforting, but the simplest explanations were usually the most accurate. And truth was never very smooth in its acceptance, which made the assumption, though distasteful, have that much more merit. We need only search for the evidence one way or the other, but it was something to work from.

"We can't rule anything out, so it's a start." My hearts warmed when Mabel gave her agreement, supporting my theory. I imagined her leading the hive with such understanding, and firmness towards truth, wherever it may come from, that any warrior would be honored to proclaim her their queen. She sighed. "We also know who we should be looking for... Luan wouldn't have boarded just any ship, she had her eye on the bounty hunter. He was a shol, as I recall."

This wasn't Mabel's fault at all. I had let the shol go, even knowing he had interest in Luan. My guilt over my planet's part in destroying Sholunus had clouded my judgement. He was working with King Sylve all along, and if I had killed him, Estreldez and Krelis would have a better chance at stopping whatever King Sylve had planned, and perhaps, Luan would still be here.

"I've met many unscrupulous types over the years," Loric said while rubbing the exhaustion from his face, "I knew the shol was lying about something, but I hadn't thought it was as devious as kidnapping Luan. Mate with her...yes. I saw that in the way he watched her, but not this. We should speak with Almder."

A long silence passed amongst everyone as we traveled back to the palace, until Loric spoke, "So, queen, then?" He grinned, but sadness still clung to his eyes.

Ignoring his prompt about her title she diverted with discussing a plan instead. "We need to contact King Sylve and gauge his reaction. We can't tell him we think he has Luan, he could just lie, and if he doesn't have her, then we've revealed that she's missing."

Her dismissal of what she was gave me doubts she ever intended to free Krelis from my mother's savagery. And with that thought came many more, instilling fears that I had never felt before, ones where this journey was the last time I would admire the way the moon's light reflected off her black hair like stars lighting the way through the galaxy. I would follow them, if she'd have me, but if she refused to lead Krelis then I would have no choice but to dethrone my mother without her help. My people could not continue to suffer.

Their conversation buzzed in the back of my mind. Distraction was a dangerous pastime, but I hadn't processed what Loric said until he repeated it for me once more, bringing me back to reality, "Prince Trenton," he used my proper name and title, not even my warriors called me that, it was Commander to them, "I'll need your warship to help track down Luan, will you be assisting our efforts?"

I lifted a brow, considering what he was asking, but remembering what he had said earlier. "Am I not to stay out of this, as well? Or is it because Estreldez does not have ships capable of withstanding an attack from King Sylve?" I knew the estrelds only had transport ships, it's why all the trade was done at their moons and not elsewhere. If a planet wanted something from Estreldez it was facilitated by Krelis or independent traders willing to go the extra step to source goods.

Loric gritted his teeth, smiling tightly. He knew as well as I did, the only reason Estreldez maintained its independence from another planet taking over was because it had a superior natural defense system with the moons, harnessed by technology that could vaporize several ships and leave estrelds and the planet relatively unharmed. And even if someone, like King Sylve, were to risk a few ships, Krelis has been defending this sector as the primary trade partner for many cycles. Queen Kai knew it was an investment for Krelis whether she invaded Estreldez or continued to benefit from the resources and profits from them by using our own cargo ships.

But an all-out war with King Sylve would be devastating to Estreldez without Krelis warships at their disposal.

"Have you changed your mind about a diplomatic mating union between Estreldez and Krelis?" Loric skillfully placed the blame of whatever broken promises there were between our planets on me, instead of the runaway turned kidnapped future Almder, Luan. It was true, the promise was broken well before she left the planet when I took Mabel to a hidden oasis within the gardens, but he didn't know that.

"Not at all," I replied, unconcerned with his slight, and suddenly my tongue got away with me, planning out several steps ahead to have my mate finally accept our bond, starting with step one, "I fully intend to fulfill a mating bond between Estreldez and myself, and the command of the Krelis Horde will be at the service of protecting the sector as we always

181

have."

"That's good to hear," Loric replied, but did not press the issue.

"You'll still mate with Luan..." Mabel stated quietly, and I did not correct her.

I had no intentions of mating with Luan, but I had every intention of having the current Almder agree to a match particularly phrased that she would think it was. She would be forced to accept the agreement when I chose another. When I chose Mabel. My mate was an analytical mind, she would not accept me if she thought it was better for me to be with someone else. She was a kind heart that would sacrifice what we have to protect the future of our planets.

My hearts were not so kind. And I had no intention of giving her up, but I would make sure the path was easier for her to come to me. Part of that path was the Almder's acceptance, even if I had to trick her to do it.

"I don't care if I must lie to your Almder, go to war with King Sylve to return Luan, and destroy my mother to clear away any objection you may have against being mine. But, there will always be obstacles and until you clear the one in your heart... I'll be right here waiting." I knew it was pointless to try to speak through our bond when I could feel the block between us, but I tried anyways. *"Kansa... let me in."*

Chapter Seventeen

Mabel

Warmth spread through my limbs, and I glanced over at Trent with his determined stride through the palace corridors. He was headed straight to the Almder to tell her of his plans. Plans to mate with Luan, I thought with irritation. Staring daggers at his firm ass, I resisted everything in me that wanted to yank on his arm, spin him around to face me, and demand that he explain himself. After what we shared in the gardens, and in the shuttle, I had developed hopes that shouldn't have been mine.

The first time was a mistake, the second time was because I lied to myself that it would mean nothing. Was there no longer a next time? I knew he had to be with Luan. I knew that in theory, but she left, and he still wanted to have her.

Loric opened the doors to the alcove, and Almder was

pacing back and forth in her distress. Her crown was in her hands as she rubbed at the jewels embedded in its tarnpul surface, one for each of her lost offspring. I felt a pang of pity for her, before I remembered that she had planned to make me feel the same pain, while secretly having Elder Ezra use my eggs, my offspring, my family, in experiments.

I still cared for Luan, and I'd find a way to help her, but I felt nothing for whatever pain Almder was going through while worrying if she'd lose another daughter.

"Did you find her?" Almder asked Loric. Had she clung onto hope that Luan didn't make it to the ship that disappeared?

"There is a team still searching, just in case, but there is no evidence that she returned from the transport pod, and it is likely Luan has fallen into a trap set by King Sylve."

Almder replaced her crown on her head, and with a nod, she accepted this information, a steely resolve on her face. "Prince Trenton of Krelis, what have you to say on the matter?" Her voice was cold, and for a moment I thought she would blame Trent for Luan's disappearance, when it was me who did not inform Almder about Luan's plans sooner.

"That is what I wished to discuss with you, Almder of Estreldez," he remained calm, and dignified in his reply, bordering on aloof, "I will retrieve my mate and bring her back to Krelis with me for a proper Kloaph Rite Ceremony. You will have the full support of the Krelis Horde's warships to ensure the safe return of Luan. All I need is your approval to proceed, bound by your blood."

"You are aware my stipulations remain the same, Prince Trenton. She must choose you in return, I will not force her to be your mate, even for the sake of peace between our planets."

My chest tightened at Almder's reply because it was

exactly what I would expect from her. She defended Luan's right to choose and knowing that she would defy all logic for one estreld's happiness was exactly why I loved her, because she loved so fully, and that extended to all estrelds. That's why she had advisors to help make sure she considered beyond her feelings, but for the future of the planet as well. My heart broke hearing what I loved about the woman I considered as close as a mother for so many years protect Luan, and not hours before she didn't do the same when it mattered most... for me.

Tears stung my eyes as I watched my Almder from behind Trent's imposing form. I knew I hid behind him, because I did not wish to bring attention to myself. I didn't want to confront my feelings over her betrayal just yet. She wished to remove my eggs, without true consent for why she was doing it. It was all a lie, when she stood there now, as she was two days ago telling me about how she knew how I felt having lost her own offspring.

What other lies was she capable of?

Fists clenched at my sides, and nails dug painfully into my palms.

Trent replied, "I will not force my mate to accept me, if that is your concern. I'm sure you've heard many things about krelins, but I am not my ancestors, and I will not abduct her."

I chewed the inside of my cheek, feeling affronted on all sides. The man who defended me on more than one occasion in but a few days stood before my betrayer speaking of being gentlemanly for another mate. Everything in me wished to flee the alcove and retreat, but despite the hurt reverberating through my very bones she was still my Almder, and I knew before I gave myself to Trent that he would not be mine.

Almder addressed Loric next, "Knowing the Prince of

185

Krelis chooses to mate with Luan, do you still offer to be sired?"

Having it said so clearly of his intentions stung more than I thought it would, even with preparing myself to hear it, to see it, to live it.

Bending to one knee, Loric bowed, lowering his head. "I offer to be sired, and will accept whatever offspring she may carry. I will care for them as they were my own. What is mine is hers, and what is hers is mine until the moon collects my dust."

"So be it," Almder accepted his offer. Trent didn't even bother to turn his attention away from her to see Loric's heartfelt proposal to be Luan's life partner, regardless of who she mates with. While Loric was confessing his love, I was pining for a guy that had literally just agreed to send his whole fleet of warships to scour the system for Luan to be his mate, not even caring that she might say no, or that she'd never stay on Krelis with him.

That's how dedicated he was to his hive.

Knowing he was doing what he had to do for peace didn't make things any easier. Who was I to get in the way of Estreldez's only hope for survival? If I came forward as a queen of Krelis, prepared to dethrone Queen Kai, I couldn't possibly beg Almder to still accept the peace treaty... How could she trust that a half-krelin she was prepared to neuter would advocate for Estreldez the same way Luan would? A mate bond with me wouldn't solidify peace between our species.

I knew that. I repeated it to myself over and over again, but I couldn't get him out of my head. A little voice kept saying, *find a way*. With a warring storm dispersing the thought with the wind.

The deal between my Almder and Trent was solidified,

and any chance I thought I had at finding another way to save our planets without Trent mating with Luan vanished before my eyes. I was in a daze as I was shuffled out of the alcove among all the warriors that had been part of the search for Luan across the palace. Plans were discussed about how soon Trent's warships would be dispatched to retrieve Luan, and what they would do if met with opposition from King Sylve.

King Sylve, his name triggered me to wake from my daze, and I realized by this point we were at the transport deck, and I had boarded a shuttle to launch towards Trent's personal ship. I hadn't realized I'd made the decision, but my feet walked of their own accord, and they weren't going to leave me behind.

Finally finding my voice once more I told Trent, "If King Sylve is involved, you can't send all your warships to find her, you'll leave this sector unguarded."

"I'm aware," he stated simply, unconcerned with what I was worried about.

"Not only would Estreldez be in danger if his plan was to lure your warships away, but so would Krelis," I tried to re-explain with more emphasis.

"That would be true, if I were doing as you said." I blinked at him with confusion muddling my thoughts. An uncomfortable state that was becoming all too familiar.

"But you just told Almder you were going to send the whole Krelis Horde to bring your mate to Krelis," I said, exasperated.

He patted the seat next to him, as the shuttle's engines roared to life, and I found myself flopping into the seat without a thought. When had we made it to the shuttle? I had blindly been following until my mind woke with a start at the mention of King Sylve and the danger that posed.

Trent smiled and leaned in close. "That is exactly what I am doing." He paused, a smolder in his golden eyes as he added with a seductive lick of his lips, "My Kansa."

"What does that even mean," I questioned with irritation at how my cheeks turned red, despite not fully understanding what he was saying, but the way he said it had my blood heating. I had heard him say it before when we were in the garden, and my legs were wrapped around his head, my cheeks burned at the memory, but I wasn't sure what the nickname meant for a krelin.

"Do you remember when I told you why our horns are called kan?"

I nodded. "It means to sense, and I've felt it, the vibrations of everything around me."

"Yes, and sa in krel means soul. You, Mabel, are felt in my soul." He pressed his horns against my forehead, connecting with my own kan, and I shivered with an indescribable sensation rushing through to the tips of my toes. "*My mate. My Kansa.*"

My eyes widened. Did he call me his mate? I heard it in my head, but he didn't say it. His lips were unmoving as I stared at him. I only wished he had, right? I melted into his touch, and for a moment, I let myself believe I wasn't imagining this whole thing and thought, *mine.*

"If you'll have me," he said. Had he heard my thoughts?

My lower lip trembled. "You're not running after Luan?" I mean, of course, we had to save her, but that's not what I meant.

"Not directly, no. And not without you."

"Just to be clear, you're—"

"Taking you to Krelis as my mate, while I have warships posted across the sector to search for Luan. If King Sylve has her, a direct approach is not going to help her, we'll have to infiltrate Necias Delta Fal. I was planning on arranging for a meeting with him anyways to incentivize a collaboration for when the trill arrive. All of this takes time to implement and prepare. Meanwhile, I'd like to show you the mating caves of Kai Mountain."

He tucked a bit of my black hair behind my ear, then slid his fingers behind my neck to lift my lips to meet his. He paused with a sliver of air between us, my heart slammed in my chest, a painful longing burning to be completed.

"Do you accept?" he asked, nipping at my lip, before I wrapped my arms around him, and our teeth clashed instead of being romantically entangled in the kiss that I was anticipating. Wrinkling my nose from the sharp knock, I groaned. He chuckled, and I smiled unable to help the happiness swelling within me, but not quite over my embarrassment. Slowly, he lifted my chin back to gently press our lips together, recalibrating, and my whole body hummed.

Between breaths I repeated, "Yes." Then kissed him again. *Yes, yes, yes,* I thought. I started to reach down his pants, when he stopped my hand. I pulled away in confusion, blinking up at him. I thought he had asked me to be his mate, and he was holding my hand in his, preventing me from touching every part of him now that I knew he was mine.

But did I?

Was he?

"It's okay that you haven't fully accepted me yet, but all of me is yours when you do. I can wait."

"I don't understand?" That didn't sound like a rejection, but he wasn't releasing my hand either. He even kissed my forehead, and positioned himself back into his chair. What was happening?

"Our bond is incomplete. I believe time in the mating caves will change this. It is tradition to take the path of trials up to the mountains instead of flying, and that by the time we reach the caves our bond will be strong enough to be blessed by Goddess Lenkal within her temple." He could see the look of shock on my face. It would be days before we reached Krelis from Estreldez.

Smiling, he hadn't let go of my hand and squeezed gently. "My warship is the fastest of the fleet, and equipped with refined Ordin fuel, we will warp there within the day. Krelis isn't far from Estreldez, mate, I will prove to you that our bond is strong, and perhaps then you will let me inside both your mind and hearts."

"I only have one heart," I corrected.

"No, Kansa, you have three." He brought my hand to his chest, and I stilled, realizing what he was saying. That his hearts were mine, and I was more determined than ever to get to this Kai Mountain of his and show him just how much that meant to me.

Chapter Eighteen

Trent

"Welcome home, Commander," my queen's silky voice punctured through the walls I built around my mind. So focused on being open to receiving the bond from my mate, I had unwittingly ignored the danger of leaving myself exposed. The connection was made, and a sickening warmth filled my mind, fogging over the unsettling nausea of the invasion to give into the bliss of a queen's affections.

"Hello, my queen," I droned, absently in my mind. A faint tickle at the back of my head, the only indication that something was wrong. Ignoring it, I enjoyed the way my mind filled with a sense of peace and happiness.

"I've heard you've been busy finding our hive a new queen. What a blessing this is," she cooed. *"Bring her to me."*

"Of course, my queen." I thought happily of how my

mother would give her blessing to my mate. What was I so worried about before? I had been so eager to take Mabel to Kai Mountain before taking her to the hive, but this made sense to bring her to see my mother first. Perhaps this once, my queen will finally give her blessing now that I was mating another queen. No one else measured up to her standards. Mabel would surpass them.

Commander Li-aq stepped out of the clearing, as we descended from the ship's transport pod to Krelis's surface. I had sent estreld warriors to make sure the moon was secured, just in case he didn't leave, and it was nice to see he had listened. He bowed before Mabel, taking up her hand in his before placing his lips on her skin. I bristled at the contact, but another wave of pleasure coursed through my mind, and a soothing buzz lulled my anxiety. My queen was still connected, and joy filled me. When was the last time my mother actually cared this much? It wasn't normal for her to give so much attention, but her presence was like a gentle stroke, and all my worries disappeared.

"My son, I'm disappointed in you, but I am nothing but forgiving, as your intentions were for the hive. I wish you'd have sought my guidance and let me in sooner. Commander Li-aq will be escorting you both."

Guilt tore through my gut, and I grunted, before my queen's soft approval returned, flooding my mind with peace.

"What's going on?" Mabel asked while removing her hand from Commander Li-aq's hold. It felt right to have her withdraw from his touch, but my tongue was too soft to answer her. Even if I could, what would I say? My mind blanked on where I was supposed to be taking her, to Queen Kai?

"My Queen Mab," Li-aq addressed reverently, "Queen

Kai, is welcoming you to the hive, and is so very excited that you've agreed to come to Krelis to help repopulate our kantos combs. We have a celebration prepared for your arrival so you may meet with all your mates."

She choked, and replied with a stutter, "*All,* my mates?"

Commander Li-aq nodded enthusiastically, and threaded her arm through his to guide her forward while I watched on in a daze. It all felt very dream-like, she was so beautiful. Her black hair twinkled in the Krelis atmosphere, like the pollen in the air knew who she was and clung to her aura just to be near. Even her skin glowed with dew, making her appear as ethereal as the goddess herself. As she moved the pollen reacted, flickering a pleasant red that complimented the green in her eyes.

Mabel glanced back with worry, but she needn't be concerned since I would follow her always. I smiled back at her, and her brows furrowed, creating an adorable wrinkle that extended down her petite nose. Every part of her was perfect.

I was speechless in her wake. Commander Li-aq spoke instead, "A queen is given everything the hive has to offer. Any mate you want is yours, and many are happy simply to please you."

"I'm not sure I'm following this correctly... Trent? What is he saying? I thought—"

"He knows as well as any krelin," Li-aq quickly interjected, "that he can't have you all to himself. A queen is a blessing to the whole hive, and he knows the consequences of selfishness."

"Consequences?" she repeated, her voice like sweet nectar for my ears, even the vibration of it in the air, made my kan warm with pleasure. I sighed, feeling my cock throb. I needed my mate. I needed her blessing.

"A queen has many mates and should one mate try to keep her to themselves... Well, it's immediate death so that the hive may thrive."

"Trent?" Her face appeared horrified, and I wanted to comfort her within my arms, but they felt so heavy at my sides. I did my best to smile at her to ease her burden. It was true that queens never mate bonded with one. They were connected to the whole hive, and a mate bond would block them from soothing all warriors without direct contact. Unmated, they claimed many to replenish the hive's spawn, and can help coordinate the fleets with ease when our planet is threatened.

The word repeated in my mind, threatened. We needed a queen more than ever. There was a war coming to the sector. I frowned, not liking the clouds in my mind, making it difficult for me to think straight. I reached out to my queen, Mabel, cupped her cheek in my hand. My skin on hers was like touching the stars, melting away my existence, leaving only her in my mind.

"Are you saying the hive would kill him if I didn't have other mates?" She pushed away from Commander Li-aq, backing away, her wings spreading out, prepared to fly or fight. Stunning, I thought, now that she was on Krelis she truly shined. How did I ever miss all the signs of what she was?

"Of course not, he is welcome to be your first mate, My Queen, but I'm sure once you meet the rest of your mates you will accept them into your hearts as well."

"She only has one," I said absently, correcting Commander Li-aq. There was a shift on Mabel's face that made both my hearts clench with pain. Had I said something she disapproved of? Perhaps, I should not have imposed and allowed her to correct him in her own words. It was impudent of me to answer for a queen. I bowed my head, hoping for mercy, when I glanced up, she glared and snapped her head around to show me her back.

"He's right, I only have one now. Let's go meet these mates," she snarled that last word, and I watched her walk off, leaving Commander Li-aq and myself behind. She was well out of earshot, not even able to hear the way her feet padded against the dirt, towards the mountains. Did she even know where she was going?

Commander Li-aq spoke with a sneer of satisfaction on his lips, "Queen Kai has no intention of releasing her hold on you until you've ruined things with Queen Mab, that's what the hive is calling her for they wish to hear her in their hearts. You thought I couldn't see what she was, what you were hiding from the hive? It's one thing to seek an estreld queen and keep her to yourself, but you lied to us all trying to keep a true Krelis Queen to yourself.

"You're lucky all I did was report you to Queen Kai, instead of telling the hive what you were up to. You'd have a different kind of greeting, and I think Queen Mab would not have been pleased with losing her favorite mate. Though," he paused to tap my chin with his palm like I was a fresh spawn out of the kantos, "don't get used to being first mate. I plan on replacing you soon enough when she sees I can give her pleasure, fill her kantos with spawn, and accept any mate she chooses with grace. Enjoy the high of the queen's attentions, Trenton, and by that, I mean Queen's Kai's attentions."

I blinked at him, his words barely registering. A dull throb at the back of my mind begged for attention, and I tried to reach for it, only for it to disappear from my grasp. It was as if this light existed in my mind that fluttered away every time I approached. What a lovely little thing, I thought, as my finger grazed it sending jolts through my horns that made my wings itch to fly. I'll catch you yet, I grinned to myself, hearing Commander Li-aq scoff in disgust didn't deter me from my goals.

You will be mine, you elusive spark. It called to me, teasing, only to be yanked away.

Chapter Nineteen

Mabel

Trent was acting strange, but really, what did I actually know about him other than how great his fingers felt inside of me? Sure, I was attracted to him. And yes, my insides melted at the sight of all his firm muscles, chiseled jawline, and that bulge in his pants that torched any semblance of a normal thought from my brain.

I should be focusing on making sure Luan was safe, and how I apparently placed myself in harm's way by thinking the Krelis warships would be deployed to protect Estreldez. Simply trusting that Trent wanted the same things as me was my first mistake. He had been so convincing. No, I was distracted with pretty words of him feeling my soul when he had simply been feeling between my sensitive folds. How stupid could I be?

As soon as we stepped foot on Krelis, he changed. He got me on the planet, and now he was done with me, or at least he didn't want to take me to Kai Mountain anymore. I'd learned from Commander Li-aq that it's where the temple of Goddess Lenkal was, and it's where bonded mates go to complete their psychic connection with each other. As a queen of the hive, I had no need to go to the mountain unless I wished to commune with Goddess Lenkal, since I would already be psychically connected with each krelin's oath to serve, making me a conduit for the whole hive.

I couldn't even imagine.

Having the whole hive in my mind? Was that how that worked?

When we arrived at the hive, it wasn't what I had expected. It was the mountain itself, and there was this silky film covering the rock that made it glow and sparkle, not exactly as the mountain I dreamed about, but it was huge, and structured like each section was created separately and then melded together in an intricate pattern that reached in all directions. It wasn't solid looking, but also not transparent either. Tunnels and tubular rooms spanned in a way that seemed haphazard, and yet beautiful.

Li-aq explained, "The hive was created by every warrior before us. Each krelin is given a section to create or repair as they please, and over many centuries it became what it is today. You may choose any pod you wish, and should you like to make adjustments, they can be arranged."

The walls moved like they were alive, breathing as I breathed, and I entered a room filled with stones I recognized from Estreldez. They've decorated the walls of this large, tubed space with jewels, and they were placed like decorations, even ones estrelds would never consider as anything other than sustenance. It was breathtaking, and the jewels glowed in a wave with the movement of the walls. Lucky, the floors did not fluctuate, or I might have been queasy. The deeper we went into the hive, the more structure there was. And we reached the center of the hive, which was a large crater sinking deep into the earth, and rising high into the clouds. I stopped and stared.

Krelin warriors flew above the opening, and others milled about on different levels of the hive, their shadows seen through the filmy membrane of rooms, or peering over balconies so high, I lost my breath. With the light filtering down through the open oculus of the self-made cave structure, the tunnels and pods appeared like bronzed gold, twinkling and grand. There was a pollen dust in the air that turned red with my movement through the space.

I was beginning to think Trent didn't have a voice, though neither did I in that moment, before he finally spoke, "This is the heart of the hive. This is where you will sway the hearts of every warrior with your song."

"Like singing?" I cringed. If they expected me to sing, they would be in for a rude awakening about all their hopes and dreams of a new queen. I did not have a melodic voice.

He chuckled, and I loved that sound. He should be the one singing to his hive for their hearts... He had mine. Why was it so easy to forget that he had lied to me about wanting to be mates? When he stood there gazing out at something like this with awe, when all I felt was terror at how real it was being asked to be queen over so many krelins... it was overwhelming, and I didn't think I could do it. He made it seem like this would be easy, and everyone would love me. Everyone but him.

"Not literal singing," he assured. "From here your kan can connect with the hive and create a psychic link with them. You'll show them how much you care, and they will trust you with their lives like I do with mine."

I punched him in the arm, he didn't even flinch from the contact. "You don't have to charm me anymore, Trent. I'm here already, and I don't have much of a choice but to go to this party the queen is throwing. Even if you're a liar, I wouldn't be able to live with myself if I left, and your hive decided to blame you, performing some kind of sacrificial ritual."

Not sure why I cared, when he obviously didn't care if I took on a whole harem of mates, but I didn't want him to die. I'd go to this party, pretend to choose some mates, become their queen or whatever, then use my influence to get the fuck out of here. At least then, I could make sure the Krelis warships were actually doing what Trent said they were going to do. Then find Luan.

As I stood before the busy, beautifully terrifying, sight of the mecca of the hive, my skin prickled like the air was electrified. Reaching up, I rubbed at my forehead, my loh burned... No, were they kan now?

"Looks like your kan are coming in nicely," Commander Li-aq complimented. "Most female warriors kan stay rooted beneath their skin, it's a sign of a queen to have them grow like they are doing now."

"Are you saying no female krelins have kan, or wings?" So, all of the krelins flying right now were male?

"Ah, you misunderstand. All krelins have kan, female's kan never break the skin unless they grow. Think of it the same as our chests, they grow with ducts for spawn for females, and males do not. As for the wings, all females are born with them, but once they sprout are usually much too frail for flying and end up being molted from their backs before they are even seven cycles old."

How horrifying, I thought. My hand instinctively reached

for my back to make sure my wings were still there. They expanded out, stretching, and an eerie silence filled the heart of the hive. Only a soft buzz of wings hovering in mid-air remained. Trent turned to truly look at me since we landed on Krelis. His golden eyes glowed, and I squirmed under the attention, even Commander Li-aq remained quiet. Was I supposed to speak?

"Uh," I began awkwardly. I winced, and lifted a hand with a ridiculous wave, while averting my eyes from the stares.

Whispers filled my ears, and they grew louder.

"That's her," some said in hushed speculation.

"She's so small."

"Do you feel that?"

"It feels warm," another said with a sigh.

"Queen Mab, give us your blessing," many chanted and it was almost like they were inside my mind, overwhelming me, before Trent stepped forward and spread his own wings out, breaking the spell.

"What was that," I gasped, clutching at my chest. A splitting headache called attention to my kan when I tried to hold my temples and was scraped by the sharp end of the horns that were now an inch long.

Trent spun around to grab my hand and I was too stunned to stop him. He lifted my hand to his lips. His tongue flicked up my wrist, sending shivers down the back of my legs, and shooting urges I shouldn't have between my thighs. He lapped up the drop of blood from the tiny scratch, and for a moment I thought I could see something like panic in Trent's eyes, before it disappeared once more.

He dropped my hand, unceremoniously, and without a word, flew up into the hive.

"Where is he going?" I grumbled and stared at my hand

that tingled where his tongue touched.

"He must have been summoned by Queen Kai," Commander Li-aq dismissed, and ushered me along the rest of the tour.

Something troubled me about Trent's behavior, but what could I do if he didn't feel the same way as me? I wanted more from him. More than what he was willing to give, but I also couldn't let go of this feeling inside that begged me to follow him. I thought he wanted more, he was so passionate about having someone to share his life and not simply someone to give him spawn.

The farther he flew away, the more my insides seemed to rip apart. I didn't like that he could make me feel this way. Finding out that my parents were either murdered, or abandoned me, in the last few days was enough to deal with. I didn't like being toyed with, and that's what this felt like. Like my guts were being twirled around for fun.

"Commander Li-aq," someone called from behind us, making us both turn our attention away from the fleeing Trent.

"Gho-ran, I thought you would stay with the ship," Commander Li-aq said with a tight smile.

"And miss the party?" The newcomer smacked Li-aq on the shoulder, though what might have been considered a friendly gesture between warriors, seemed more like an unwelcome aggravation by the way Li-aq stiffened with the contact.

"It isn't an open invitation, Gho-ran," he dismissed, "you should return to your commander's ship."

"Li-aq," he dropped all formalities of commander, and continued, "there isn't a party that I'm not invited to."

"It's for potential mates only," he said while his wings bristled, and a clucking sound vibrated around us that gave me an uncomfortable itch behind my ears.

"Then I guess all I need is Queen Mab's permission then," Gho-ran bowed before me with a mock flourish while extending his hand to me, "I, Gho-ran, second to Commander Trenton of Krelis, request the honor of attending your Mating Kloaph, as well as escorting you to the best chamber of the hive, while Li-crap returns to serious matters of importance to Queen Kai."

My eyes widened at the very slight, but distinct change in sound when he addressed Li-aq's name, which referred to him as crap. I had to bite the inside of my cheek to stop myself from laughing, and though I didn't know anything about Gho-ran, his candor and dislike of Li-aq was enough evidence to seek out his company, even if he weren't someone close to Trent. It didn't hurt that I wanted to pick his brain about what he knew about the Prince of Krelis.

"I've already picked out her chamber, next to Queen Kai, where she will want for nothing," Li-aq interjected before I could accept or deny, and he unwittingly gave Gho-ran the final blow that made my decision very clear. I wanted nothing to do with being that close in proximity to Queen Kai without investigating what was going on first.

"And the accommodations you have in mind?" I prompted Gho-ran, who read the situation as plain as if I had shouted my distrust of the queen from the top of the hive.

"They are on the opposite side of the hive, and have the best views of the mountain, My Queen."

"That sounds lovely," I agreed and took up his offered hand.

"You've crossed a line, Gho-ran," Li-aq threatened, but seemed reluctant to upset me by denying what I accepted. "Queen Mab, if you should change your mind, I will return to the heart within the hour to escort you to a queen's chamber."

His wings burst open in a rush, and he bolted up in the direction Trent had left, leaving me with Gho-ran.

My new escort chuckled and kissed the top of my hand before righting himself. "Follow me, so we may speak freely."

I nodded, and through many tunnels that kept my eyes occupied, he finally stopped at a dead end, and I narrowed my eyes, thinking perhaps I'd been too hasty once more in giving him even a small bit of trust over Commander Li-aq. Then his wings buzzed, lifting him up, and he left me with no pre-amble or warning.

Flexing my back muscles, I allowed my wings to extend, but I had no practice in flying. They fluttered and flapped, but as I ascended, I smacked against the membrane of the hive several times, and by the time I made it to another opening at the top, I was practically upside down, and feeling nauseous. Gho-ran gave me a crooked smile and grabbed my hand to pull me through the new tunnel, and I quickly folded my wings back, collapsing to the floor.

"Real funny," I gritted, as he laughed, assisting me to my feet. Sweeping at my robes on instinct from the dust I was used to from the plains between the palace and the research center, I realized there wasn't any on the ground of the hive's tunnels. Curiosity made me scratch at the walls and see if the membrane flaked or not. It didn't. Whatever it was made of was stronger than any fiber I'd seen before, yet it appeared thin, and fragile. "There's no dust," I thought out loud.

"There wouldn't be," Gho-ran replied as if I were speaking to him. "The hive is designed with the heart circulating the air through the flexible membranes and sweeping any dust along with it. Trent would know more about how it works, I never really thought much on it myself, but he shoved me out of his rooms once when I was inviting him to seek out a mate. Too busy with whatever the hell he

204

was doing, he wished for me to be swept up into its current and fly off." He chuckled heartily at the memory and thought of how similar Trent was in his dedication to his hive as I was to my clan. That same dedication was why I was so frustrated with him and betrayed by the knowledge that I'd fallen into his trap.

"He seems like the type to prioritize others," I grumbled. Others... not including me. It left a tangy grit in my mouth to know that his betrayal was more than simply tossing me into a party of krelins wishing to mate with me, but also a sign of his devotion to the survival of his hive. Could I fault him for bringing me here under the pretense of wishing to be my mate, it wasn't completely false, was it? He'd still be considered my "first mate" as Commander Li-aq had explained. I shivered at the idea of having Li-aq as any one of my mates. There was just something about him that irked me. Perhaps it was the way he leered or even the way his eyes appeared milky like he wasn't even looking at me at all some of the time.

I could end this pointless debate about if Trent was even worthy of sympathy for his actions if I knew he actually planned on saving Luan from King Sylve, or if that was a lie as well.

"You're the second in command, and technically the Commander of Trent's ship in his absence, correct?" Gho-ran nodded and gave a wry smile while he led me farther down the corridor. "When you return to your ship, I assume after the party, what are your orders?"

He stopped at a door that was layered thicker than any door I'd passed so far. The membrane was designed with webbing that created a picture of wings, krelin wings that were black like the membrane had been burned, yet survived. Gho-ran touched the door and swiped. The membrane sucked up into the walls, opening into a large room. The furnishings were organic like the hive, but there were also bits of technology here and there, and even jewels from Estreldez that were used to create a piece of art on the wall next to a large bed with black silken sheets. It felt... lived in.

"The ship will wait for you and Commander Trent to join the rest of the fleet in their patrols of the sector. He believes it will be easier to find Luan, once he personally connects with Lord Zorn, and strikes a deal with King Sylve's biggest competitor on Necias Delta Fal. Plus, your spawn will be safer in the hive, than on a ship. I'm sure you'll return before they are ready to have your blessing into the hive."

Spawn... blessings... Lord Zorn? My brain had to process through the data dump he'd just chatted about like it was nothing to blink an eyelash at. I didn't want to come across as stupid for not knowing who Lord Zorn was, but whoever he was, he wasn't mentioned in meetings I had been part of. I only knew of King Sylve because Luan and Loric spoke of him in heated discussions in the library. My advisory job was specific to interviewing and correlating data about the mating cycle.

My mouth opened to ask, then closed once I thought better of it. Whoever he was, he was associated with King Sylve and that couldn't be a good thing. I decided to wander the room instead, and my eyes landed on the jugs sitting in the corner with tubes sticking out, and filtering into another jug. They were the same containers used to transport nectar, I had a few just like them in my room on Estreldez. I smiled to myself, feeling lucky that there should be some nectar waiting for me in the chambers here. If there was ever a time to have a bit of help relaxing it was now. Krelis nectar helped ease the tension in my muscles and take the edge off my worries so I could focus, or... not focus so I could sleep.

I looked around for a glass to pour the nectar into but didn't find anything near the jugs. How did they expect people to drink it with nothing to pour into?

"Allow me," Gho-ran offered while grabbing a disc from the table. He placed the disc on the tip of his finger, and lifted it to his mouth before he clucked, and hissed. A clear string snapped from between his teeth, attaching to the disk, and he spun it round, forming a bowl with his... saliva? He ground down with his back teeth, cutting the string once it was complete. Grabbing the tube from the nectar jug, he unstoppered it to fill the bowl while commending the maker of the nectar, "This is some of the best nectar in the hive."

He handed me the bowl, my hands automatically accepting it before I could object. Gho-ran was already making another bowl to serve himself. I wrinkled my nose. I was already a little grossed out that I had an affinity for nectar that included the blood of krelins to make, and now I was being offered the drink in a bowl made of some strange substance that came from Gho-ran's mouth. I poked at the bowl, expecting it to be sticky, but it was smooth, and felt like silk, yet hard like stone.

Gho-ran was already drinking from his bowl, before he glanced over, finally realizing my hesitation. "It's fermented long enough, I assure you. Many krelins would battle to drink this stuff, only a few batches are made every cycle, and most of them get shipped out in trade before they are even offered to the hive."

"Why would it get traded off world before being offered to the hive?"

"Ah," Gho-ran downed his nectar, and sighed, "the brewer of this nectar had a crush on an off-worlder that had a penchant for smuggling nectar. He liked knowing his batches were being enjoyed by someone who appreciated his efforts and was kind to his warriors when he was away."

"Oh," I thought, now feeling awkward about drinking the nectar if whoever brewed it preferred it to be given to someone else. I was about to place it down on the table, before Gho-ran tilted the disk back towards my lips.

"Don't waste it, it can't be put back into the gorn once it's tapped out. Plus, I'm sure he wouldn't mind sharing his nectar with the queen of the hive, don't you think?"

"I'm not—" I started to object before he interrupted again.

"I'm not sure that I would want to accept such a job either, too much responsibility, but I'm glad that you're considering it. And just so you know," he tapped another bowl of the nectar for himself, "No matter what anyone in the hive tells you, our warriors live a long time, if they aren't stupid and get killed that is. What I'm trying to say is, you don't have to accept any of the mates at the party if you don't want to. You can just as easily bless other mates to do the work for you, instead of taking on the whole repopulating the hive on your own wings. That's what I would do," he said with a shrug.

"I can do that?" I found myself sipping from the bowl on instinct, once the intoxicating smell reached my nose. Ignoring that the bowl was made from some biomatter from the back of Gho-ran's mouth, my eyes lit up at the sweet and tangy nectar warming down my throat.

He smiled his agreement and then eyed the nectar in my hands as I greedily took another gulp. "What do you think of the subtler notes of the brew?"

"It's delicious," I admitted. It tasted just like my favorite nectar at home, except better, if that were possible. "All the nectar I've had on Estreldez doesn't even compare."

He lifted a brow, before he slapped his knee, and placed his bowl down on the table. "Right! I have the same problem with nectar we bring with us on the ship. As soon as you bring the stuff into orbit the flavor alters slightly, like it isn't quite as fresh as drinking it from the gorn in the hive. It loses a bit of something in the transport. Perhaps the pressure does something to it. I can have the same nectar on the ship as in the hive, and it's just not the same. You have a discerning palate, My Queen."

"You don't have to call me that," I said, finishing off the bowl. "What do they call this nectar, so I know what to ask for next time?"

"I will call you whatever you wish, Queeny, just name it. As for the nectar, the hive calls this batch the Black Vein Nectar. Anyone who's tried it says that it gives them the strength of many warriors and swear by its aphrodisiac abilities in charming potential mates." He gave a brow wiggle and added, "Do I seem more appealing?"

"Uh, no," I let slip without thinking about being diplomatic, and he merely spluttered a laugh at my blunt honesty. "The Black Vein," I repeated before I scrambled to turn the jug around and look for the signature that was on every batch of nectar I traded for on Estreldez. Gho-ran watched with amusement as I patted the jug down like a lunatic, then my hand snagged on what I was looking for. Every jug of nectar of the homebrew I bought whenever it was available had a distinct emblem etched into the surface, and I recalled it was usually a black lace-like branding, like a krelin wing with black veins...

"I've had this before," I mumbled to myself. This was the home brew I was given a sample of and had a difficult time repurchasing. No wonder, I thought, if this nectar was so popular that there was a whole story behind it on Krelis. Why hadn't the trader, Ong, told me about this story? I turned to Gho-ran. "How is that possible?" I suddenly felt sick that I had stolen this nectar from it's intended recipient countless times over the last cycle.

He rolled his eyes at me, but waved his hand dismissively. "Lots of things can happen during transport, perhaps you were the recipient of black-market goods, or," he snorted in bemusement, "an infamous krelin has a crush on you, but either way, as Queen of Krelis, you can have whatever hivebrew you want. I'm sure any warriors you ask will happily learn the art of nectar brewing and offer it to you. There's a dive brewery in the canopy of the Helmer Woods with a wide selection of nectar, called the Ki-Hive, you can try an array and find a favorite, but it attracts all kinds of krelin..."

"I've tried quite a few different brews," I said, staring longingly at the Black Vein nectar jug. I didn't want to drink more, knowing it was so rare, and secretly thinking about how I would smuggle it out with me when I left the hive.

"Well, I won't keep you, you'll probably want to rest before the party in your honor. I'll be back to escort you, if you don't find a better offer. And don't forget what I told you, Queeny, there are many ways to serve the hive, and I'm happy to lure your potential mates in my direction should you need a distraction. Happy to assist." He winked at me, and I couldn't help smiling at his charm as he offered to take the heat of other people's interest on to himself. It was laughable, and yet welcomed.

"I'm sure you would be," I joked.

"It will be most inconvenient, of course," he mocked with a flourished bow. "But I am nothing if not devoted to the hive, and if the queen has need of my body to take care of her mate prospects, then I must do my part."

"For the good of the hive, naturally." I smirked, watching him back away and exit from the room. It was comforting to know I wouldn't be going to this party without someone running interference, but I doubted one krelin would be enough to distract all the mates attending. My smile fell, and the warmth of the nectar was taking effect, making my body melt in a lovely way that had me crawling into the bed. Even the sheets smelled divine, and welcoming.

I closed my eyes, seeing Trent in my dreams. A single tear slipped down my cheek, absorbing into the pillow that conformed to my head like a cloud made of foam and silk. I needed him to tell me what Gho-ran had said so simply moments before, that I didn't need to mate with others, and if I wanted to bond with him at Kai Mountain then that's what we would do. But that isn't what he said. He wasn't at my side, merely the illusion of him in my mind.

"Come back to me," I thought with all my might before the heaviness of sleep took me.

Chapter Twenty

Trent

Confusion fogged my brain as I glanced around to see I was in the queen's chambers, my mother lounging before me with a gleam in her dull yellow eyes.

"Come back to me," a gentle voice thrummed through me. A sudden sharpness of clarity made me aware that I didn't wish to be here, and it took all my self-control not to immediately retreat to my rooms as my second eyelids snapped in place to clear the fog further.

Where was Mabel? I didn't dare make any quick movement to distract my mother from her delighted ramblings. On quick survey, it didn't appear Mabel was anywhere within the queen's quarters, and that was a blessing. All my mother needed was first contact with Mabel to have an easier time entering her mind to control her. I wouldn't let that happen until more of the hive had a chance to feel the draw of a new queen. The more support Mabel had, the higher her chances of pushing out my mother's influences.

"As the first mate to a queen, don't you think you should give the other mates a chance to bond with her, Trenton?" She didn't wait for me to reply before continuing, "I knew you would understand the importance of putting the hive first, over your own attachments."

At least, I knew her plan would not involve harming Mabel beyond controlling her for the purpose of the hive's repopulation. That gave us time.

"You'll return to your rooms for the remainder of the night, and you can visit her once she's chosen at least one other mate."

"Who?" It was unlike my mother to leave any room for choice about who she expected Mabel to have as a mate.

"Me," Commander Li-aq said, entering the chambers.

"Ah, Commander Li-aq, have you escorted our new queen to her chambers?"

He wore a smug smile but, after my mother's question, it flattened to stone. "Queen Mab has decided to take up different chambers temporarily. I thought it prudent to allow her a bit of freedom for now. Once I offer myself officially at her mating Kloaph, I will escort her to her new chambers with your blessing."

"I see," she was displeased with the delay, but placated by Commander Li-aq's explanation. "It's important that you begin the mating process as soon as possible. Make sure she's surrounded by your musk during the ceremony, and that you offer her your personal nectar to drink throughout the night. That should be sufficient, but my blessing will be the final incentive to have a few of her eggs drop. Bring them to me

213

while she's sleeping off the pleasure of the completed Kloaph Rites."

"Of course, My Queen, it is my honor."

I saw white, everything blurred with a burning flame of hatred that begged for me to rip the wings from Commander Li-aq's back and shove them down my mother's throat for the ancient treachery she was planning on my mate. These were tactics of the old ways when our ancestors were little more than animals grunting and clucking to continue our race without anything but body language, and our emotions transferred through the bond. It was taboo to musk a mate without stating your intentions first. And then to give her a nectar made from his own blood was a lethal combination with musk from the same krelin, it was no better than drugging her.

And my mother left nothing to chance in her plans... she fully intended to use her blessing to influence Mabel while her guard was down. All it took was a moment of weakness, and she could pump Mabel's brain with natural chemicals that would cloud her higher functioning. She would be in a haze, with Commander Li-aq guiding her towards the feeling of losing control and letting him make her body scream with pleasure that should only be mine.

My wings buzzed, and I couldn't stop the clucking of my glands in the back of my throat reacting to my anger.

"Don't antagonize him, Commander Li-aq," my mother laughed, even as drops of blood dribbled down my knuckles as I fisted my hands, "You'll have to learn to get along with each other once our new queen accepts him as a mate as well."

"My Queen? I thought you approved of Queen Mab having me as her first mate?" Li-aq kept his tone calm, but he was obviously perturbed by sharing my mate with me. The feeling was mutual. The only reason why he still had wings this moment was because I knew my mother thought I was still under her control, and I wished to keep it that way. The only one mating with Mabel would be me, when I steal her from this hive, and take her to Kai Mountain like I originally planned.

"Of course," she dismissed. "I'll send Trenton away on his missions off-world, and you'll have our new queen all to yourself, as well as any other mate that I choose for her. But what a powerful krelin a queen's touched warrior and a queen would make, don't you think?"

"Yes, My Queen," Li-aq droned, while I seethed. I was nothing more than a male who had inherited a queen's venom. Nothing but a tool.

I'd seen enough dazed warriors under my mother's influence to know that just because she had control of them, didn't mean they didn't have moments of defiance if what she asked of them was out of character. They would follow through, unwillingly, but sometimes they would protest while they did it.

"She is mine," I hissed my objection of this whole plot of hers.

"Oh, my dear son," she nodded mockingly, "She will be in time, just wait your turn. Now, go to your chamber and sleep. There is no need for you to trouble yourself while our new queen attends to her duties to the hive. You're both dismissed."

Commander Li-aq watched me return to my chamber, making sure that I followed orders, but stopped at what he assumed was the only exit in this dead-end of the hive. I had done many renovations to my space over the cycles, and making sure I had a rooftop deck that overlooked the whole hive was one of them. I'd go into my chamber, and exit out the roof deck, and enter in through the heart of the hive if I had to in search of where Mabel was. It would be like testing myself before we entered the caves of Kai Mountain, seeing how well I could sense our bond. I would follow wherever it led me.

So, when I entered my room to find her lying in my bed, I stilled in shock. Was I hallucinating? The door closed behind me, and I heard noises from the roof. Quickly, all I thought about was protecting my sleeping mate, so I flew through my space, and my ki snapped out stopping just short of stabbing whoever dared enter my room.

"Move and you will suffer a slow death should my poison enter your blood stream," I warned.

"Too late, brother, I already drank your nectar recently, and I'm immune for at least the next few hours still. I drank an extra serving just to be sure." He pushed my ki stinger aside, cutting his skin, allowing drops of my black poison to enter his body with no care in the world.

"Gho-ran..."

"As your second in command, I've been waiting a long time for someone like her to come along. A new queen," he laughed heartily, "Fuck, it's a miracle, and we can finally shunt our mother out of our hive. As long as you don't fuck it up, that is."

Was he saying what I thought he was saying? "Brother..."

He smacked me on the shoulder with glee. "I knew from the moment I tried your nectar cycles ago. It's why I worked so hard to become your second in command. So, I could be ready to help you once there was a chance to topple the crown so to speak. You thought I liked all this responsibility," he scoffed. I stared at him stunned and he proceeded to make himself at home within my chambers, lounging on a chair, and kicking back, while wiping his blood on his chest like it

216

was a tiny papercut. "You don't know how long I've waited to finally tell you. Well," he paused thinking about it, "I guess you do, since I just told you cycles before I was your second, and that was several cycles before now..."

"Just shut up," I snapped, needing some space and silence to think. He was always a chatty one, and overly jovial towards me, which I found odd in the beginning until it grew on me over the cycles. It was like lifting a mask from my eyes, to look at him now, and having thought about the possibility of having blood family that escaped the fate my mother would have given spawn that didn't meet her standards. He survived.

After a few minutes of quiet he couldn't take the only sound being the pacing I made across my room, while the soft hum of Mabel's breath lifted and fell in deep sleep behind us. Gho-ran was never really one for controlling his mouth, though he seemed to do just fine when the pressure was on for him to lead the warship when I wasn't present. I trusted him, and now there was a bit more sense to why I could tolerate his annoyances.

"I had this whole plan of taking the time to make my own nectar. Having you try it. You know, give me pointers and stuff, only for your eyes to grow wide with recognition of being connected by blood and we would bond and all that nonsense. You're really messin' with my plans."

"I think you did that all on your own," I pointed out, considering he was the one that decided to tell me now, while my mate slept in the bed behind us. "You said your father was hooman..." I shook my head, trying to wrap my mind around his admission. Then if he was hooman... he would be even more susceptible to my venom. "For your sake you better not be lying on drinking the nectar or being my blood." My poison would still make any krelin sick regardless of if

217

they drank my nectar, but if he was my brother by blood, then the poison wouldn't be as affective, and adding the nectar would make him immune for a time. But I still couldn't account for how his hooman half would react. It was only a drop that entered his system, so as long as he was truthful, I hoped he'd be fine. "Why tell me now?"

"Right." He leaned forward with a serious expression that I was now searching for the hints of familiarity that I'd missed over the cycles he'd been by my side. "I thought that would be obvious."

"I'd like you to confirm it," I stated bluntly.

He frowned, but complied, "Queen Mab is too new to the hive to match up with Queen Kai, even with her waning influence. You need to complete your bond, so you can block any attempts at controlling the new queen, not that I trust you to do a good job of that when I saw how zoned out you were earlier. That's why I decided to intervene a bit."

"I didn't take into account, opening myself up to the bond with My Kansa," I made a point to mention she was mine, because I didn't like the way he glanced over my shoulder at where she lie there sleeping, and his tone about intervening spoke of a fondness he was developing for her, "also opens my mind up to being influenced by Queen Kai if she's actively probing. I've pretended I was still under her thrall when the effects broke, but she'll notice soon enough, and double her efforts."

"So, to complete your bond, you run the risk of breaking it while Queen Kai tries to bring her under her control."

Sighing with frustration, I rubbed at my face, knowing I'd have to speed up my plans. "Mabel isn't safe here, until she gains the support of the hive."

"Sure, sure," he dismissed, and I felt my anger from before boil, my patience was wearing thin. It was like he didn't care about Mabel's life, and I didn't care if he was my blood or not, I took a foreboding step forward. He threw up his hands in surrender. "We both know her life is in danger. That's just fact, right? I was going to say, the fastest way to gain the hive's respect is to prove to them that she can lead."

"She doesn't know how to control her kan like that." A more selfish part of me knew that for her to connect the hive and have us work as an immutable force together would require her to open her mind to not just me... but to the hive.

"That's why I'm here," Gho-ran said grinning like a fool, relaxing like this was some game. A game with lives at stake, including my mate's.

"And why is that exactly?"

"I'm your blood, and she just drank your nectar not that long ago in a bowl made from my glands. She has a bit of both of us in her as she sleeps—"

"You had no right," I bellowed, before I heard her stir behind me, and I softened my voice, "What are you playing at, Gho-ran?"

"I've proved my blood connection with you, by staying alive, and without illness after deliberately taking your venom. I've also proved my loyalty to you, by not making any moves on your mate while she sleeps before you arrived. I also brought her to this room instead of wherever Li-aq planned on taking her."

I scowled at the mention of Li-aq, thinking of his under-winged plans to seduce and addle my mate into submission.

Gho-ran continued, "Brother, I will call you that from now on, since that is what we are, brothers. I've been waiting in the shadows for a time to finally seek my revenge on our mother for what she did to our sister, and what she did to the last queen to rise."

A sister? I stayed still, not daring to breathe as he

219

explained, "We were twins... it's why I even survived, because there was only one kantos and I was not awakened immediately after our sister. I've named her Panala, since no one else dared to name a queen dead at spawning. She had kan sprouting from her first light, and a sign of a powerful queen to be, despite being only half krelin. Our mother tossed her to the heart and left the kantos to be cleaned up by whoever came next."

"For such a quiet spawn, you turned out to be talkative," I joked with a tight smile, trying to lighten the mood, but there was nothing funny about what he was saying. He was accusing our mother of more than merely sending our warriors out to die in needless wars under the guise of protecting our sector, our planet, but of deliberately putting our hive in jeopardy by murdering a future queen. And proving that she had mated with a hooman around the time..., calculating how many cycles Gho-ran was, the time she stopped being able create more spawn.

I had gauged the appropriate response based on the many cycles we had served together aboard the ship. Gho-ran would not wish for me to pity him, but I had to respect the loss of our sister. I cleared my throat to add, "You chose an apt name for our sister. Panala. Heart of the Goddess. Our mother will answer for her crimes against the hive." I promised.

"I believe the only reason why your mate is not dead is because Queen Kai realizes that her connection to the hive is failing. Her only shot at keeping the hive together and keeping her position is to turn Queen Mab into a mindless breeder, while she rules in her."

"I will not let that happen," I hissed, my throat glands clucking in warning. I knew his assumption to be correct. I'd heard it for myself. She fully intended to pick and choose mates for her benefit, and political sway with the hive. Starting with Commander Li-aq.

"Yah, I'd rather not take your word for it. You have an entire horde of warriors willing to fight for you to become the next leader of the hive. No offense to your mate, our new queeny, or anything, but she doesn't need to sway the hearts of the hive today. You do. Horn up, and protect your mate, protect this hive. You need to show everyone at tonight's party that you are first mate to Queen Mab and claim your Kloaph Rite to take her to Kai Mountain, show them that you are not controlled by Queen Kai, and take your place as Prince in more than name, or perhaps you'd rather I do the honor myself?"

"She hasn't fully accepted me," I admitted with shame.

"Who's fault is that? Have you told her about the nectar?"

I pressed my lips together flatly. How did he know about that? He saw the momentary shocked reaction at his knowledge and scoffed.

"You think I don't have you followed? You are my best bet on not living in fear of our mother discovering that our sister had a twin, and finally being able to tell the hive the truth. To honor Panala. Of course, I knew what you were up to when you disappeared to check up on the trade transports. I didn't follow you the first time, but after you said the chief had things handled, and yet you continued to go spy on the trade to Estreldez, I couldn't ignore it."

"I thought she was the Jewel of Estreldez, covertly dealing with a problem with the trade between Krelis, but I had been wrong."

"You weren't wrong," he corrected me. "She did handle a problem with the trade routes by treating the chief with kindness, and chatting about Krelis, and Estreldez through shared nectar. Doesn't matter if she was spying or not, our queeny was learning about what our warriors wanted, and helped soothe their souls even from another planet. And you were drawn to her even then. Don't think I didn't notice how the chief paused before asking questions, and how his eyes glossed over.

"You, Commander, were falling for our queen before she even knew who you were. Doesn't matter that you didn't know who you were speaking to. Perhaps your *sa* did."

"Enough," I blustered. "I can't force her to complete our bond, and I can't let her go to the Kloaph party either. Queen Kai has made it clear she will go to any lengths to control Mabel, the whole thing's a trap."

"So what if it is? I've already got the horde ready to swarm the party in your defense on command."

"I will not risk more lives," I turned down the offer. I knew we would win a fight, but at what cost? The hive would be torn apart.

"Then tell your kansa what she means to you, and what is needed for her to claim control of the hive. I spoke with her, and she still has no idea that you're the one that made the nectar for her, or that all those conversations she was having with the Chief of Trade, Ong, were mostly with you using him as a proxy. Enough hiding, brother, enough stalling, enough waiting for the right moments." Gho-ran was standing now, his hands gripping at his braids ready to tear them out in his impatience.

Recalling all the conversations I had with the mysterious woman who traded for my nectar through my Chief of Trade, there was a singular confession that I believed would convince her that I told the truth. She never revealed anything about her parents, which is why I thought she was being careful as the only daughter of Estreldez's Almder, but she did speak of other things.

I sat at the edge of the bed, brushing away black hair from her cheek so it didn't cover her closed eyes. There was a subtle twitch in her jaw, near her ear, and I felt our connection through my kan pulse. "How much did you hear?" I asked her, sensing she was awake.

"Enough," she whispered, but kept her eyes closed.

She still refused to fully admit that she was awake, and I wasn't sure if it was because she didn't want to talk about what it meant that I was the one talking to her through my Chief of Trade, or perhaps she wished to ignore that she'd heard anything at all. I didn't know which one made me more irritated, but I couldn't stop my hearts from beating just a little faster as I admired her soft features. She was stubborn, and I admired that about her, yet I didn't enjoy being on the side of uncertainty and distrust directed from her. I knew I deserved it after ignoring her earlier, and I hoped she'd understand I wasn't fully myself.

"Sa means soul in krel, doesn't it?" she asked, and her green eyes stared up at me from thick black lashes. My hearts stilled, and I merely nodded my confirmation. There was something in the way she watched me that melted my insides, and I didn't wish for her to stop. I at least knew she heard that much of our conversation. She heard that my hearts, my soul, knew we belonged together before I let my mind accept it. What would she say next? I waited, and when I saw her eyes begin to leak, I couldn't stop myself from scooping her into my arms.

Her nose rubbed into my chest, and I whispered into her hair, "Whatever your choice, both my hearts will beat for you. Always, My Kansa."

"What is wrong with you?" Mabel smacked my chest with her fist, but it was as weak as a nit bug, barely noticeable, before she clung to my shoulder armor, pulling me closer to her. I understood this better than I understood any other emotion she could have given me in that moment. The instinct to protect yourself, and the desire to be protected. I felt the same as I held her in my grasp. Wishing to keep her close to protect the hearts she held, and warring with the need to push her away so I didn't harm her. Being my kansa mate made her a target, and without the hive's support... she would be in danger.

"I don't deserve you." It was my fatal flaw, being raised by a queen that saw me as nothing more than a tool. And as such, I was incapable of providing what my kansa had every right to, a life filled with happiness and peace. The hearts I give to her were damaged, cold, and hardened, but they were all I had to give.

I could feel Gho-ran observing us, and I regretted that I couldn't even give her privacy or time to process what was being asked of her. Would she accept me as her mate, and face my mother together? Or would I be sending her away with my brother to escape to my ship alone?

My answer came swifter than I could even have hoped.

Mabel's words hummed in my mind, "*Those are the words of a man not expecting to return. I won't let him go up against his mother on his own.*"

Warmth spread through my kan, and I was suddenly aware of Mabel's small form huddled up on my lap as I sat on the edge of the bed. When I had wrapped my arms around her, it was her upper body that I clung to. At some point between her throwing her fists at my chest, and pulling her closer, she had crawled onto my lap. Her hips adjusted, and I closed my eyes willing myself not to get excited while Gho-ran was observing us mere feet away. My cock twitched, and Mabel stilled.

"*If I reached for him, would he let me feel him this time?*" Her

224

thoughts entered my mind, and I realized quickly that she was unaware she had formed this connection with me. My mate had a dirty mind, and I was eager to explore this further. And yes, I wanted nothing more than to have her wrap those fingers around my cock, guiding me to her sweet center, but I'd have to tell my new-found brother to fuck off first. Her hand began to trace down my chest, and I groaned, knowing exactly where she was headed.

Gho-ran cleared his throat, and I cursed when his own thoughts entered my mind as well, "*Should I tell her she's using her hive connection, or should you?*"

Fuck, I thought, as much as I didn't wish to end the feeling of having her in my mind, sharing this with someone else wasn't my idea of a good time. Everything in me wanted her thoughts to only be for me, that she was accepting the bond, making her my kansa. I could only pray to the goddess that she was only projecting within this room, and not to other hive warriors.

"*My Kansa,*" I spoke through our bond, "*I would love to do all the things you desire, but I need you to direct your thoughts to only me. Follow where you feel my voice coming from and dismiss all others.*"

She pushed away to stare up at me with flushed cheeks. I shouldn't have smiled at her embarrassment, but even this was such an endearing look on her.

"You heard my thoughts?"

"So did I," Gho-ran announced himself, and I clucked my throat glands in warning. I wanted his presence to disappear from her thoughts, not for him to bring attention to it. She ignored him, and for that I was thankful. For someone so talkative, I recognized he avoided saying anything about his hooman spawn maker, and given how much he had already revealed, I felt bringing attention to it was not necessary.

Though, I was debating this choice to let well enough alone as he invaded what should have been a private moment with my mate. When he was ready, he could tell me more of who the hooman was, and how they became involved with our mother. I suspected Gho-ran might not even know himself.

"You're the voice I heard before..." she said staring at me with wide eyes. "It's always been you. I thought I imagined it."

Mabel flung her arms around me and crashed her lips into mine. My hearts felt so full, and my wings buzzed behind me with emotions I couldn't express at her affections.

"Mine," her thoughts so loud that nothing but her voice filled my mind, and nothing but the need to feel more of her consumed my very soul. I stood from the bed and trailed my hands down her backside to lift her legs around my hips. She complied, and her own wings fluttered so fast, she was lighter than air in my arms, nearly lifting my own feet from the ground.

Chapter Twenty-One

Mabel

Trent's lips worked against my own in a fury of passion. I could feel his essence within my very bones, and now that I knew all those times I'd heard his voice in my head was actually him, and not my imagination, everything was different. It was like a switch clicked in my mind, and the thread that held his voice reached out and wrapped around my heart tugging me closer.

I hadn't really noticed it before, until he told me to follow his voice, but there were other wisps that tingled at the edge of my mind. Earlier I had touched the closest ones. One I realized now was his, and I never wanted to let go.

"Don't let go," Trent's voice reaffirmed my thoughts. It was bewildering, and I wondered how much he actually heard and made a mental note to figure out how to filter

things so he didn't know everything. There were some things best left a mystery, like how much I wanted to undress him immediately, there was no reason he had to hear that, it ruined the fun for when my fingers wandered to the clasps at the front of his pants.

"*Queeny, as much as I appreciate the extra dose of pleasure you've decided to share with me, I have preparations to make for the Kloaph Rites,*" I heard Gho-ran's voice in my mind, and it thrummed from the other wisp I had touched earlier... It's the only way I could think of explaining the feeling I got in my mind when I heard people's thoughts. Distracted, Trent could feel that I was stunned for a moment and pulled away to nip at my lip.

"*Come back to me,*" his tone was dark and filled with promises that I would make sure he fulfilled.

I grabbed hold of the strand that I felt Gho-ran's voice come from in my mind, visualizing it while I did it, and I heard him moan as I did. Trent turned us in his direction, and Gho-ran was biting his own hand.

"You cannot fool me with that trick," Trent glowered at him, "You are not weak, and you can end the connection yourself."

Gho-ran shook out his hand with a wry smile. "You caught me. It's been a long time since I've felt the endorphins of a queen's affections, and I like how it feels." He watched me with a gleam in bright eyes that looked so much like Trent's. "My apologies, Queeny, as a dedicated warrior to your hive, I'm at your disposal. I look forward to the next time you gift me with your touch."

He took a low bow, and the wisp in my mind vibrated sending a strange warmth through my limbs. Trent hissed, and that familiar clucking from his throat that I now knew warded off other krelins when directed at them, but when he used them on me sent shivers down my legs in a delicious way. Gho-ran laughed and exited the chamber his last words pulsed in my mind, "*My Queen, it's been my pleasure.*"

Then the connection fluttered away from my reach yet didn't fully disappear. It was like it was in a container within my mind, and if I really wanted to get to it, I could, but for now it was stored away safely. Confused by his flirtation, I didn't know how to take it, but I trusted he wouldn't do anything against my wishes, so I let it go.

"Trent," I said, tugging at the warmth I felt wrapped around my heart, drawing his attention back to me. His second eyelid cleaned over his golden stare, and I watched in fascination. Even something that was automatic for him was remarkable to me. The way he looked at me, the distraction of Gho-ran already passed, and the whole world fell away around us. Here I was about to ruin the moment with something both of us knew to be true. "Taking over the hive isn't going to happen overnight."

"No," he agreed. Kissing my forehead sweetly, he kept me close as my wings folded back behind me. "It will be a process. Our immediate concern is to stop Queen Kai from giving you her blessing, and regaining Commander Li-aq from her influence. She'll find someone else to replace him, but it will delay her plans and you'll have more time to gain more supporters."

I liked how he said it was our concern, including me in his plans.

"You know I was raised in the offspring clan garden with Luan," I began, remembering what I'd told the Chief during a few of the times I'd been convinced to share a bottle of nectar before departing from the trading post.

"It's why I confused you for being the Jewel of Estreldez."

I nodded understanding the confusion. I had

inadvertently given clues about my identity to the Chief that were just as likely to be Luan as they were me. Almder was busy much of the time, so Luan was raised with the rest of the clan's offspring. Unlike many of the others raised alongside us, we didn't have any estreld to come pick us up before the darkside of the moon's rotation. As we became older, Almder requested Luan's presence more often, and I was dragged along with her.

Smiling at the memory, we used to be inseparable. These days Luan barely confided in me at all, and the one time she did, I felt pressured to keep her secret to her own detriment.

"Elmon was good to all of the offspring. I used to think she was my mother, and she did care for me and Luan, but over the cycles I realized that I was an occupation to her, more than a daughter. I still call her mother sometimes. She was kind to me, and because of her, I had many estrelds on rotation that sought to entertain me when Luan was busy. It was how I was introduced to Elder Ezra, and worked my way up towards being an advisor to the Almder."

"You spoke of Almder like she was your own mother," he recalled, and I nodded while nuzzling into his chest.

"It wasn't until I was older that I realized she cared for," I stopped abruptly, not knowing if it was even true anymore. Everything she's ever done for me was colored with a sticky film of betrayal. All those times she defended me, and insisted I be her advisor over others because I had proved myself, despite my lack of loh and being so young. She'd reprimanded those that objected to me working in the palace. She arranged for tutors to guide me in my studies that would not have been available to me otherwise. I spent many rotations in her alcove with her as she lead our clan.

It all settled differently now, after she ordered Elder Ezra to breed my eggs without my knowledge. I had avoided thinking about it, but I couldn't help think that Almder had done all those things because she knew what I was and planned on using my offspring to advance her own goals with Krelis. Was I merely a bargaining plan from the beginning? The only person who truly thought of me as family was Luan, and even she was pushing me away.

"Shhh," Trent soothed, feeling my turmoil through our bond.

"You can't ask me to be Queen of Krelis," I begged. Even someone like the Almder, who I thought was kind and wise, was capable of unthinkable things in the name of the clan. I didn't want to be put in a position that forced me to choose between my morals and the planet's future. What made everything so frustrating was that as much as it hurt, I was leverage that a leader couldn't ignore. Would I do the same? I swore to myself that if I were her, I would explain the benefits to the clan for someone to cooperate. But what if they refused?

I refused, didn't I?

"That's exactly why you'd be a queen worthy of the hive, My Kansa. You do not seek to control anyone. With your heart, you would lead our warriors without the need to force them to do anything. Fear is what drives Queen Kai's rule. I used to think that it was fear for the hive's future, but it's her own that she fears losing." He sighed before reminding me, "I will never force you to do anything against your wishes. Though I think you would make an excellent Queen of Krelis, you are not required to take on such a responsibility. We can stick to the plan. Use your connection to the hive to sway Commander Li-aq, to protect you from my mother's plans. I'll reclaim an abandoned hive on the other side of Krelis for those wishing to leave Queen Kai, and slowly we will liberate any of the hive that are unwillingly held by my mother's

231

influence. You needn't do anything but be by my side."

Of course he would still need to lead his hive. Regardless of if I became queen or not. I pulled away from him, and lifted my hands to cup his face. He was willing to face that alone, and guilt tore through me, but I couldn't bring myself to accept being queen. He will be a great leader for Krelis, I knew that because if he were a different man, he would have stopped me from trading with his Chief of Trade as soon as he discovered what I was doing.

Smiling up at him as best I could, I gave him what I could, "I've been an advisor to Almder for a few cycles now. The role seems a bit more demanding on Krelis, but I take my job very seriously." My hands trailed down his neck, and along his firm pectorals, tracing over one of his nipples. His breath caught, and those golden eyes hooded with desire.

"I would be a fool to dismiss such dedication," he teased, and I could feel his interest grow as he grabbed my ass, pressing himself against me.

"Trent, I'm serious." I shoved at him.

"So am I." His hardened length rubbed against me, and I nearly came undone right there.

"Prove it," I said, nipping at his lower lip. I wasn't exactly sure what I was asking for, but he delivered nonetheless.

"I'll prove to you that I can find you anywhere, My Kansa. If that is what you want, we will leave now, and I can have Gho-ran take charge of undermining my mother's infestation before we must face the coming war."

Before I could object to dismissing the real threat that was Queen Kai, he was already flying through a hidden tunnel that led out the top of his rooms. As we launched up, my whole body seized, electricity coursing through my veins like fire. Trent wrapped his wings around us and landed hard on his back to protect me as we crashed into the roof of his chambers. I tried to move, but was stuck beneath his wings, and the soft look on Trent's face told me he was passed out. Adjusting within his arms, I could finally see a tall woman staring down her nose at us with a grim expression of disgust.

"I know you're awake, spawn of Leahme. You're lucky my son is quick to shield you, but not quite fast enough to have seen the traps. I've known about his little roof-top escape for some time now, but I couldn't let him screw up my plans for your Kloaph Rites. I wasn't expecting to catch both of you, but it saves me the trouble of figuring out where you were." She sneered at me before addressing someone out of eyesight from where I was stuck beneath Trent's wings, trapped inside of some electrified netting. "Put my son back on his ship, and make sure the navigation places him in front of one of King Sylve's spy ships from the recent survey report. As for our new queen, she needs to be prepared for her mating rites." She paused to glance back at me. "Please don't disappoint me like your mother. Queens don't survive long without the support of the hive, and I'd hate for them to turn on you."

A strange sound came from my throat that I wasn't used to, and Queen Kai narrowed her eyes at me. "Sounds like a personal problem," I muttered. She should be taking her own advice. If it was the hive I should have been scared of, then she should be more afraid than me.

"Your mother thought that as well. All the way up to the very day of her death," she threatened, and my whole-body chilled despite being held in Trent's warm, limp arms. I tried to tug at the connection between my heart and his, begging him to wake, but nothing stirred.

"*Trent, please.*" I pressed my forehead to his, our kan touching, sending jolts of warmth through my limbs.

Chapter Twenty-Two

Trent

Please, Mabel's beautiful voice repeated in my mind like a mantra. The last thing I remembered was being shocked by a net that prevented me from taking her to Kai Mountain to complete our bond. I turned over, squeezing my arms tight to pull her back to me, but my arms were empty. Bolting up right, both my hearts sped up erratically in search for her, but that tug of our bond was weak. She was not in this room. Wherever this was, it was not with her.

I winced as I opened my eyes, my vision still fuzzy at the edges of my vision. My muscles flexed, still aching from the charge of being electrocuted. That was the only way anyone would have bested me in a duel, tricking me while distracted. Yet they kept me alive. That was their first mistake. Whoever took Mabel would not be so lucky when I caught up with them. The bond was incomplete, but not absent. I would find her.

Metal was beneath me, cold and uncomfortable. *Fuck*, I thought, this was not the hive. I was on a ship that would take me off-planet, if I wasn't already. How long was I out?

"Oh good, you're awake," a voice I recognized, but hadn't expected to hear for many cycles said before they revealed themselves. Gaven... "You know, I thought you'd do a better job at protecting Mabel, and I did debate, liberally, on whether I should help you, or simply be the one to swoop in myself."

"What a hero you are," I snapped, putting pressure on my head where it throbbed like someone had punched me when I was out.

"She loves you," he said with a wrinkle of his nose. "I saw the way she clung to you when they pried you both apart to throw you in here. I won't try to understand why, but if it's the last thing I do for her, I will make sure you return."

"You were there, and you did nothing!" I charged at him, unable to keep my temper down. He sidestepped and disappeared into the distorted metal of the ship's luggage compartment.

He tsked with his tongue. "You're still not ready, once you're recovered, we'll leave, but you should know as someone in your position that sometimes the most successful course of action is to wait and plan instead of rushing into an ambush. Then again, perhaps that isn't something you do... since you're here."

The mockery in his tone set my nerves on edge and I spun around the room, clucking my tongue so my kan could search for him. There, I thought, and extended a hand to grab him by the throat. I couldn't see him, and he had the advantage of seeing me coming, so my hand wrapped around his wrist, protecting him. He smiled, his illusion gone, but not the sting of the heat sizzling the flesh from my fingers. I held firm, uncaring of the pain.

"You have a limited source of radiation away from your moons, Sky Bender, best you save it for something other than games," I warned. He lowered his wrist, and my grip went along with it. I gritted my teeth against the burns, but knew they were only temporary.

"We aren't in space," he assured. "I made sure the shuttle routed a course back into Krelis atmosphere. They assumed correctly that you would be passed out long enough that you would dock at the ship before you could do anything about turning around. I'm sure there would have been guards waiting for you upon your arrival, but they didn't account for me canceling the coordinates before we ever docked."

I released him.

"We're on Krelis..."

"Yes." He rubbed his wrist from how hard I had gripped him. I flexed my ki stinger in my forearm, as if I were simply examining my burned flesh, but making sure he was aware that stopping my hand from choking him would not have stopped me from stabbing through his throat if that was my intention. He grunted, as if he were clearing phlegm and then continued, "When you're ready we can grab Mabel, and get off this rock."

The last thing I saw when I shielded Mabel from the fall, was my mother's deadly eyes. "You'll take Mabel," I amended the plan. "I can't leave until I've settled a debt."

Gaven lifted a brow. "Finally going to nut up and lead your hive?"

"I have a queen to kill."

Regardless of who would lead the hive, it could be Ghoran for all I cared since I knew Mabel was reluctant to carry such a burden, I couldn't allow my mother to harm another krelin, let alone my kansa. The bond between us was weakened, I could barely feel the faintest of light that had curled around my hearts since meeting her.

Going to her was all I could think about, but, as much as it pained me to admit, Gaven was correct. It didn't do my mate any good to be caught in a trap, and she was strong enough to hold her own until I figured out if Gaven's little disappearing act worked farther than his own skin.

Chapter Twenty-Three

Mabel

Having Trent be snatched away from my very fingers, his body limp and vulnerable, was the worst feeling I had ever experienced. I could do nothing, and everything in me shut down. A blank void filled my eyes as I was dragged from the departing shuttle and taken to the mountains of Krelis by flight, hanging from two warriors. Not even my wings had any fight left in them.

What would they do with him? Would he be okay?

Queen Kai finally spoke as we reached an entrance that glowed, my attention jolted recognizing this place from my dreams. Either side of the trail was guarded by krelin warriors, their wings spread out and blocking any exit. The female warriors had their stingers out, and crossed as they watched me with a sick kind of reverence. A few warriors even hovered above should I have decided to fly towards escape. Not that I was practiced in flying to be successful in my attempt. I was just as likely to crash into the ground or fly right into their grasps. Combat training would be my best bet out of here, but they were likely more trained than me, and I was outnumbered, and the queen was at my side.

"Spawn of Leahme, in honor of your Kloaph Rites we bless you." All of their wings flexed at the same time sending a storm of musk spores assaulting my nose, making me cough and choke. I stumbled forward, disorientated. My hands flailed out grasping for purchase anywhere. Finally, I found something to cling to.

Blinking through the haze, I saw the sneer of Queen Kai as she yanked my head back by my hair. As I gasped, she poured a liquid down my throat, and it overflowed from my mouth. I spat, and coughed, but she held my head firmly in place. It was a struggle to close my mouth to stop the drink from being forced into my very lungs. She kneed me in the stomach, making me suck in the thick nectar down my aching throat to my stomach, and airways. My head was tossed from her grip, and I scrambled on the ground, choking on the nectar that went down my windpipe.

Queen Kai spoke again to the gathered krelins. "With this nectar you grow in union with the hive!"

Grunts formed a haunted sound around me and feet stomped in a matching rhythm that my heart matched in measure. My body thrummed, and the dust of everyone's musk settled for me to see a large krelin cast in the shadow of the mountain's glow, wearing a mask of gold. His wings spread out and his own musk filtered through the wind towards me. The warmth in my belly distracted from wanting to hold my breath, and when it hit my nose, I close my eyes and moaned.

"Trent?" I muttered. Was that him? I'd only ever felt this way around the marvelous, imposing force of the Prince of Krelis. He was of similar build, and this warmth was undeniable. Then he turned from me and walked into the cave, being swallowed up by the green glow. I reached out to him as if to stop him from leaving, but he was gone.

Queen Kai's chuckle echoed against the mountain, and she addressed her warriors, "As is tradition, she isn't to leave this cave for two weeks for completing the Kloaph. Guard the entrance. No one in, and no one out. You can trade your posts and join the celebration at the hive when your replacements arrive."

I heard their replies bouncing around in my mind, "*Yes, My Queen.*" Lights pulsed on the edges of my vision, what I used to think was my imagination part of me knew intrinsically was the hive bond. I could see them all, and one in particular wrapped around my heart... but it didn't lead into the cave where Trent escaped to. No, I shook my head, remembering the feeling of him being ripped away from me and disappearing into the sky as the shuttle departed.

My head throbbed, and an enticing, strong light beckoned me into the cave. I crawled towards the green glow, and when I got there my heart seized. Heat and desire clouded my thoughts, images of Trent's hands exploring my body made me shiver. He was in there, I convinced myself. My mate was lost, and I needed to find him. When I passed over the threshold, I collapsed and saw my dreams come to life.

Trent smiled at me, and without a word motioned for me to follow. With whatever strength I had left I stood. My wings fluttered behind me to keep me on my feet. Then I chased him down the tunnels, losing track of him around the bend.

I'd been here before. Touching the walls, they felt familiar, like I had returned from a long journey and this was home. There was a pulse through the ground, green, glowing veins that led me the opposite direction of where I had been heading. A tug in my gut wanted me to continue where I'd lost track of Trent, but then the cave thrummed louder in my head, piercing through my horns.

I relented and went down the other fork in the tunnels for what seemed like hours and yet only minutes. All concepts of time were gone. The tunnel became more narrow, and I had to shimmy sideways to continue.

Why was I so determined to continue?

Then my jaw dropped as the passage opened up into a hidden hot spring within the mountain. Steam rose up in puffs through cracks in the ground, and yet the only warmth was in my newly formed kan on my forehead, and deep within my chest. I clutched at my shirt, willing the pressure to ease. Instead my vision blurred, and from the walls white smoke billowed, rolling off the waters of the pool until I was stepping into a cloud of dense plumes of sticky vapors clinging to my skin and robes.

Not once did I even think of turning back the way I came. Drawn into the room, I stepped into the waters. My robes were soaked and heavy, and I peeled them away until all that was left was me and the spring. A drop in the surface of the spring startled me, but my wings opened on instinct, gently swaying to keep me afloat without any efforts from my arms or legs. The natural feel of being in the water made me wonder whether krelins used to be creatures of the depths. The way the water never truly absorbed into the fibers of the wings, and how my shoulders seemed to relax much more than when I tried to fly in the air. I closed my eyes, and the fog of the room resembled the way the lights of my connection to the hive did in my thoughts.

Reaching up from the water, I played with the wisps which were cold to my fingers. I smiled as they warmed with my touch. And then I heard them speaking.

"*Do you feel that?*"

The two wisps seemed like they were entwined together, and I liked that. As soon as the thought of how perfect they were formed, the wisps glowed and they were no longer separated. That was the way they were meant to be. I knew that deep in my bones.

"*I feel you...*" the wisp said, but I knew it wasn't directed to me.

"*Kansa.*" they said together, and that word made me flinch back, the wisps floated away from my fingers, and I clutched at my own heart. Light warmed my heart, and I clung to it.

"*Where is she?*" I heard Trent's voice demand.

Then Queen Kai replied, but they were nowhere in sight, "*Building an army of powerful warriors as we speak, I suspect. She seemed quite taken with Commander Li-aq when I saw her last.*" Her dismissive tone was dripping with a kind of smug achievement that made me cringe. Whatever benefit I wanted to give her for being the mother of the man that occupied my mind and heart was lost, and a true understanding that she was never a mother to him, just as my mother was never there for me hit hard.

"*What? Nothing to say?*" she teased, and there was a tug at my heart that thrashed against my ribcage. "*I had so much planned for you, Trenton. I'd make sure her next cycle of eggs were from your seed before you left to claim Estreldez. You were going to be a hero, dying valiantly defending Krelis alongside your warriors as I rebuilt this hive from spawn up. Monuments would be erected in your honor.*" Her tongue clicking vibrated through my mind like an unwanted pest. "*I see now that you are still too selfish to see what needs to be done for the future of the hive, and this will be the last of your defiance. May Lenkal keep you as you join Leahme in the eternal dust.*"

She was killing him... I gripped at my tight chest, feeling my heart slow.

A heavy despair made the water cold, and my wings stiffened as I sunk beneath the surface. "No," I screamed, letting my lungs fill.

Chapter Twenty-Four

Trent

All it would take is one touch, and I knew my journey would end here. Queen Kai's efforts to enter my mind thundered at the back of my mind, a constant battering seeking a moment of weakness to take control. Images of Mabel glaring at me intertwined with moments where she let me give her pleasure surged to the front of my thoughts. How could I expect my kansa to let me inside her mind, and accept our bond when I've done nothing but cause her discomfort, and showed her with my actions that all I cared for was her body. Of course her mind protected itself from me. I was a parasite leeching the warmth from her very soul.

Something in me snapped, and I knew the best I could do for her was be the Black Prince that everyone expected of me… the Queen's Revenge.

"Why?" I begged of Queen Kai, still struggling with the decision I made to come here and end this with the venom dripping down my ki, readied at my sides to plunge into one of her hearts. It wouldn't matter if we shared blood, or that her blackened hearts somehow survived the wound... without my nectar in her system the poison would take her.

"You are too young to understand, but the shol did." She looked down her nose, shaking her head with that all too familiar disapproval in her darkened eyes. With a sigh, she decided to enlighten me with her twisted reality before she gave me the final push into the waters of Lenkal's embrace. "The shol knew." Pausing for a long moment, she gazed off as if she were reliving the haunted past of decimating an entire species when she was not much older than I was now.

"What does this," I motioned around us, but my reach was farther than what we could see, reflecting on her recent decisions to control the hive, to attack the estrelds, and even to kill her own spawn, "have to do with the shol? You've already seen that the planet is uninhabitable, and whatever is left of them is scattered so far into the universe that they will all but die off."

"Everything, my son—"

"I am not your son," I cut off, not wishing to have anything to do with her. I was disgusted with my own black veins, given to me from a queen that cared little for me or our hive.

She ignored my outburst and continued, "I will honor your essence by taking you into my body from once you came. Did you ever once ask yourself, son." She called me son pointedly to get under my skin, and I held firm in my attention to keep her out of my mind. I couldn't afford to let her rattle me further. Focus, I repeated to myself as pain radiated through my kau, down my neck, and webbed out to the very fiber of my bones at the tips of my fingers. "Why did we take over Sholonus? Why be so unrelenting with the shol?"

"They were resistant to our musk, and the bonds they shared with their mates healed them from those with venomous ki. Their teeth could pierce through our thick scales, and their strength could rip our wings from our backs. Everyone knows they were designed in perfect harmony to destroy krelins."

"And yet, we outnumbered them, and infiltrated their planet for a successful eradication. I ask you, why?" She insisted with an air of annoyance that I hadn't questioned things sooner.

She wasn't making any sense. The obvious answer was that she was greedy for Sholonus resources and didn't like the risk they posed to the hive, but I was missing something, so I allowed her to continue.

"My naive spawn, you think I destroyed a species because they were a threat? No, I destroyed a species because they infected our hive! They came to our planet under the guise of peace! I was young, and as naive as you are now. I let the molt fever into our hearts."

"How?" I shook my head, unbelieving of her explanation, and still irritated she would even try to excuse the choice to destroy the shol, long before I was spawned.

"Do you think the krelin were always stunted in our fertility? We were the threat to *them*, and they acted accordingly, infecting our nectar reserves," she said this last part quietly, a deathly and palpable heaviness to her claims that was filled with anger that never left her since the day her kindness was torched with betrayal. "We flourished. Just look at the many hives Krelis used to have, all but abandoned."

A crazed intensity lifted her features and her eyes all but

glowed as she continued, "Ordin Crystal will change everything... Leahme's spawn will change everything. I've already seen how it's cleansed our nectar and given us a queen unaffected by the molt fever. We will rebuild. Our hives will grow."

"You expect me to believe any of this?" I took a step forward, ready to end her madness. "You killed Queen Leahme, and you are killing this hive!" A nagging voice begged to hear her out, to know her truth, even if it was twisted with hate. My eye twitched, but I relented.

"I am saving our hive! Leahme died the moment she refused to accept any other mate but her estreld. She was dooming us all. I won't make the same mistake with her spawn. Ordin Crystal is not enough to cleanse our planet from the molt. You can't be selfish! For the future of our hive, I can't let you ruin everything by keeping our only hope to yourself! Even if that means I must destroy my own blood, I won't let you doom us as Leahme did."

"Doom us," I repeated with every bit of restraint I could manage. "Are you so blind? So consumed with your own savior complex that you can't see what you're doing? You are the one dooming our hive," I seethed. "I've seen it, no," I corrected quickly, "I've felt it myself. Estrelds' radiation can cure our blight without the need for this, *this*," I shook my head, "death, and manipulation. Was it even the molt fever that took Queen Leahme to the heart of Goddess Lenkal?" I had to know, I needed this confirmation to help push me to what needed to be done. I still couldn't bring myself to kill my own mother, even with that crazed glimmer in her eyes that spoke of a future of death and chaos.

"She was going to leave us," she said under her breath, her gaze far off like she couldn't even see in front of her own nose. I approached, my ki readied at my sides while she was

247

distracted with the ghost of the past. "She was going to leave me just like him..."

I paused, stunned by her last words and the way they tugged at the very center of my gut. There was pain there, and loss. Her eyes locked onto mine and she found my moment of weakness within her own, recalling how it felt to have Mabel retched from my grasp. It was love, however twisted it had become. She may never have loved me... yet she loved our Queen Leahme, loved this *him*. I could only assume she meant Gho-ran's father... the hooman.

Tendrils latched into my mind, hearing her words resonating through me, "*I did my duty to the hive, sacrificed to bring about prosperity and new life.*" Queen Kai gripped at her leather scales across her chest and closed her eyes. I could feel it within, burning through my veins... her ache. Her suffering throbbing and stabbing through my skull, crippling me to my knees. "*She was the warmth after years of frost. She gave me strength to rejuvenate our hive. I tried to stop her...*"

Her hands turned over, this way and that, as she examined them like they were separated from her body. Perhaps they were. Whatever connection she had with the hive was fading, and though she still had the strength to keep me on my knees, her hold on the hive was not what it used to be. She was not what she used to be. Her eyes lingered on her own ki, where poison dripped off the tips of the stingers. It wasn't hard to connect the dots. Queen Leahme didn't die of the molt like the stories were told.

Did it matter if it was an accident, or out of anger?

Did that erase all the wrongs she'd committed since?

I bowed my head to face what fate she had for me. I was no better than her. Driven by hate... and love, the line between them was so gray and shrouded in darkness. Then her ki pressed into my chest drawing a drop of blood as she hovered there. Her head rested atop my own, kan touching kan, as she filled my mind with her final gift of pumping my body with a queen's euphoria, blinding me with a pleasant warmth before the end.

I saw the memory she latched onto when she gave pleasure to the hive.

A man laughed, and in his eyes I saw the same cheeky humor of Gho-ran. How could mother not see the similarities between them? He was smearing dirt across his brow as he raked a garden of strange planets that I'd never seen on Krelis, then the leaves crumbled and turned to ash. The light from the man's eyes dulled to a milky gray, and signs of molt fever colored his once dark skin. How was this possible? A hooman dying of the molt?

The pain I expected to feel when the poisoned stinger entered my hearts never came.

My vision was blurred, my body numb, but with heavy eyes I saw the same vacant stare reflected back at me as Queen Kai pulled away. She collapsed in a heap of sobs before me, tears streaming down her cheeks, and a stiff smile on her lips. Her ki never entered past my chest guard scales.

"My son, you are our final hope. Convince our queen of what needs to be done. There isn't time. She's found the heart of Lenkal. Save her. Save Krelis when the trill come for us."

"What are you saying?"

"So much warmth," she said holding her head in her hands, "She'll destroy us all, just like her mother." Turning her own ki on herself, she plunged the stinger deep under her ribs, and up to her hearts. I scrambled across the floor to reach her, cradling her head in my arms.

"What have you done?" I rocked her, only now realizing I didn't have the strength to kill my own mother. I came here to escape my own fate, knowing one of us would die. Had I been so foolish that I would rather die than see Mabel with another male? My mind was slowly clearing from the haze Queen Kai's influence had on me. She smiled up at me with a dribble of blood leaking from the edge of her lips.

"Naive spawn, what do you think will happen when the trill discover we've found a cure to the molt fever without first fortifying our warfleets? Queen Mab, must take on many mates. You can not keep her to yourself. I wished to hide her, to have her compliant and safe like I did her mother. We needed more time. They are coming, you know this. King Sylve knows this. They will come, and they will think just as the shols did. We are a threat. As long as there was only one queen, one successor, and our numbers were bound by molt, we were controllable. But she's found the heart and is reaching out to the hive. I have no choice but to return to the dust of Lenkal to save us all. We can't take the chance they do the same to us as they did to the shol."

I blinked in confusion, my second eyelids relubricating.

"The shol were strong, an equal match to our strengths. We didn't defeat them by force alone."

"The trill," I said finally seeing the pieces clicking together.

"We did the same thing to the shol that they did to us... a poison they couldn't cure, even with their healing," she choked on her own blood, filling her lungs.

"They don't have to defeat us in battle, they can just let us die off." I didn't agree with how my mother was going about things, but I could understand the pressure she was under. I looked at the black veins running through my forearms, and black veins now spreading through her own, creeping up her neck and across her jawline.

My mother was a survivor, our genes fought off the molt fever, and she kept another generation going with the help of

Queen Leahme, but she didn't trust that burden on any other's shoulders. She took the whole of the hive on herself, and that was her error, I realized. I was making the same one.

I tried to face this all by myself, willing to die or kill to unburden myself from everything. Wash my hands of the hive's troubles. Now, Mabel was doing the same. Facing the hive by herself, somewhere within the caves of Kai Mountain. If Queen Kai wasn't lying... Mabel found the heart of the mountain, that not even she could access. We had more trials to face to protect the hive, and Estreldez, from what was coming.

I wouldn't let her do it alone.

"Leave me," my mom gave me permission to let her die alone, giving me the only smile that ever truly reached her eyes. Perhaps the only act as something more than my queen, but the one to give me life. She had a chance to kill me... and she didn't. Now, she was letting me go.

I had to follow my bond with Mabel, and pull her from the waters of Lenkal, or she'd be lost forever. Resting my mother's head on the floor of her chambers, I closed her milky eyes with my palm.

The party I'd snuck through on the way here, was completely still. Every krelin I passed was in a kind of stasis, with vacant expressions glossed over as they stared up at the skies. The ones in flight still had their wings buzzing to keep them afloat, but their minds were lost to the birth of a new queen.

Why was I spared?

Pushing faster, I flew through the heart of the hive, and made my way to Kai Mountain. Eerie silence urged me on. The last known queen to enter the waters stayed there for many cycles, by the time she re-emerged from the mountain she was feral, and there was nothing left of her mind. Queen

Kanweh, the one said to have given life to our kan... the source of the hive's bond and a queen's ability to control it.

When I reached the entrance to Kai Mountain's glowing caves, the guards were just as the rest of the hive, moaning and enjoying the high of the most powerful connection to a queen we'd had in centuries of cycles.

Yet, I was immune... Through the mist a figure emerged. Mabel stood before me, wings spread like the goddess herself, and black hair floating in the wind of her floating form, like she was still submerged in water. Her emerald eyes glowed like she was part of the mountain.

She turned, with a smile on her ethereal lips. Her toes barely tapped the ground as she darted into the mountain, wings spread and fluttering, luring me to follow. I knew that's what I should do, because as soon as she disappeared into the fog, every instinct in me intensified. My hearts throbbed and tugged me forward.

"*Mine*," I thought, and I gave chase.

Chapter Twenty-Five

Mabel

Gel filled my lungs just like the medical pods I'd heard about in far-traveling galaxy ships, allowing me to breath despite being submerged. The confusion I felt from earlier disappeared and my body shivered with clarity, no longer drawn towards the light that had lured me into the caves to begin with. I could still see the wisp of that connection as I closed my eyes, but it wasn't the one that wrapped around my heart. I knew that now. Grabbing hold of the bond, it nearly broke within my fingers. When I clucked my tongue, the vibrations seemed to solidify the light under the waters, and I tried once more. Pulling myself to the surface. Coughing up the gel, it glittered on the smooth green rock of the cave as I panted, clinging to the edge.

My mind buzzed with noises, like a low chatter of too

many people talking at once. I winced, and reached up to hold my head, only to feel my kan had grown once more, and curled back along my scalp like a twisted crown.

The pressure around my heart throbbed, and one voice in particular became more clear than the others, "*Focus on me, Kansa, just me. I'm coming.*"

He was alive, I nearly sobbed with relief.

"*Queen Kai...*" I thought, still unbelieving of what was happening. This was all a horrible hallucination.

"*She took her own life, you're safe,*" Trent assured, but it wasn't my safety I cared about.

"*Are you real?*" I couldn't hope that I was still asleep in his bed this whole time.

I crumpled to the ground, curling in on myself with my wings spasming behind me as the noise in my head intensified. "Arrrghaaa," I groaned with an overwhelming surge of emotions that didn't feel like my own.

"*Listen to my voice,*" he screamed louder than the rest before a calming clucking echoed through the cavern that drowned out the chatter vibrating through my mind.

"*Feel,*" the word resonated and faded.

That's what my kan were now, the sense of the whole hive, and there was no turning it off, I thought with defeat. I would go insane. I shivered and wallowed in the mist of the oasis hidden deep in the Kai Mountains, accepting my fate to succumb to the chaos of my mind, lost to the thoughts of others.

"*I'm a wretched soul, but you are not the hives' queen, you are mine. Do you hear me Kansa! Do not retreat from me.*" A yank jerked in my ribcage, and I gasped at the strength of the jolt. He had to be alive, this wasn't a trick of my mind, and even if it was, I would live here in this illusion for eternity.

"*If you are a wretched soul, then so am I. Forsaking my clan, running from the hive, I am wretched. And it's you I can't escape from. I don't want to.*" I clutched at my chest, and crawled across the ground, begging my body to cooperate. Trent was always truth, even when I doubted him.

I thought about all the reasons why I wanted him that had nothing to do with how my heart sped up when he was near. "*You listened to me. You supported me. You never once believed that I was broken, even when I thought you did. I know that now. And it was me who gave up on us when you needed me most. I should have seen the way your eyes were distant. I should have known you weren't yourself. I should have known you needed me.*"

"*I still do, Kansa,*" he said as his hands scooped me up into his arms. He felt so real, the mist clung to him like colored stars on his skin. "I can't do this without you."

My eyes widened at the sound that felt so close. Hands scrambled up his chest, and cupped his face to confirm he was solid. If he was an illusion, he fooled me, and I didn't care as long as he was mine.

"Why?" I sobbed, and he flinched at my question like it haunted him.

His kan touched against my own, and the noises of the hive quieted to a dull hum at the back of my mind. His voice was like a soothing balm keeping the battle within my mind at bay. "With my mother gone, someone will have to lead the hive. It doesn't have to be you," he quickly added so I didn't misunderstand, "I will take you to a safe sector of the universe if you ask it of me, far away from the cries of the hive, where their voices cannot haunt you. We can live simple lives, and others will take up the burdens of what is coming. You've freed the hive, and you need not give anymore."

I knew what he was doing. He was supporting me once more, at the cost of everything he believed in. He did it before and he's doing it again. He tricked the Almder into agreeing to his cleverly worded treaty about bringing his mate back, he had no obligation to find Luan, bridge the peace between planets, or defend the sector against King Sylve's ships before the trill came to re-establish their claim on what was theirs by name... The Trillume Galaxy.

My lip quivered thinking about how this whole time he never wanted to burden me with taking over being Queen of Krelis. We were supposed to come to Kai Mountain to solidify our bond, and here we were in the heart of the mountain prepared to flee if I decided to disappear into ignorance. He wouldn't blame me for it, but I would. I had something Krelis needed to fight against King Sylve, and to deny the buzz at the back of my head was to abandon them all.

I wasn't my mother. I couldn't do it.

"Mabel," Trent spoke softly, hesitant.

"Say it," I urged, when he wouldn't continue what he started.

"Your mother was a kind krelin, I should be so honored to be gifted by Queen Leahme more than once in a lifetime. Once when she blessed my life into this world, and again when her daughter became part of my soul." I was sobbing, tears streaming on his shoulder from where I clung. He explained what his mother said about Queen Leahme, and his suspicions about her death. I stayed cradled in his arms for a long time, as he kept his kan touching my own to quiet the voices of the hive.

With a hiccup, I finally spoke, "I don't believe in fate, but I don't have to believe in it to be thankful that you're part of my life and we discovered this cave."

"What is going through that mind of yours, kansa?"

I forced a smile and pulled my face away from his chest.

"I know what this place is, and why the queens can reach the whole hive across distances even through space."

He blinked at me, probably never questioning why it was ever possible as it was always something he lived with since being spawned. It always was. Trent grinned back at me, wiping moisture from under my eye with his thumb. "My mother admonished me for never questioning more than simply her rulership over the hive, and I felt foolish. I understand now more than ever that I was always a warrior, there to defend and waiting for the day you would come along to open our minds. Tell me, why was my mother's reach even present on Estreldez, regardless of where she was in the universe?"

He wasn't mocking me, he was genuinely eager for what I had to say, and for the first time in all my years as an advisor I felt... heard.

"This pool is full of nanobots, and I think all of Krelis has them... floating in the pollen we breathe. It's possible the molt is caused by faulty technology reacting poorly to biomaterial in the body. I've been in a medpod before, and I know what it feels like to be submerged in one."

"That doesn't account for hearing our thoughts, and no other species visiting is able to join the hive mind," he disagreed, it was like I was talking to a fellow researcher challenging to help me flush out my thoughts, not to disparage me, but to clarify.

I nodded fervently, wrapping my mind around the new theory with all the observations I'd made. "Right, I think that has to do with krelins specifically and how they, we," I corrected, accepting that I was one, "interact with the nanobots. Naturally, krelins communicated through sound waves with their kan before they spoke." I added through my thoughts, "*Somehow the nanobots have translated patterns in the*

257

way our kan produce sound waves when we think, and perhaps it's similar to morse code... krelin code."

He laughed and lifted me up into a twirling embrace, our wings buzzing with the motion. "The nanobots could connect over long distances because there was always a ship, or technology within reach for them to connect with, pinging from one connection to the next until it established a hold." Trent paused, narrowing his brows in thought. "But the queens..."

"I can't answer everything, but I suspect it has something to do with a queen's ability to sense and feel more. But, you said so yourself that you could communicate through Chief Ong... you aren't a queen."

He nodded his understanding and pressed his kan to mine. A hum vibrated through my mind. *"Nanobots or not... you are."* He took my breath away. Even if I didn't want the responsibility of queen, when he said it, I wanted nothing more than for him to tell me I was his queen. My lips lifted to graze across his, and he moaned. All the noise of the hive's nanobots trying to communicate with me was nothing but a dull echo, forgotten to the thrum of my heart synchronizing with his before I couldn't stand the distance any longer. I lifted to meet his lips as they crashed into mine, both of us having the same thought, *"Mine."*

It was like our minds melted together, and just like that moment I saw those bright wisps of light becoming one... so did we. One bright light in my mind, and it created a bubble around my sanity, keeping everyone else's thoughts out. I sighed in relief, and joy as his tongue slipped along mine and we pushed and teased in equal savagery. I needed to feel him, only him.

"Trent," I whimpered against him as I sucked in air to dive back into touching every part of him, with my mouth, with my hands, and... I realized now... my mind. It was somehow easier to accept that I could hear him, knowing it had something to do with technology and not some fated soul bonding that I had no control over. This was my choice, and every other kansa mate out there had to make the same choice that I did... to accept that this connection was more than chemistry... more than nanobots. It was love, born from the fires of trial and forged in the heat of adversity. Everything, and everyone told us this shouldn't be, but though pheromones and nanobots helped guide us... *we were a choice.*

"And I'd choose you every time," he rasped before plundering my mouth once more, making me moan.

My hands trailed down his torso, and he didn't stop me from reaching for the treasure beneath his leathers this time. I stilled before I undid the flap that would expose himself to me. He groaned, lacing his hands behind my head, and through my black tresses to press his lips firmly to mine, working against me in tandem as I opened for him, capturing a moan of my own with his kiss. This all still felt too much like a dream, freezing me in place, I didn't want the illusion to die.

One of his hands trailed down my arm, sending shivers to my toes, until he grabbed my frozen hand and yanked it where it wanted to be all along, feeling the flutter of his mating scales straining against the leathers of his pants. His cock was the girth of my hand, rounding out at the edges of my palm. He wasn't exaggerating when he said he was concerned about if he'd fit. I'd have been worried it wasn't possible if it weren't for what we did in the gardens. Remembering how full he made me, had my insides leaking liquid heat down my thigh. The feeling of moisture trickling between my folds was triggering my nerves to fire, and I clenched, needing to feel the pressure of some kind of friction to relieve myself.

I needed him inside me, nothing else would fully satiate this hunger for removing every micro space between us. And the scales that fluttered against my palm had me nipping at his lip, eager to devour every morsel of his flesh. My back loh burned where my wings moved so fast, they were nothing but wind urging me forward, closer to destroying the very air that kept us apart. Mist sparked around us lighting up red amongst the greens and purples of the cave, the nanobots as electrified as we were.

The heel of my hand rubbed his hardened length, and I mewled, imagining his flexible scales expanding and buzzing against my sensitive flesh. Glands at the back of his throat clucked sending vibrations through my kan down to my very core like he was already touching me. His hand still cupped over my own, and worked in rhythm before he slid a finger between my folds.

I couldn't take the layers between us, and he hadn't even entered me with a single finger yet. My clit vibrated as he lightly slipped up and down, teasing little circles around my entrance. Poking just the tip before sneaking away to rub my clit to make it sing. My hand seized as I desperately tugged at the flap of his pants to remove his scaled leather pants, but there was more to removing them than I remembered, because he was the one to take them off last time. I'd interviewed countless mates and giggled to myself internally at estrelds that complained about the garments of off-worlders not being as accessible as our traditional clothing. Panting, and feeling my climax build as I struggled to relieve him of his own garment made me curse under my breath, "Fuck."

"Not until you come in my hand, Kansa," he replied

gruffly as he nipped at my ear, his other hand pressed against my lower back to keep me in place as I writhed against his ministrations like my clit was a temple of worship, and I was his goddess. "Let me taste you," he begged while trailing kisses down my neck. He lingered in his descent to suck a nipple between his lips, his tongue swirling around it, and tugging just enough to make me gasp.

I whimpered as his cock left my reach, and I had yet to release it from its confines. Only now did I notice that my feet were barely touching the ground, and he stopped petting me to lift my legs over his shoulders as I floated in the air, his beautiful grinning face kissing up my thighs. For a moment, I thought I would fall, and I grabbed the closest thing I could as if that would stop me from careening backwards when I lost all focus and couldn't control my wings. My hands gripping his kan, the horns sending a thrill through my fingers, up my arms, and straight to my pulsing core distracted me enough to realize that I didn't need to control my wings at all. It was all instinct, and I was too spun up to do anything but buzz with excitement, I wasn't touching the ground anytime soon.

With a flick of his tongue between my slick folds, I knew I wasn't going to last long. Then he pushed a knuckle at my entrance, and rotated it back and forth as he sucked on my clit. I was undone. My back arched, and I pulled on his kan as I spasmed with a scream, squeezing my eyes shut.

He flicked his tongue over my clit and growled out, "Look at me."

I forced my eyes to open and stare into the golden suns filled with so much warmth that I bit my lip, moaning my release into his mouth.

"You are perfect," he said while lapping up any vistage of my juice from my thigh, and sucked up along my throbbing folds, making my clit vibrate and start building that ache once more. His knuckle pushed at my entrance, stopped by the base of his other fingers. Would he prepare me like he did before? I whimpered thinking about it, but I wanted to experience all of him, and as much as I wanted to do that again many times over, I craved to feel complete, to feel like there was nothing between us.

It was my turn to beg, and I would, "This is torture. Please..."

"Please what?" He smirked at me, withdrawing his finger with a quick yank, then teasing little circles while tapping.

"*Fuck me,*" I begged through our bond.

"*As you wish, kansa,*" he replied while delicately removing my legs from his shoulders. I whimpered at the distance, but I knew it was only temporary. I didn't give him the chance to remedy this cold air between us, and I ripped at his pants to undo that blasted flap that gave me so much trouble, and he laughed so fully it made my heart thrum with joy. I didn't care that I was inexperienced with actually doing any of this myself. I was willing to put in the work and gather a life-time's worth of data on the subject of just him.

The pants finally submitted, and I preened with accomplishment as my prize popped from its prison and greeted me eagerly. I practically purred to touch him again. Still floating, I wrapped one of my legs behind his ass, and hooked my heel to guide him to my heat. Scales fluttered in anticipation, and I giggled as they sent thrills through my core as he slipped between my folds and his head rubbed against my clit, slipped past my entrance. I shivered with delight, and took his hard cock in my hand, rubbing his smooth head along my slit, smearing his precum and my juices before settling him at my entrance. I pulled him closer with my heel under his ass, and yanked his kan towards me so I could taste myself on his lips.

Again, he slipped from my entrance, too large to not need assistance, and my inside walls clamped down needing to feel him inside me, only making things more difficult to get what I desired. I chuckled and cursed but shoved two fingers between myself and spread like a v before I slowly eased out, keeping the tension and angling his cock within me as I stretched around him with such satisfaction and relief, I mewled in triumph.

His hips rocked in, and out until he slipped farther. He whispered between our breathless kisses, "This won't be quick, my love. Once I'm seated the scales will lock. Are you—"

I cut him off by thrusting my hips up and sinking him in another inch deeper with a groan. The scales fluttered inside of me, and made me rock back and forth, feeling the feather-light touch ignite the nerves inside my core.

"Fuck," he cursed into my hair, and gripped my ass for purchase. My walls stretched and molded to his hard cock until he was fully masted within me, the scales expanded, making me clench around him and he stilled with a moan. "You're so fucking perfect, Mabel."

I smiled into his shoulder, as I clung to him through the waves of sensations pooling inside of me. With every thrust he pulled back and the scales would catch and tug in the most delicious way before he plunged back to fill me so completely every muscle was coiled up, readying to explode. It was seconds before I was panting and scratching at his back around his wings and convulsing around his cock in ecstasy. I shyly bit my lip in embarrassment, and I could hear him in my mind, "*Give me all of you. Don't pull away.*"

Emboldened, I rocked my hips against him as he gripped my ass to pull me tight against him, increasing the pressure on my clit as it vibrated, sending jolts through my limbs all the way to my fingertips. My kan was warm and tingling and I spoke to him about every thought I had, opening the floodgate to everything I was.

"*My kansa,*" I finally called him what he truly was to me, my mate, and forever part of my soul. "*If we ever had soul mates on Estreldez before, we never had a name for it, but if we did... I'd say it would include my heart being fused with yours, both of them. I'll forever have three hearts. Lupane, one of many hearts. That's what I'd call you.*"

"*They are yours, forever.*"

Trent wrapped me in his arms, his hands moving from my ass to hold onto my shoulders as he moved his hard cock in waves with the pulsing of his scales fluttering against my walls. Until he tapped the furthest most part of me quick and hard over and over, sending a burning tingle through my nerves that made me flail in a crazed, but delightful manner. It was chaos that I didn't wish to have curtailed. It was fire I didn't want extinguished, and it was light that illuminated every dark desire from the depths of my soul. I was so filled and he hit a button inside of me that kept forcing wave after wave of sensations that I thought I could die happily from until he whispered against my lips with a groan, "*Forever.*"

The scales on his cock hardened, and a pulsing barrage of his cum hit that pleasure center in a way I didn't think I could feel anything better, until I did, and my whole body went limp in his stiffened hold. His fingers trailed lightly along my back in a loving gesture, and they helped me ride the ebbing tides of that heightened release dripping between us. I couldn't tell where my cum ended and my sweat of our heated bodies began. Every muscle in my body relaxed and turned to jelly. Even my wings stopped fluttering, just a twitch every so often with the pulse of his cock inside of me.

I could ask for nothing more. And I became suddenly tired and yawned into his shoulder with a blissful smile of being fully satisfied. Luckily, his hold was tight, and he guided us back down to the smoothed-out rock of the cavern. His wings flexed and folded back, disappearing like a stary night, still glittering in the mist. He was so handsome, and I realized I mostly only enjoyed his eyes this whole time. Well, visually speaking. I very much, enjoyed every second of his cock throbbing inside of me, but I took the time now to really take in every curve of his muscles, built like the warrior he'd been trained to be. And his kan, the horns... I stopped to stare at them. Markings glowed upon his kan that I hadn't noticed before. I traced my finger along the length, and he shivered.

"You have them too, my mate," he said then kissed the tip of my nose before adjusting our angle to see my reflection in the water. There was a ripple to the surface, but it was clear enough to see a glowing pattern along the black horns that had curved around my temple. "Forever," he repeated, and I agreed.

And I knew that these were marks burned into our horns by the nanobots when I accepted him into my mind. We were mated, and I grinned up at him with a devilish smile. My hips moved against his cock, still seated within me. I knew he was knotted inside, and he wouldn't be going anywhere, and he was mine.

"Remind me how long a krelin fucks for, my hearts." Because I wasn't just one heart anymore... all three were mine, as they were his. Forever.

Chapter Twenty-Six

Mabel

We couldn't give ourselves the full two-weeks of light cycles in Kai Mountain like what we would have been given on any Kloaph Rite of a freshly mated couple. There was too much to do. While the voices in my mind were quieter, I could still sense the unease of the hive. They knew there was something wrong with their queen, and they also knew I was there, yet just out of reach. I had a duty to Krelis, but I needed to help Luan. Despite the troubles that were ahead I couldn't stop smiling at the beautiful man beside me.

There was one thing that wasn't stated in any of the files about a krelin male...

After the first mating of a light cycle... their spines stayed soft, only knotting once. Once his spines relaxed... they stayed that way while his cock stayed hard inside of me. I shivered at the memory, and he chuckled, squeezing my shoulders against him so he could whisper in my ear, "Careful, Kansa, the images you evoke in my mind give me the urge to abduct you to my chambers to make them reality."

Biting my lip, I never thought I would be one of those mates that publicly displayed my lust like those at the mating ceremony, but in the moment... I would not have cared who was watching, and I wasn't sure I could wait until his chambers if we started anything. I shivered, and only in words, my body still buzzing, begged for him to let me finish what needed to be done with promises of later, "What I have planned for you isn't quick." I had wicked plans to add more data about his magnificent cock with further testing. He groaned, and I playfully pushed him back so I could concentrate.

Wings opened and flexed behind us, as I stepped off the ledge and ascended into the air with Trent in tow. The lights at the edge of my mind's vision came into focus and I drew them in, while I flew to the center of the hive's heart.

"Our queen," some voices buzzed with relief at feeling my presence once more.

Trent stayed by my side, squeezing my hand in reassurance that I would not be doing this alone.

"Look at her kan, they are shaped like a crown..."

"She is blessed by Goddess Lenkal," another said, and there was a hum of agreement. I was honored that they thought so highly of me, but things were not going to be as they were. I would not rule alone, and if anything, with our plans, neither Trent nor I would hardly rule at all.

"We've lost Queen Kai, and I am not here to replace her, but you should all know that there are threats coming to Krelis. The Molt Fever is a sickness brought on by faulty nanobots that were planted into our ecosystem." I didn't know when I became part of the hive, or if I ever truly was separated from them to begin with. I couldn't be sure without further tests whether the nanobots that caused the Molt Fever were faulty, or if that was their original purpose... but I was going to find out. "The trill of Trillume will be coming, King Sylve of the outlaw planet Necias Delta Fal will come, and we will need to work together to defend our planet and rebuild our hives."

It wasn't a slip of the tongue, I meant to make it plural. We needed more queens... No, we needed more delegates to form new hives, and figure out what to do with the nanobots on Krelis. Something about the Glorbin Flower, Ordin deposits, helped disrupt or alter the technology to stop decaying within the krelin's bodies. There was still so much to unpack, I thought, and it would be overwhelming if I didn't feel the peace at knowing I wasn't alone. This was on us all. And somehow that made things a little easier to digest.

We put Gho-ran in charge of finding delegates for new hives, to help spread the responsibilities. But mostly to stay behind and keep his kan on alert for any signs of Commander Li-aq. No one had seen him since he went into the mountain, and Queen Kai's body went missing. Trent assured me that he saw the light fade from her eyes, and I believe him, but it didn't stop the queasy feeling I got thinking about it. I knew it was likely someone came across her body before we returned and honored her with devouring her remains, but what effects would that krelin have by digesting her venom...? And with her being a queen, it didn't add up that she would be consumed by one krelin alone, if at all.

As we left to rejoin the hive warship, I looked over my shoulder at the planet I hardly got to explore, and the hive that now felt like my home, a part of me. "Will they be okay?" Guilt gave me pause before stepping foot on the shuttle.

"You would feel it if they weren't," Trent said gathering me up in his arms, kissing my kan. The sensation of heat spread straight to my core, and I clenched my thighs. I had no idea how sensitive horns were, and I wondered if I'd hurt him those times I clung to his. I frowned, and he spoke through our bond, "Every touch you give is pleasure, My Kansa."

I shook my head and smiled. It was still hard to believe this wasn't some crazy delusion of my own making. And having him understand me so completely was strange, and yet welcomed. My implant connected with the shuttle communication, and a familiar voice distracted me, "Mabel, thank the moons. I've been trying to get a hold of you since you're the advisor assigned to Krelis, and communications with Prince Trent. I have urgent communication from Luan. She's injured, and not within reach of a radiation source capable of helping her heal... she may not make it back to Estreldez. We need Krelis warships to intercept the Viper Raul of King Sylve's fleet. Krelis has tarnpul reserves, bring as much as you can to help her."

Hazel hardly took a breath as she spoke, and when she did the silence was eerie, filled with a heavy hope that I would save the Jewel of Estreldez from King Sylve. How did Luan get caught up with the outlaws so fast? And she was injured... Trent could sense the anxiety building within me, and he spoke in my stead, easily heard by the speakers in the shuttle.

"I'll have my ship loaded with tarnpul, though I'm unsure how much of it is charged with the moon's radiation. We were already setting course towards Necias Delta Fal. We'll do what we can to bring her back," he said sounding so confident. Of course he would, he was a Commander of the ship and used to being in charge. This queen thing was new to me. I was used to relaying information, not figuring out what to do with it.

"That's not true," Trent objected to my thought that must have got away from me, "You correlated data every day, developed plans, and recommended next steps as an advisor. It's the same thing, only you don't have to waste time waiting for approval of what you know needs to happen."

I flushed at the compliment, and it was odd having someone that believed in me so fully. It was nice. I nodded with a renewed confidence in myself and spoke to Hazel, "As much as it pains me to say this, Luan will not agree with it, but we need to make a treaty with King Sylve, and unite this sector before the trill arrive. But I don't trust him, so we also have to find a way to infiltrate his network, if it's even possible... Do we have people like this?"

Luan would not want to make any alliances with an outlaw planet, but what choice did we have?

Trent laughed. "You have been sheltered in your research center, My Queen. Yes, we have warriors trained for such things. Do you not remember krelin history?"

I frowned. I knew krelin history a bit too well. It wasn't pretty. The humor fell from his face, and I knew he would take care of putting a team together that would make sure any treaty was followed regardless of whatever King Sylve said.

"Queen?" Hazel repeated the title, still connected through the shuttle communications.

"Queen Mab of Krelis," Trent intoned with a flourish for emphasis. I pressed my lips together in a pucker at the title. He knew I accepted what I was, but I wouldn't rule the whole planet on my own. This was a team effort, and I would have delegates, Gho-ran was already seeing to arranging for everyone.

"Do you wish for me to connect you with Almder?" Hazel offered hesitantly.

"No, now isn't the time to figure all of this out. If what you're saying is true, then we must hurry. I'll talk with Almder once I have Luan by my side."

"As you wish, Queen Mab." Hazel agreed like I was her superior, and not the same warrior and advisor she'd spoken casually to not days before. I didn't like it, but before I could say anything the connection was gone. I'd have to have a chat with her when time allowed. We had plans to arrange on how we would approach King Sylve, and how we would set up contingencies if he refused or couldn't be trusted to keep his promises.

I clung to Trent's leather chest plate, and one of his flaps adjusted revealing the tip of something lace-like under his armor... Plucking it from between his skin and the armor, was a delicate wing that warmed at my touch. Trent cleared his throat.

"I was going to tell you later, when things were settled."

"Tell me what?" I held the wing up in the air, seeing it glitter in the light. It was beautiful, reminding me of the same emblem he burned into the gords of his home-brewed nectar.

"It's uh..." It was odd for him to stumble over his words, and a bit endearing. I grinned up at him. "It's an onla, a traditional gift from a krelin warrior to his mate."

"So, it's for me then?" Happiness spread through my chest, and I held it against my chest.

He was still squirming, and I smacked him to shake whatever he was still keeping inside to loosen out of him. I could feel inside his thoughts for what it was, but I didn't like pushing myself inside his mind unless he wanted me there.

Finally, he said, "It's an offering to make a kantos for our offspring."

271

I stilled, having been too distracted to think of that kind of future. "Right now?" There was too much going on. We couldn't right now, could we?

"Whenever you choose, My Kansa. I dream about them too," he admitted softly, nuzzling the top of my head. Them, the two offspring I saw running around that looked just like him. I smiled at the thought, and tradition would continue with the estreld markers taking after their mother. If I had been paying more attention to my own dreams I would have noted the offspring didn't have several loh like Luan at all. In my dreams they were mine, a boy and a girl... the thought popped into my head... twins. One day we would have twins.

"Just like their kapa," Trent added. I stared at him in shock and recognizing the confusion he explained, "I thought you overheard more of my conversation with Gho-ran than you must have. He is my brother, and he was also a twin to our sister Panala. It would run in the family. Kapa is a krelin term for an elder blood bond offspring may rely on. He has been a trusted second, and will make a great kapa to our offspring."

I grinned so big, watching my tough warrior of a man speak about our future that proved to me that he had been thinking about this for a while. "And when did you make this onla offering?"

"After the first time I tasted you, and my mind struggled to understand what my body already knew... you were my choice, My Kansa. I carried that with me, even when I thought I lost you and forced myself to see if Luan was the woman I came to make my mate. It was you all along, at every turn and twist of fate, and will always be you for every choice to come."

I hadn't expected him to say so much, to delve so deeply into my heart, yet he did. I loved him more for it. How was it possible to care so much in so little time? I didn't know, and such a question would normally drive me to collect more data and correlate this into a plan to replicate these results with other mates, but now I truly understand why my questionnaires were so difficult to answer. This feeling was unexplainable.

My lip quivered, and I couldn't form words, but my mind told him what I could, "We aren't the mates we planned for, but we are the ones we need. I hope our dreams come true, my hearts, so we need to come up with the plan of our lives to convince King Sylve to work with us and be incentivized to keep his word, so we can focus on making our dreams come true."

"Mine is already standing before me," he said in that sultry dark voice that made my knees weak.

Why couldn't he just say he loves me like a normal male? But that thought didn't stop me from swooning at his words. There was still some time between now and the shuttle docking at the ship, and I gripped his kan in my hands and pulled him down to my lips.

"I don't want to stand anymore," I purred.

His golden eyes hooded with lust, and an electrified warmth passed through my hands that tugged on his kan down to my pulsing need between my thighs. I knew he could feel the same thing, we were connected, and the back of his throat clucked making me shiver as the vibrations met my sensitive new horns marked with our mate bond. I needed him inside of me, with no barrier in body or soul between us.

"Allow me to prepare your throne, My Queen." He licked his lips, and I squealed in delight as he dove down to sweep his arms under my knees and bury his face beneath my robes. My wings ignited, stopping me from the backward trajectory, but I knew he wouldn't have let me fall. A hand secured me behind my back as I sat on his face, and he nuzzled his nose between my wet folds, a few pieces of fabric still stuck between us in his haste.

I laughed, and he growled as he tore the offending barrier away with his teeth and rubbed his tongue along my slit. Hanging on to one of his kan, I ran my fingers through his blond-white hair and wrapped his braid around my palm, enjoying the sensation of soft strands between my fingers, and a rough tongue made for extracting pulp from plants against my clit.

"You are the rarest flower of them all," he voiced to me in his head, reminding me that I could hide nothing from him when I'd open myself to him like this.

I shuttered as he sucked, and his thumb put pressure at my entrance. Not knowing what to do with my legs, they curled up, and my knees squeezed together almost like they were trying to push him away as I bucked into his mouth.

"You know how I get when you try to run away, My Kansa. I won't let you escape another time." He smiled, pulling away slightly to spin a clear pulpy gel from his lips just like I'd seen Gho-ran do to make the bowls for nectar. I highly doubted he'd be making a bowl for us, and as the string got longer the wickedness in his golden eyes only heightened my awareness of him. I tried to read his mind, but he was clever in his evasion. "Patience," he'd say. "Do you trust me?"

"With my soul," I told him.

He took the silky string and laced it behind my lower back, then took a step back, his hands trailing down my thighs the string slipping through until he reached my knees. Then he wrapped the string that was hardening in the air, becoming less malleable the longer it was in the air, around my knees.

274

"Now, where was I?" He grinned devilishly before spreading my legs once more, and waiting painfully long as my hips thrust up towards him before he said, "That should do it." Then he dove in with a savageness that would make one question if I had not drugged him into a starved state. I ached, and squirmed, but as soon as my knees tried to close on his again... they did not move.

The tension in my muscles as I writhed against my bonds was the only evidence that my body could not contain itself, but it did not move. The pulp he produced was hardened and too tough to bend anymore, allowing him full access without my unruly knees trying to bar him once again. I laughed and threw my head back enjoying the freedom to allow myself to push and pull against the restraint without worrying about harming him. The extra pressure caused by my strained muscles built my orgasm even higher.

It's too much, and all he was using was his tongue and his thumb pressing at my entrance, barely even dipping in, and out. Over, and over again. Faster, and faster until I was screaming his name.

"Fuck, yes," I mewled as I spasmed, my inner walls clenching and ebbing with the flow of my release. He drank my juices, and moaned as the shuttle dinged, docking at the ship.

My eyes widened, not wanting to share this moment with anyone, and only now asking myself how long the pulp bonds would keep me bound up.

Trent bit into his lip to draw a drop of blood and licked it, before drawing his tongue along strategic points on the string, softening the pulp until he broke it with a twist of his hands. I floated back to touch the floor, and adjusted my robes, only to notice that the bottom of my robes were torn. What a sight I was, and I didn't care.

"After you, Commander," I cooed, motioning to the door.

He cleared his throat, and adjusted his stance a bit. My eyes wandered to his crotch and I smiled at the bulge of my mate's excitement. Let them see, I thought. He grinned showing off his sharp teeth. I'd take care of that later, we had the rest of our lives.

"Together," he said, offering me his hand.

And I agreed. The queen in tattered robes, and her king covered in her scent with a cock armed and ready to stab through his pants. I chuckled remembering the time he said I'd know if he wanted to stab me, and he was right. I did know, there was no question, and I was eager to feel every inch of him for the rest of my cycles. But first, there was a jewel to save.

Enjoyed reading *Her Alien Prince*? Smash the star button the zon on Goodreads.

Grab Her Alien Exchange for freesies, and be notified when the next book in the Trillume Universe launches when you join my newsletter:

What to read next?   Read about Luan and Vareo:

A jewel to steal. A planet to save. A leader to love?

I'm supposed to be taking rulership of my planet when I find myself sneaking aboard an off-worlders' ship.

It's just my bad luck the last known Shol male is a compatible mate, when being with him could jeopardize my entire species. I am a ruler, and it is my clan duty to mate for survival... not love. He can't be mine if I wish to protect my planet from invasion.

I can't keep him, but my mating loh react to his touch, and everything in me wants him to be mine.

A sci-fi fated-mates alien romance from Sky Roberts, first of the Treasures of Trillume series. This steamy, page-turning romance between an outlaw alien and the strong female ruler that wants him, will have you devouring every morsel towards their HEAFN.

Read on Kindle Unlimited
Continue reading for a sneak peek at:
Her Alien Savior and Her Alien Insurgent coming soon

Chapter Twenty-Seven

Epilogue: Gaven

If it weren't for the way Mabel's green eyes glowed with a light I hadn't seen in cycles, I'd have retired to a simple life of being sired to a brilliant estreld... or was it krelin now? The horns curving around her temple grew into an intricate crown befitting of her new role as Queen of Krelis. She was happy, despite the troubles both her and the prince would have to face. There was much to discuss, and I hadn't fully given up on being part of Mabel's life, even if it was in a different capacity now.

Almder contacted expecting to speak with Prince Trent, but what she got instead was staring at some of her darker decisions as the leader of Estreldez, facing Queen Mab after attempting to stunt her growth, and prevent her from ever truly knowing of her own offspring. It was a wicked decision made in fear with earnest intentions. All the most horrific events of the universe usually started that way.

But I was keeping a secret, not wanting to distract them from finding Luan, because I knew if I said something they would stay on Krelis. I could take care of this myself, it was what I was trained for.

Queen Kai was still alive, and the previous Commander Li-aq scooped her up and flew off. Not having wings myself, following them wasn't really an option, but they wouldn't stay hidden for long, and I'd be here. I wouldn't be waiting for them to make their move, Queen Kai was injured, and they'd need supplies. At the very least, I knew they wouldn't be able to leave Krelis without Gho-ran knowing about it.

I didn't get the nickname of Sky Bender because I popped out of camouflage to enforce compliance of our treaties. It was because I was around to punish those that acted against the better interests of peace... and though I didn't fly, I saw everything.

I just didn't see her... getting in my way.

Having a human exchange come to Krelis at a time like this was bad luck, but she kept getting herself involved and I couldn't keep my distance. Fuck whatever plans I had, I had no choice but to keep her at my side and out of trouble while I stopped Queen Kai and Li-aq from destroying the hive while Mabel was gone.

Book Three: **Her Alien Insurgent** Next in the Treasures of Trillume Series, don't forget to join the newsletter to get updates and sneak peeks at this release as well as a free book, Her Alien Exchange! https://sendfox.com/lp/m85g8r

And you can check out Book One of the Alien Warrior Series, Her Alien Exchange: Her Alien Savior. Continue Reading:

Her Alien Savior

Riley

I took in a breath and sat down, staring at the numbers highlighted on the screen. This is like any other job, I tried to convince myself. There was nothing left for me on Earth, and this was an opportunity to be adored and get any job placement training I wanted.

I dug my nails into my pants, creating indents in my thighs, unable to contain my nerves. Once my number came up, I'd be scanned, and my DNA would be paired with an alien host family.

"Number Alpha G, Lema U, Four Hundred and Sixty!" a male called out over the intercom system. I was almost up; I'd been notified when my application was close to being chosen to arrive on time. The room was filled with people hoping to be recruited into the human exchange program.

Just think, an entire year of experiencing another culture. Maybe I'd like it so much that I wanted to stay.

"...Seventy!"

I jumped up, lifting a hand. "Me!" I squealed, and the man

beside me scrunched his brows up, like I was the alien in the room for being excited to be here.

The girl next to me shook her head at my fidgety nature and remarked, "You know the chance that you'll get to visit the Trillume Galactic placement center is like a fraction of a percentage."

That's where most everyone wanted to be accepted at. It was the elite of all exchange programs. The aliens there were mostly humanoid, and large, and sexy as sin. Most of the men in this room waiting for placement were none too secretly praying to be placed there because the females on Trillume were tall, voluptuous, and super into human men. Something about how powerful they felt in comparison to a human male, and how much they enjoyed looking after them. Almost as if we humans were pets, but very well-treated pets.

I shrugged. Not my thing, but to each their own kink. I wasn't trying to mate with the aliens, I just wanted to learn everything I could about their technology and feel… useful.

"It says here your name is Riley Spearit," he said with a wrinkled nose as he quirked a brow. It wasn't the first time someone had made fun of my name, but the derision was new.

"Yes." I staggered my voice as if asking a question. Yes, it was my name resolutely, but the way he said it made me almost doubt myself about being here.

"Like a despondent spirit?" He wouldn't let it go.

"No? But that does sound more creative than simply having parents that were really into this old singer from like the stone ages that was like a king or something. Riley was his daughter," I rambled. "Also, it's not spirit, it's Spearit, like as in my ancestors way back when were like warriors with spears or something, and apparently were really good at spearing things."

"Right… Let's get this over with." He was not impressed and waved a pen over my body, then pressed it to my arm without any preamble, taking a DNA sample. It pinched quickly, and I flinched.

"Aren't you friendly," I mocked. He was not very happy about his job if this was how he treated all the applicants. I guess it was a long and busy career choice, constantly processing millions of people. Okay it was probably trillions of people, all of them excited about space travel, the new frontier, learning about new species.

"Please sign this waiver. We are not responsible should you have any adverse effects from joining the Human Exchange Trade—H.E.T.—or any dissatisfaction with your time, up to and including potential illness or death. You should know we take every precaution for every human's safety and have lightyears of advanced medicine to assist your success, but we can't account for everything. This is a note from the Trillume Galactic Empire, do you agree?"

He swiped the air to transfer the agreement to my implant, which displayed on my overlay viewer through my contacts that were provided to me as soon as I signed up to be assigned. It was happening; I was so close to being assigned to an alien host family! The contract scrolled on for quite some time. I scanned the important bits, trying to quickly get to the end.

The hosting species would never want anything bad to happen to a human in their care. It would destroy the trust built up over this exchange program. So I wasn't worried about the double reassurance paragraph that made sure I read every word and forced me to sign that section alone before continuing to the overall agreement. It was important they made sure I acknowledged that space travel is dangerous, and they can't be held responsible if I decide to go against any regulations and eat something poisonous to humans or do something stupid and die. Because most aliens thought we were stupid, and humans were likely to harm their fragile bodies simply by existing.

I got it, our bodies weren't as resilient as alien ones. Whatever. I was tougher than I looked.

Signing the contract, I gave my guide a determined stare that I hoped said "Bring it on!" But it was just as likely that all he saw was a small human girl, dressed in a standard issue space leotard, about to face an adventure I'd cry about and insist on returning to Earth before my exchange was up.

Not happening, bucko!

A ding sounded in my ears, letting me know my application was completed.

"Right, so your information has been distributed with your personal data hidden until you've been accepted, then you accept the exchange offer. It can take—"

He's cut off when another notification grabs both of our attention. I was flagged for assignment… so quickly.

I was practically hyperventilating.

My guide stared at me, dazed for a moment, as if he was confused by it as much as I was, before he said, "Join me in the briefing room, Miss Spearit. My name is Joel, and I'll be your placement adviser for the time being."

"What does this mean?" I asked excitedly.

"It means there is an exchange opportunity posted and your data fits the request, so you'll be briefed. If you accept, then there is yet another approval process by the hosts to confirm your placement."

Joel was all of a sudden acting much sweeter towards me, and I'd take it. He led me to a conference room down the hall, behind the employee-only sliding doors that whooshed as I passed. The ground glowed yellow, then green—possibly making sure I was authorized to be there. I glanced around at all the pictures on the walls of other humans with their exchange hosts, some smiling and some not. There were a few exchanges not well-suited to humans, and those were flagged after people returned with their reports.

We were human advocates; not only did we learn, but we also helped bring back intel for Earth. It was a win-win.

I stared at one photo on the revolving screen display in particular. Which species was that?

"Those are the necia, a warrior species in alliance with the Trillume. They've been flagged as a bit too rough of an exchange for those on their first voyage. Only warriors are usually recruited—humans with talent in warfare, weaponry, and with exceptional strength. The necia make up most of the Trillume warrior fleets sent out to keep the peace between species in their system."

I cringed at that explanation. Their system, as if the Trillume owned all planets in this galaxy and the next several surrounding. I mean, they weren't completely wrong, it wasn't like anyone could stop them from invading any single planet if they decided to be dicks about it. Luckily for us, they seemed to be very diplomatic about everything, allowing humans to continue to manage our own planet with little interference.

"Don't worry, they don't assign females to their battle fleets, even if most of their missions are pretty boring considering no one wants to mess with the Trillume Galactic Law."

Suddenly, a stubbornness came over me that I was all too accustomed to but Joel would probably baulk at. So what if I didn't have muscles like those necia warriors? The whole point of the exchange was to train and learn. I bet you I'd be just as good of a warrior as any other human sent there.

"I checked 'all' on my application, so maybe I'll meet the necia one day," I replied casually.

"The females are quite aggressive... and territorial over their males. It's actually not uncommon for the necia females to be stronger than the males. It's why mostly male humans are sent and not females... due to the likelihood of being killed in a duel for dominance. Their culture has, uh, tribal laws that the Trillume don't interfere with." Joel cleared his throat, and the room grew dark to highlight the display of a planet labeled AsunGor.

"It's beautiful." I gazed at the gaseous planet filled with bright colors. Where our oceans were blue and lands green and brown, theirs were a deep purple, yellow, and orange. Swirls of red clouds painted the atmosphere. Anything outside of Earth was other and strangely captivating.

"ASunGor, but that was for a different assignment."

A new image appeared of a planet I was a bit more familiar with considering all the hype about the H.E.T. across all recruitment centers. Trillume.

It was massive compared to the size of Earth, making our sun's size seem normal at 109 times wider than Earth. It was no wonder Trillume was considered home to more species than the Trill, becoming home to aliens that had lost their own planets, and making it the base of galactic law within any known star system, lumping Earth's galaxy into the fold of the Trillume Star System, T.S.S.

I stared in awe for a moment until the planet zoomed in and I got an overhead view of the main city, putting our own sci-fi movies to shame. There were quadrants creating habitats agreeable to many different species surrounding the city in domes that were created with forcefield nano nets that controlled every aspect of the environment without obstructing the view of the green sky.

Was I dreaming? Was I going to be given an assignment on Trillume?

"I'm only showing you this because something in your file was flagged, but I wouldn't get your hopes too high on this one. I've had plenty of flagged applicants be rejected once they've accepted the host."

"I'm confused, I selected 'all' under the training exchange, so they should be expecting any human to be requiring training on whatever job they are offering..."

Joel sighed like this wasn't the first time he'd had to answer that question. That didn't give me a bunch of warm fuzzies about my chances.

But this was Trillume we were talking about! No matter what my assignment was, it was the hub of many species, and on my off time I could explore everything! There was even a sexy, alien sex palace if humans wanted to have some fun with no strings attached. I could only imagine the kind of kinks people discovered there.

Those necia alien warriors came to mind, and, though I wasn't a prude by any means, I wasn't really one to visit a sex palace either. Did the warriors even visit those kinds of places? They had to, right? They must get lonely after a long assignment patrolling the galaxy for law breakers.

I shook my head of the thought. I wasn't visiting an alien sex palace. I repeated that to myself, hoping that if I said it enough times, my curiosity wouldn't get the better of me. But all those hard muscles... the necia males didn't even wear shirts!

Joel cleared his throat to regain my attention. I smiled lamely, as if he couldn't see the blush on my face signaling exactly where my mind went.

"There is a scientist researching reproductive studies on various species that are on a population decline, and he has requested a human to assist their research biologically, but also intelligently. They will train on research basics, handling their technology, and evaluating results."

"Sounds important," I said, intrigued by the idea of helping another species. But biologically speaking, I'd be an awful specimen for child-rearing of humans. I couldn't have children, but damn if I wasn't going to help other aliens have theirs. Something deep inside of me ached, and I felt my eyes get scratchy and watery.

Choking back my emotion, I knew I had to get this assignment.

"You've been part of the other human's dismissals, right? Let's be real, Joel. What do you know?"

He squinted at me like I'd grown another head before he rubbed his temples. "I couldn't care less one way or the other if you get this placement, but I'll tell you what I know. It's become a bit of a running joke around the recruitment centers that a human gets flagged once a day for this job and not a single one gets through the final approval.

"But I wouldn't worry about it, having your file flagged even once makes you a more desirable candidate for placement. You'll get an assignment within a day of being dismissed. There is a whole sector of aliens that will only choose from the flagged humans."

"That seems odd, wouldn't it make us less desirable to be chosen and then dismissed?" I wondered out loud.

For the first time, Joel smiled and lowered his voice. "Between you and me, every alien has different preferences, and even being considered for a Trillume placement makes others want you more. And really, all the aliens are obsessed with humans; it's our government that regulates the H.E.T. and only allows humans in and out. There is a strict no alien exchange in place until Earth is more comfortable that their laws would be followed, and no invasions like sci-fi horror stories would occur."

I nodded. That made sense. There was probably a limit to how many humans were allowed to leave at any given time to any given planet. So Trillume was the most sought-after placement, and there weren't many accepted. Could that be caused by humans deciding to stay in their placements longer than the exchange year?

"Do you know how many humans are allowed on Trillume per the treaty agreement?"

Joel shrugged. "They don't release that kind of information to the public, or even the recruitment centers."

So, he didn't know, or he wasn't going to tell me. I guess we weren't all that chummy since he'd first decided on a glance that I wasn't worth his time. But someone on Trillume thought differently.

ALIEN WARRIOR PREQUEL

HER ALIEN EXCHANGE

SKY ROBERT

Grab Her Alien Exchange for free

SKY ROBERT

S.M. McCoy Writing as Sky Robert for Spicier Smuttier Romances

Sky Robert is a mom of two tiny humans in training, narrates audiobooks for fantasy/sci-fi indie authors, and when she isn't writing (which is MOST of the time) you can find her consuming copious amounts of coffee, promoting indie authors, reading alien smut, fantasy, sci-fi and romance books, chowing down on Indian butter chicken, and when she actually hangs out with people in person, in real life, outside of the internet (gasps), she's playing board or card games. All around nerd, lover of the strange, and all things fantastical.

More from the Treasures of Trillume Universe:
Jewel of the Alien Bandit
Her Alien Prince
Her Alien Insurgent (In progress)

Necia Alien Warriors: (Part of the Trillume Universe)
Her Alien Exchange Grab it free!
Her Alien Savior (Coming 2023)
Her Alien Warrior
Her Alien Captor

Also by S.M. McCoy

The less steamy fantasy romances
https://linktr.ee/authorsteviemarie
www.steviemarie.com
sign up for S.M. McCoy's Newsletter here.

Divine Series:
Blood Crescent Book One: Published 2018
Blood Rebirth Book Two: Published 2019
Blood Queen Book Three: Published 2021
Available on Audible and Kindle Unlimited

Acatalec Series:
Keys of Acatalec Prequel: TBA
My Abett Book 0.5: Published 2022
Kingdom of Acatalec Book One: Published 2022
Available Wide on all Retailers including audiobook
Acatalec Chosen Book Two: TBA
Acatalec's Sword Book Three: TBA

A hijacked alien exchange, and the criminal alien warrior she'd risk her life for.

Riley:

What happens if your exchange program with another alien planet gets hijacked by a warrior that says your contracted host is a criminal? And you're required to help him infiltrate, and apprehend them, or else? Well, I guess that's what happened to me, but it was difficult to know who to trust when being a human meant I was treated like a second-class alien, and injected with nanobug trackers like a criminal, myself. All of that would be pretty difficult to handle if I was doing it on my own, but I wasn't the only one to get roped into this mission, and the warrior assigned to protect me during my mission was not only hot, but used to be commander of this ship before he was defeated by the current necia warrior in charge.

Grab Her Alien Savior on my author direct store:
https://payhip.com/BrokenBooksPublishing